DRAGONSONG

ANNE McCAFFREY

DRAGONSONG

HARPER HALL OF PERN TRILOGY

INTRODUCTION BY TAMORA PIERCE

SAGA PRESS

LONDON SYDNEY **NEW YORK** TORONTO NEW DELHI

SAGA PRESS

A Division of Simon & Schuster, Inc.

1230 Avenue of the Americas, New York, New York 10020

This book is a work of fiction. Any references to historical events, real people, or real places are used fictitiously. Other names, characters, places, and events are products of the author's imagination, and any resemblance to actual events or locales or persons, living or dead, is entirely coincidental.

Text copyright © 1976 by Anne McCaffrey

Introduction copyright © 2015 by Tamora Pierce

All rights reserved, including the right to reproduce this book or portions thereof in any form whatsoever. For information address Saga Press Subsidiary Rights Department, 1230 Avenue of the Americas, New York, NY 10020

SAGA PRESS and colophon are trademarks of Simon & Schuster, Inc.

For information about special discounts for bulk purchases, please contact Simon & Schuster Special Sales at 1-866-506-1949 or business@simonandschuster.com.

The Simon & Schuster Speakers Bureau can bring authors to your live event. For more information or to book an event, contact the Simon & Schuster Speakers Bureau at 1-866-248-3049 or visit our website at www.simonspeakers.com.

Cover illustration copyright © 2015 by Stephan Martinière

The text for this book is set in Bembo Std.

Manufactured in the United States of America

First SAGA PRESS paperback edition February 2015

10 9 8 7 6 5 4 3 2

The Library of Congress has cataloged the hardcover edition as follows:

McCaffrey, Anne.

Dragonsong / by Anne McCaffrey.—1st ed.

p. cm.

Summary: Forbidden by her father to indulge in music in any way, a girl on the planet Pern runs away, taking shelter with the planet's fire lizards who, along with her music, open a new life for her.

ISBN 978-0-689-30507-8

[1. Pern (Imaginary place)—Juvenile fiction. 2. Dragons—Juvenile fiction. 3. Dragons—Fiction. 4. Science fiction.]

PZ7.M122834 Dr3   1976

[Fic]   75-030530

ISBN 978-1-4814-2580-3 (pbk)

TO BETH BLISH
who stands first in line for a dragon—behind me!

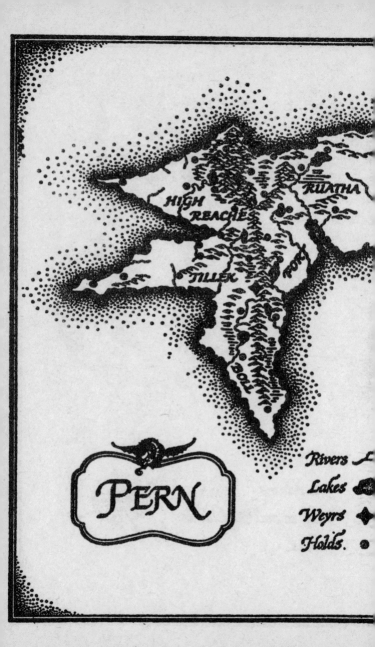

RUATHA

HIGH
REACHES

TILLEK

BOLL

Rivers
Lakes
Weyrs
Holds.

PERN

BITRA

LEMOS

LGAR

BENDEN

IGEN

KEROON

Half
Circle
Sea Hold

NERAT

N.

〰 *Hill Lands*

⩕ *Mountains*

☰ *Plateau and Tablelands*

▭ *Plains*

At Half-Circle Sea Hold, in Benden Hold
Yanus, Sea Holder,
Mavi, Sea Holder's Lady
Menolly, their youngest child and daughter
Sella, the next oldest daughter
Alemi, the third son of six

Petiron, the old Harper
Elgion, the new Harper

Soreel, wife of First Holder
Old Uncle, Menolly's great-grandfather

At Benden Weyr
F'lar, Weyrleader—bronze Mnementh
Lessa, Weyrwoman—queen Ramoth
N'ton, a wingleader—bronze Lioth
T'gellan, wingleader for Half-Circle Sea Hold—bronze Monarth
T'gran, dragonrider—brown Branth
T'sel, dragonrider—green Trenth, bronze fire lizard Rill
F'nor, wing-second—brown Canth, gold fire lizard Grall
Brekke, queenrider—queen Wirenth, killed, bronze fire lizard Berd

Manora, Headwoman of the Weyr's Lower Caverns
Felena, her second in charge
Oharan, Weyr Harper
Mirrim, fosterling of Brekke (3 fire lizards)
                green   Reppa
                         Lok
                brown   Tolly
Sanra, in charge of children in living cavern

Masterharper Robinton
Masterminer Nicat

Menolly's fire lizards:	gold	Beauty
	bronze	Rocky
		Diver
	brown	Lazybones
		Mimic
		Brownie
	blue	Uncle
	green	Auntie One
		Auntie Two

INTRODUCTION

My first manuscript for teenagers was turned down by three editors. Then my agent persuaded the third editor to meet with me and discuss the changes she felt I needed to make in the book before we sent it to anyone else. She agreed, and then we met. That was how I became one of the great Jean Karl's discoveries as she edited my first eight books.

I sometimes wonder if I could have talked to her so easily if I had known that long before me, she had worked with Anne McCaffrey.

For years as I grew up, I searched for writers with strong female heroes. They were hard to find, and too many of their characters surrendered their love of adventure to become settled. I began to write my own girl heroes out of sheer frustration, but I wanted to read ones who were better written than mine. In the 1970s, more female (usually adult) heroes began to appear, but the majority of these strong women were either gay or celibate. Glad though I was to see more female heroes, I was neither gay nor celibate. Also, these adult heroes tended to pursue careers that reflected their sexuality. The warriors protected women or enclaves of women; the priestesses and mages tended to serve goddesses and female-only agendas. It wasn't until I read Anne McCaffrey's *Dragonflight* that I found what I was looking for: female heroes who were sexually active with men and who pursued lives and careers out in the world of all sexes. I can't begin to say how much I needed to see these kinds of books. I continued to read her work as I wrote and published with Jean, not knowing until later that Jean had published my favorite McCaffrey books, *Dragonsong* and *Dragonsinger*.

I have to confess that even if I had known at the time that Jean *had* edited McCaffrey, I couldn't have asked what it was like to work with her. It would have been just as easy to ask Elizabeth I if she had ever called Henry VIII "Daddy." It was enough for me to know we had shared editors!

Although *Dragonsong* and *Dragonsinger* are my favorite McCaffrey books, *Dragonflight* told me I wasn't alone in my goals for my own fiction, and *The Mark of Merlin* showed me that ordinary characters could be every bit as haunting as extraordinary ones. But I still reread *Dragonsong* and *Dragonsinger* once every year or two, and it's been about thirty years.

It begins—it must always begin for me—with the characters. Menolly is what I love in a girl hero: stubborn, hard-working, self-doubting, kind to animals. Despite the harshness of her world and her family, she keeps trying to see the better parts, even when she is treated more like a disgrace than a daughter. She has a brother who loves her, and a sister who never stops complaining; a mother who does her best to ensure she neither plays nor sings again, and a mean old teacher who teaches her everything he can despite her much-maligned sex. And, of course, there are the Dragonriders and their allies, very busy people who nevertheless take time to be kind to a newcomer; characters with their own concerns, lives, and fleshed-out tapestry.

The themes in these books are themes I responded to and ones I carry on in my own work. Menolly's down-to-earth labors in her family's Hold and on her own showed me how vivid the most mundane work (making sweet balls and numb-weed) can make a story and make a point about a character. The many frustrations of creating hook and line and preparing fish illustrate how desperate a character is never to return home. When Menolly makes her own pipes, she triumphs over her wounded hand, finds a way to lure her brother, and entertains the fire lizards. She doesn't bemoan her lack of a Gander Mountain or a Walmart: She makes it, salvages it, or does without.

Menolly employs her natural world to her own advantage, something I think is valuable for any hero, female or not, who is dumped in a hostile environment. She puts what she's learned to use. She pays attention, a quality that serves her well—most of the time.

McCaffrey's characters aren't perfect. Menolly makes mistakes, and she learns from them. Her beloved Harper makes a mistake that results in her living in the wild, just as her brother's reluctance to follow up on a clue leaves his sister unfound. Her sister whines and flirts with the new Harper, showing us a personality as unattractive as she hopes her face is pretty. These are the characters I aspire to, ones who readers recognize and understand.

Dragonsong also taught me about the bone-deep issues that can be covered in a novel for teenagers. I had not read much of the book the first time before I realized that Menolly was abused, physically and emotionally. I had never seen emotional abuse—the continual belittling and denigrating of a child—depicted in a novel before. Hiding Menolly's music, forbidding her to sing, forbidding her to teach, criticizing everything she says and does, until she flinches when someone even speaks kindly to her . . . These are the devices that abusers employ to wear a human—a child—down to a spiritless shadow. A writer like McCaffrey, in identifying them, can show the reader what they really are. As a child I had no writer like this to point out what emotional abuse was. Menolly learns that she has been alone too long and that her courage and her dreams are valuable things for her to fight for, and for readers to fight for. If I had known Menolly, perhaps I never would have let my mother's belittling of my stories drive me to rip them up, or after one awful fight, to be unable to write original fiction for five years. If I had known Menolly, I would have recognized my situation in hers. I would have shaped for myself a fire lizard's cave where I could hide. I know that now I do that for young people who are like I was, people who need characters like Menolly, Piemur, and McCaffrey's other struggling teenagers. McCaffrey teaches that writers can transmit role models, ideas, dreams, and courage in our tales, and whenever I need a refresher, Menolly's tale is the one I read.

TAMORA PIERCE,
AUTHOR OF THE BESTSELLING
TORTALL AND CIRCLE UNIVERSE NOVELS

FOREWORD

Rukbat, in the Sagittarian Sector, was a golden G-type star. It had five planets, two asteroid belts, and a stray planet it had attracted and held in recent millennia. When men first settled on Rukbat's third world and called it Pern, they had taken little notice of the stranger planet, swinging about its adopted primary in a wildly erratic elliptical orbit. For two generations, the colonists gave the bright red star little thought, until the path of the wanderer brought it close to its stepsister at perihelion.

Then, the spore life, which proliferated at an incredible rate on the Red Star's wild surface, spun off into space and bridged the gap to Pern. The spores fell as thin threads on the temperate, hospitable planet, and devoured anything organic in their way, seeking to establish burrows in Pern's warm earth from which to set out more voracious Threads.

The colonists suffered staggering losses in terms of people scored to death, and in crops and vegetation wiped out completely. Only fire killed Thread on land: only stone and metal stopped its progress. Fortunately it drowned in water, but the colonists could scarcely live on the seas.

The resourceful men cannibalized their transport ships and, abandoning the open southern continent where they had touched down, set about making the natural caves in the northern continent habitable. They evolved a two-phase plan to combat Thread. The first phase involved breeding a highly specialized variety of a life-form indigenous to their new world. The "dragons" (named for the mythical Terran beast they resembled) had two extremely useful characteristics: they could get from one place to another instantly by teleportation, and when they had chewed a phosphine-bearing rock, they could emit a flaming gas. Thus the flying dragons could char Thread to ash midair and escape its ravages themselves.

Men and women with high empathy ratings or some innate telepathic ability were trained to use and preserve these unusual animals, partnering them in a lifelong and intimate relationship.

The original cave-Fort, constructed in the eastern face of the great West Mountain range, soon became too small to hold either the colonists or the great "dragons." Another settlement was started slightly to the north, by a great lake, conveniently nestled near a cave-filled cliff. Ruatha Hold, too, became over-crowded in a few generations.

Since the Red Star rose in the East, it was decided to start a holding in the eastern mountains, provided suitable accommodations could be found. The ancient cave-pocked cones of extinct volcanoes in the Benden mountains proved so suitable to the dragonmen and women that they searched and found several more throughout Pern, and left Fort Hold and Ruatha Hold for the pastoral colonists, the holders.

However, such projects took the last of the fuel for the great stonecutters, originally thought to be used for the most diffident mining since Pern was light on metals, and any subsequent holds and weyrs were handhewn.

The dragons and their riders in their weyrs, and the people in the cave holdings, went about their separate tasks and each developed habits that became custom, which solidified into tradition as incontrovertible as law.

By the Third Pass of the Red Star, a complicated social, political and economic structure had developed to deal with the recurrent evil of Thread. There were now six Weyrs, pledged to protect all Pern, each Weyr having a geographical section of the northern continent literally under its wings. The rest of the population, the Holds, agreed to tithe to support the Weyrs, since these fighters, these dragonmen, did not have any arable land in their volcanic homes, nor did they have time for farming while protecting the planet from Passes of the Thread.

Holds developed wherever natural caves could be found: some, of course, were extensive or strategically placed near good water and grazing, others were smaller and less well placed. It took a strong man to keep frantic, terrified people in control in the Holds during Thread attacks: it took wise administration to conserve food supplies for times when nothing could be safely grown. Extraordinary measures controlled population, keeping its number healthy and useful until such time as the Thread should pass. And often children from one Hold were raised in another Hold, to spread the genetic pool and keep the Holds from dangerous inbreeding. Such a practice was called "fostering" and was used in both Hold and Crafthalls, where special skills such as metalworking, animal breeding, farming, fishing and mining (such as there was) were preserved. So that one Lord Holder could not deny the products of a Crafthall situated in his Hold to others, the Crafts were decreed independent of a Hold affiliation, each Craftsmaster at a hall owing allegiance only to the Master of that particular craft who, as the need arose, took likely students in as fosterlings.

Except for the return of the Red Star approximately every two hundred years, life was pleasant on Pern.

There came a time when the Red Star, due to the conjunction of Rukbar's five natural satellites, did not pass close enough to Pern to drop the dreadful spores. And the Pernese forgot about the danger. The people prospered, spreading out across the rich land, carving more Holds out of solid rock and becoming so busy with their pursuits, that they did not realize that there were only a few dragons in the skies, and only one Weyr of dragonriders left on Pern. In a few generations, the descendants of the Holders began to wonder if the Red Star would ever return. The dragonriders fell into disfavor: why should all Pern support these people and their hungry beasts? The legends of past braveries, and the very reason for such courage, became dishonored.

But, in the natural course of events, the Red Star again spun close to Pern, winking with a baleful red eye on its intended victim. One man, F'lar, rider of the bronze dragon, Mnementh, believed that the ancient tales had truth in them. His half brother, F'nor, rider of brown Canth, listened to his arguments and came to believe. When the last golden egg of a dying queen dragon lay hardening on the Benden Weyr Hatching Ground, F'lar and F'nor seized the opportunity to gain control of the Weyr. Searching Ruatha Hold, they found a strong woman, Lessa, the only surviving member of the proud bloodline of Ruatha Hold. She impressed young Ramoth, the new queen, and became Weyrwoman of Benden Weyr. And F'lar's bronze Mnementh became the new queen's mate.

The three young riders, F'lar, F'nor and Lessa forced the Lord Holders and the Craftsmen to recognize their imminent danger and prepare the almost defenseless planet against Thread. But it was distressingly obvious that the scant two hundred dragons of Benden Weyr could not defend the widespread and sprawling settlements. Six full Weyrs had been needed in the olden days when the settled land had been much less extensive. In learning to direct her queen *between* one place and another, Lessa discovered that dragons could teleport *between* times as well. Risking her life as well as Pern's only queen, Lessa and Ramoth went back in time, four hundred Turns, to the days before the mysterious disappearance of the other five Weyrs, just after the last Pass of the Red Star had been completed.

The five Weyrs, seeing only the decline of their prestige and bored with inactivity after a lifetime of exciting combat, agreed to help Lessa, and Pern, and came forward to her time.

Dragonsong begins seven Turns after the Five Weyrs came forward.

CHAPTER 1

Drummer, beat, and piper, blow
Harper, strike, and soldier, go
Free the flame and sear the grasses
Til the dawning Red Star passes.

Almost as if the elements, too, mourned the death of the gentle old Harper, a southeaster blew for three days, locking even the burial barge in the safety of the Dock Cavern.

The storm gave Sea Holder Yanus too much time to brood over his dilemma. It gave him time to speak to every man who could keep rhythm and pitch, and they all give him the same answer. They couldn't properly honor the Old Harper with his deathsong, but Menolly could.

To which answer Yanus would grunt and stamp off. It rankled in his mind that he couldn't give voice to his dissatisfaction with that answer, and his frustration. Menolly was only a girl: too tall and lanky to be a proper girl at that. It galled him to have to admit that, unfortunately, she was the only person in the entire Half-Circle Sea Hold who could play any instrument as well as the old Harper. Her voice was true, her fingers clever on string, stick or pipe, and she knew the Deathsong. For all Yanus could be certain, the aggravating child had been practicing that song ever since old Petiron started burning with his fatal fever.

"She will have to do the honor, Yanus," his wife, Mavi, told him the evening the storm began to slacken. "The important thing is that Petiron is properly sung to rest. One does not have to record who did the singing."

"The old man knew he was dying. Why didn't he instruct one of the men?"

"Because," replied Mavi with a touch of sharpness in her voice, "you would never spare him a man when there was fishing."

"There was young Tranilty . . ."

"Whom you sent fostering to Ista Sea Hold."

"Couldn't that young lad of Forolt's . . ."

"His voice is changing. Come, Yanus, it'll have to be Menolly."

Yanus grumbled bitterly against the inevitable as he climbed into the sleeping furs.

"That's what everyone else has told you, haven't they? So why make so much of a necessity?"

Yanus settled himself, resigned.

"The fishing will be good tomorrow," his wife said, yawning. She preferred him fishing to stomping around the Hold, sullen and critical with enforced inactivity. She knew he was the finest Sea Holder Half-Circle had ever had: the Hold was prospering, with plenty for bartering set by in the storage caves; they hadn't lost a ship or a man in several Turns either, which said much for his weather-wisdom. But Yanus, at home on a heaving deck in foul weather, was very much adrift when taxed with the unexpected on land.

Mavi was keenly aware that Yanus was displeased with his youngest child. Mavi found the girl exasperating, too. Menolly worked hard and was very clever with her fingers: too clever by half when it came to playing any instrument in the Harper Craft. Perhaps, Mavi thought, she had not been wise to permit the girl to linger in the old Harper's constant company once she had learned all the proper Teaching Songs. But it had been one less worry to let Menolly nurse the old Harper, and Petiron had wished it. No one begrudged a Harper's requests. Ah well, thought Mavi, dismissing the past, there'd be a new Harper soon, and Menolly could be put to tasks proper to a young girl.

The next morning, the storm had cleared off: the skies were cloudless, the sea, calm. The burial barge had been outfitted in the Dock Cavern, Petiron's body wrapped in harper-blue on the tilter board. The entire Fleet and most of the Seahold followed in the wake of the oar-driven barge, out into the faster moving current above Nerat Deep.

Menolly, on the barge prow, sang the elegy: her clear strong voice carrying back to the Half-Circle Fleet; the men chanting the descant as they rowed the barge.

On the final chord, Petiron went to his rest. Menolly bowed her head, and let drum and stick slide from her fingers into the sea. How could she ever use them again when they had beaten Petiron's last song? She'd held back her tears since the Harper had died because she knew she had to be able to sing his elegy and you couldn't sing with a throat closed from crying. Now the tears ran down her cheeks, mingled with sea spray: her sobs punctuated by the soft chant of the steersman, setting about.

Petiron had been her friend, her ally and mentor. She had sung from the heart as he'd taught her: from the heart and the gut. Had he heard her song where he had gone?

She raised her eyes to the palisades of the coast: to the white-sanded harbor between the two arms of Half-Circle Hold. The sky had wept itself out in the past three days: a fitting tribute. And the air was cold. She shivered in her thick wherhide jacket. She would have some protection from the wind if she stepped down into the cockpit with the oarsmen. But she couldn't move. Honor was always accompanied by responsibility, and it was fitting for her to remain where she was until the burial barge touched the stones of Dock Cavern.

Half-Circle Hold would be lonelier than ever for her now. Petiron had tried so hard to live long enough for his replacement to arrive. He'd told Menolly he wouldn't last the winter. He'd dispatched a message to Masterharper Robinton to send a new Harper as soon as possible. He'd also told Menolly that he'd sent two of her songs to the Masterharper.

"Women can't be harpers," she'd said to Petiron, astonished and awed.

"One in ten hundred have perfect pitch," Petiron had said in one of his evasive replies. "One in ten thousand can build an acceptable melody with meaningful words. Were you only a lad, there'd be no problem at all."

"Well, we're stuck with me being a girl."

"You'd make a fine big strong lad, you would," Petiron had replied exasperatingly.

"And what's wrong with being a fine big strong girl?" Menolly had been half-teasing, half-annoyed.

"Nothing, surely. Nothing." And Petiron had patted her hands, smiling up at her.

She'd been helping him eat his dinner, his hands so crippled even the lightest wooden spoon left terrible ridges in the swollen fingers.

"And Masterharper Robinton's a fair man. No one on Pern

can say he isn't. And he'll listen to me. He knows his duty, and I am, after all, a senior member of the Crafthall, being taught up in the Craft before him himself. And I'll require him to listen to you."

"Have you really sent him those songs you made me wax down on slates?"

"I have. Sure I have done that much for you, dear child."

He'd been so emphatic that Menolly had to believe that he'd done what he'd said. Poor old Petiron. In the last months, he'd not remembered the time of Turn much less what he'd done the day before.

He was timeless now, Menolly told herself, her wet cheeks stinging with cold, and she'd never forget him.

The shadow of the two arms of Half-Circle's cliffs fell across her face. The barge was entering the home harbor. She lifted her head. High above, she saw the diminutive outline of a dragon in the sky. How lovely! And how had Benden Weyr known? No, the dragonrider was only doing a routine sweep. With Thread falling at unexpected times, dragons were often flying above Half-Circle, isolated as it was by the bogs at the top of Nerat Bay. No matter, the dragon was awing above Half-Circle Hold at this appropriate moment and that was, to Menolly, the final tribute to Petiron the Harper.

The men lifted the heavy oars out of the water, and the barge glided slowly to its mooring at the far end of the Dock. Fort and Tillek might boast of being the oldest Sea-Holds, but only Half-Circle had a cavern big enough to dock the entire fishing fleet and keep it safe from Threadfall and weather.

Dock Cavern had moorings for thirty boats; storage space for all the nets, traps and lines; airing racks for sail; and a shallow ledge where hulls could be scraped free of seagrowths and repaired. At the very end of the immense Cavern was a shelf of rock where the Hold's builders worked when there was sufficient timber for a new hull. Beyond was the small inner cave where priceless wood was stored, dried on high racks or warped into frames.

The burial barge lightly touched its pier.

"Menolly?" The first oarsman held out a hand to her.

Startled by the unexpected courtesy to a girl her age, she was about to jump down when she saw in his eyes the respect due her at this moment. And his hand, closing on hers, gave silent approval for her singing of the Harper's elegy. The other men stood, too, waiting for her to disembark first. She straightened her shoulders, although her throat felt tight enough for more tears, and she stepped proudly down to the solid stone.

As she turned to walk back to the landside of the Cavern, she saw that the other boats were discharging their passengers quickly and quietly. Her father's boat, the biggest of the Half-Circle fleet, had already tacked back into the harbor. Yanus's voice carried across the water, above the incidental sounds of creaking boats and muted voices.

"Quickly now, men. We've a good breeze rising and the fish'll be biting after three days of storm."

The oarsmen hurried past her to board their assigned fishing boats. It seemed unfair to Menolly that Petiron, after a long life's dedication to Half-Circle Hold, was dismissed so quickly from everyone's mind. And yet . . . life did go on. There were fish to be caught against winter's hungry months. Fair days during the cold months of the Turn were not to be squandered.

She quickened her pace. She'd far to go around the rim of

the Dock Cavern and she was cold. Menolly also wanted to get into the Hold before her mother noticed that she didn't have the drum. Waste wasn't tolerated by Mavi any more than idleness by Yanus.

While this was an occasion, it had been a sad one and the women and children and also the men too old to sea-fish observed a decorous pace out of the Cavern, making smaller groups as they headed toward their own Holds in the southern arc of Half-Circle's sheltering palisade.

Menolly saw Mavi organizing the children into work groups. With no Harper to lead them in the Teaching Songs and ballads, the children would be kept occupied in clearing the storm debris from the white-sanded beaches.

There might be sun in the sky, and the dragonrider still circling on his brown, but the wind was frigid and Menolly began to shiver violently. She wanted to feel the warmth of the fire on the great Hold's kitchen hearth and a cup of hot klah inside her.

She heard her sister Sella's voice carrying to her on the breeze.

"She's got nothing to do now, Mavi, why do *I* have to. . . ."

Menolly ducked behind a group of adults, avoiding her mother's searching glance. Trust Sella to remember that Menolly no longer had the excuse of nursing the ailing Harper. Ahead of her, one of the old aunts tripped, her querulous voice raised in a cry for help. Menolly sprinted to her side, supporting her and receiving loud protestations of gratitude.

"Only for Petiron would I have dragged these old bones out on the cold sea this morning. Bless the man, rest the man," the old woman went on, clinging with unexpected strength to Menolly. "You're a good child, Menolly, so you are. It is Menolly, isn't it?" The old one peered up at her. "Now you just give me a hand up to Old Uncle and I'll tell him the whole of it, since he hasn't legs to leave his bed."

So Sella had to supervise the children and Menolly got to the fire: at least long enough to stop shivering. Then old auntie would have it that the Uncle would be grateful for some klah, too, so when Mavi entered her kitchen, her eyes searching for her youngest daughter, she found Menolly dutifully occupied serving the oldster.

"Very well then, Menolly, while you're up there, see that you set the old man comfortably. Then you can start on the glows."

Menolly had her warming cup with the Old Uncle and left him comfortable, mournfully exchanging tales of other burials with the aunt. Checking the glows had been her task ever since she had grown taller than Sella. It had meant climbing up and down the different levels to the inner and outer layers of the huge Sea Hold, but Menolly had established the quickest way to finish the job so that she'd have some free time to herself before Mavi started looking for her. She had been accustomed to spending those earned minutes practicing with the Harper. So Menolly was not surprised to find herself, eventually, outside Petiron's door.

She was surprised, however, to hear voices in his room. She was about to charge angrily through the half-open door and demand an accounting when she heard her mother's voice clearly.

"The room won't need much fixing for the new Harper, so it won't."

Menolly stepped back into the shadow of the corridor. The new Harper?

"What I want to know, Mavi, is who is to keep the children up in their learning until he comes?" That voice was Soreel's, the wife of the First Holder and therefore spokeswoman for the other Hold women to Mavi as Sea Holder's lady. "She did well enough this morning. You have to give her that, Mavi."

"Yanus will send the message ship."

"Not today, nor tomorrow he won't. I don't fault Sea Holder, Mavi, but it stands to reason that the boats must fish and the sloop's crew can't be spared. That means four, five days before the messenger gets to Igen Hold. From Igen Hold, if a dragonrider obliges by carrying the message—but we all know what the Old-timers at Igen Weyr are like so let's say, Harper drums to the Masterharper Hall at Fort is another two-three days. A man has to be selected by Masterharper Robinton and sent overland and by ship. And with Thread falling any time it pleases, no one travels fast or far in a day. It'll be spring before we see another Harper. Are the children to be left without teaching for months?"

Soreel had punctuated her comments with brushing sounds, and there were other clatters in the room, the swishing of bed rushes being gathered up. Now Menolly could hear the murmur of two other voices supporting Soreel's arguments.

"Petiron has taught well . . ."

"He taught *her* well, too," Soreel interrupted Mavi.

"Harpering is a man's occupation . . ."

"Fair enough if Sea Holder'll spare a man for it." Soreel's voice was almost belligerent because everyone knew the answer to that. "Truth be told, I think the girl knew the Sagas better than the old man this past Turn. You know his mind was ranging back in time, Mavi."

"Yanus will do what's proper." The finality in Mavi's tone firmly ended that discussion.

Menolly heard footsteps crossing the old Harper's room, and she ducked down the hall, around the nearest bend and down into the kitchen level.

It distressed Menolly to think of anyone, even another Harper, in Petiron's room. Obviously it distressed others that there was no Harper. Usually such a problem didn't arise. Every Hold could boast one or two musically able men and every Hold took pride in encouraging *these* talents. Harpers liked to have other instrumentalists to share the chore of entertaining their Holds during the long winter evenings. And it was also the better part of wisdom to have a substitute available for just such an emergency as Half-Circle was experiencing. But fishing was hard on the hands: the heavy work, the cold water, the salt and fish oils thickened joints and calloused fingers in the wrong places. Fishermen were often away many days on longer hauls. After a Turn or two at net, trap and sail line, young men lost their skill at playing anything but simple tunes. Harper Teaching Ballads required deft quick fingers and constant practice.

By putting to sea to fish so quickly after the old Harper's burial, Yanus thought to have time enough to find an alternative solution. There was no doubt that the girl could sing well, play well, and she'd not disgraced Hold or Harper that morning. It was going to take time to send for and receive a new Harper, and the youngsters must not lose all progress in the learning of the basic Teaching Ballads.

But Yanus had many strong reservations about putting such a heavy responsibility on the shoulders of a girl not fifteen Turns old. Not the least of these was Menolly's distressing tendency toward tune-making. Well enough and amusing now and again in the long winter evenings to hear her sing them, but old Petiron had been alive to keep her to rights. Yanus wasn't sure that he could trust her not to include her trivial little whistles in the lessons. How were the young to know that hers weren't proper songs for their learning? The trouble was, her melodies were the sort that stayed in the mind so a man found himself humming or whistling them without meaning to.

By the time the boats had profitably trawled the Deep and tacked for home, Yanus had found no compromise. It was no consolation to know that he wouldn't have any argument from the other holders. Had Menolly sung poorly that morning . . . but she hadn't. As Sea Holder for Half-Circle, he was obliged to bring up the young of the Hold in the traditions of Pern: knowing their duty and how to do it. He counted himself very lucky to be beholden to Benden Weyr, to have F'lar, bronze Mnementh's rider, as Weyrleader and Lessa as Ramoth's Weyrwoman. So Yanus felt deeply obliged to keep tradition at Half-Circle: and the young would learn what they needed to know, even if a girl had the teaching.

That evening, after the day's catch had been salted down, he instructed Mavi to bring her daughter to the small room off the Great Hall where he conducted Hold business and where the Records were stored. Mavi had put the Harper's instruments on the mantel for safekeeping.

Appropriately Yanus handed Menolly Petiron's gitar. She took the instrument in a properly reverential manner, which reassured Yanus that she appreciated the responsibility.

"Tomorrow you'll be excused from your regular morning duties to take the youngsters for their teaching," he told her.

"But I'll have no more of those finger-twiddlings of yours."

"I sang my songs when Petiron was alive and you never minded them . . ."

Yanus frowned down at his tall daughter.

"Petiron *was* alive. He's dead now, and you'll obey me in this . . ."

Over her father's shoulders, Menolly saw her mother's frowning face, saw her warning headshake and held back a quick reply.

"You bear in mind what I've said!" And Yanus fingered the wide belt he wore. "No tuning!"

"Yes, Yanus."

"Start tomorrow then. Unless, of course, there's Threadfall, and then everyone will bait longlines."

Yanus dismissed the two women and began to compose a message to the Masterharper to go when he could next spare the sloop's crew. They'd sail it to Igen Hold. About time Half-Circle had some news of the rest of Pern anyway. And he could ship some of the smoked fish. The journey needn't be a wasted trip.

Once in the hallway, Mavi gripped her daughter's arm hard. "Don't disobey him, girl."

"There's no harm in my tunes, mother. You know what Petiron said . . ."

"I'll remind you that the old man's dead. And that changes everything that went on during his life. Behave yourself while you stand in a man's place. No tuning! To bed now, and mind you turn the glowbaskets. No sense wasting light no eye needs."

CHAPTER 2

Honor those the dragons heed
In thought and favor, word and deed.
Worlds are lost or worlds are saved
From those dangers dragon-braved.

Dragonman, avoid excess:
Greed will bring the Weyr distress:
To the ancient Law adhere,
Prospers thus the Dragonweyr.

It was easy enough, at first, for Menolly to forget her tuning during the Teachings. She wanted to do Petiron proud so that when the new Harper came, he'd find no fault in the children's recitations. The children were attentive: the Teaching was always better than gutting and preserving fish, or net mending, and longline baiting. Then, too, winter storms, the severest in many Turns, kept the fishing fleet docked and the Teaching eased the boredom.

When the fleet was in, Yanus would stop by the Little Hall where Menolly held her class. He'd scowl at her from the back of the Hall. Fortunately, he'd only stay a little while because he made the children nervous. Once she actually saw his foot tapping the beat; he scowled when he realized what he was doing and then he left.

He had sent the message sloop to Igen Hold three days after the burial. The crew brought back news of no interest to Menolly but the adults went around looking black: something about the Oldtimers and Menolly wasn't to worry her head, so she didn't. The crew also brought back a message slate addressed to Petiron and signed with the imprint of Masterharper Robinton.

"Poor old Petiron," one of the aunties told Menolly, sighing and dabbing affectedly at her eyes. "He always looked forward to slates from Masterharper. Ah well, it'll keep till the new Harper comes. He'll know what to do with it."

It took Menolly a while to find out where the slate was: propped up conspicuously on the mantel in her father's Records room. Menolly was positive that the message had something to do with her, with the songs that Petiron had said he'd sent to the Masterharper. The notion so obsessed her that she got bold enough to ask her mother why Yanus didn't open the message.

"Open a sealed message from the Masterharper to a man dead?" Mavi stared at her daughter in shocked incredulity. "Your father would do no such thing. Harpers' letters are for Harpers."

"I only remembered that Petiron had sent a slate to the Masterharper. I thought it might be about a replacement coming. I mean . . ."

"I'll be glad when the new Harper does come, m'girl. You've been getting above yourself with this Teaching."

The next few days were full of apprehension for Menolly: she conceived the idea that her mother would make Yanus replace her as Teacher. That was, of course, impossible for the same reasons that had forced Yanus to make her the teacher in the first place. But it was a fact that Mavi found all the smelliest, most boring or tedious jobs for Menolly once her teaching duty was done. And Yanus took it into his head to appear in the Little Hall more frequently.

Then the weather settled down into a clear spell and the entire Sea Hold was kept at a run with fish. The children were excused from the Teaching to gather seaweeds blown up by the high tides and all the Hold women set to boiling the weed for the thick juice in the stalks: juice that kept back many sicknesses and bone ailments. Or so the old aunties said. But they'd find good out of any bad and the worst of any blessing. And the worst of the seaweed was its smell, thought Menolly, who had to stir the huge kettles.

Threadfalls came and added some excitement: the fear in being Holdbound while the dragons swept the skies with their fiery breath, charring Thread to impotence. (Menolly wanted to see that grand sight one day, instead of just singing about it, or knowing it was taking place outside the thick stone walls and heavy metal shutters of the Hold's windows.) Afterward she joined the flamethrower crews that checked for any possible Thread that might have escaped dragon flame. Not that there was much for Thread to eat on the windswept bare marshes and bogs around Half-Circle Sea Hold. The barren rock palisades that made Half-Circle bore no greenery at all, winter or summer, but it was wise to check the marshes and beaches. Thread could burrow into the seagrass stalks, or slide down the marshberry and seabeachplum bushes, burrow into the roots, multiply and eat anything green and growing until the coast was as bare as rock.

Flame-crewing was cold work, but it was a distinct pleasure for Menolly to be out of the Hold, in the rough air. Her team got as far as the Dragon Stones to the south. Petiron had told her that those stones, standing offshore in the treacherous waters, had once been part of the palisade, probably hollowed with caves like all this stretch of cliff.

The crowning treat for Menolly was when the Weyrleader, F'lar, himself, on bronze Mnementh, circled in for a chat with Yanus. Of course, Menolly wasn't near enough to hear what the two men said, but she was close enough to smell the firestone reek of the giant bronze dragon. Close enough to see his beautiful eyes catching all colors in the pale wintry sunlight: to see his muscles knot and smooth under the soft hide. Menolly stood, as was properly respectful, with the other flame-thrower crews. But once, when the dragon turned his head in a lazy fashion to peer in her direction, his eyes whirled slowly with their changing colors and she was certain that Mnementh looked at *her*. She didn't dare breathe, he was so beautiful!

Then, suddenly, the magic moment was over. F'lar gave a graceful leap to the dragon's shoulder, caught the fighting straps and pulled himself into place on the neck ridges. Air whooshed around Menolly and the others as the great bronze opened his fragile-looking wings. The next moment, he seemed to be in the air, catching the updraft, beating steadily higher. Abruptly the dragon winked from view. Menolly was not the only one to sigh deeply. To see a dragonrider in the sky was always an occurrence: to be on the same ground with a dragon and his rider, to witness his graceful takeoff and exit *between* was a marvel.

All the songs about dragonriders and dragons seemed inadequate to Menolly. She stole up to the little cubicle in the women's dormitory that she shared with Sella. She wanted to be alone. She'd a little pipe among her things, a soft, whispery reedpipe, and she began to play it: a little whistle composed of her excitement and her response to the day's lovely event.

"So there you are!" Sella flounced into the room, her face reddened, her breath rough. She'd obviously run up the steep stairs. "Told Mavi you'd be here." Sella grabbed the little pipe from Menolly's fingers. "And tuning, too."

"Oh, Sella. It's an old tune!" Menolly said mendaciously and grabbed her pipe back.

Sella's jaw worked with anger. "Old, my foot! I know your ways, girl. And you're dodging work. You get back to the kitchen. You're needed now."

"I am not dodging work. I taught this morning during Threadfall and then I had to go with the crews."

"Your crew's been in this past half-day or more and you still in smelly, sandy clothes, mucking up the room I have to sleep in. You get below or I'll tell Yanus you've been tuning."

"Ha! You wouldn't know a tune if you had your nose rubbed in it."

But Menolly was shedding her work clothes as fast as she could. Sella was just likely to slip the word to Mavi (her sister was as wary of Yanus as Menolly) about Menolly piping in her room—a suspicious action on its own. Though Menolly hadn't sworn not to tune at all; only not to do it in front of people.

However, everyone was in a good mood that night: Yanus, because he'd spoken to F'lar the Weyrleader and because there'd be good fishing on the morrow if the weather held. Fish always rose to feed from drowned Thread, and half the Fall had been over Nerat Bay. The Deep would be thick with schools. With Yanus in a good mood, the rest of the sea holders could also rejoice because there'd been no Thread on the ground at all.

So it wasn't any wonder that they called on Menolly to play for them. She sang two of the longer Sagas about dragons; and then did the Name-Song for the current wingleaders of Benden Weyr so her Sea Hold would know their dragonmen. She wondered if there'd been a recent hatching that Half-Circle mightn't have heard about, being so isolated. But she was certain that F'lar would have told Yanus if that were so. But would Yanus have told Menolly? She wasn't the Harper to be told such things as courtesy.

The sea holders wanted more singing, but her throat was tired. So she played them a song they could sing, bellowing out the words in voices roughened by wind and salt. She saw her father scowling at her, though he was singing along with the rest of them, and she wondered if he didn't want her—a mere girl—to play men's songs. It galled her because she'd played them often enough when Petiron was alive. She sighed at this injustice. And then wondered what F'lar would have said if he'd known that Half-Circle Sea Hold was dependent on a mere girl for their harpering. She'd heard everyone say that F'lar was a fair man, a farseeing man, and a fine dragonrider. There were even songs about him and his Weyrwoman, Lessa.

So she sang them, in honor of the Weyrleader's visit, and her father's expression lightened. She sang on until her throat was so tight that not a squeak would come out. She wished that some-one else could play to give her a rest but, as she scanned the faces of the holders, there wasn't any of them who could beat a drum properly, much less finger a gitar or pipe.

That was why the next day it seemed only logical for her to start one of the children learning the drum rolls. Plenty of songs could be sung just to drumbeat. And one of Soreel's two children still in Teaching was sensitive enough to learn to pipe.

Someone, Sella perhaps, Menolly thought bitterly, informed Mavi of Menolly's activity.

"You were told no tuning . . ."

"Teaching someone drum beats is not tuning . . ."

"Teaching anyone to play is Harper business, not yours, m'girl. Just your good fortune Sea Holder is out in the Deep or you'd have the belt across your shoulders, so you would. No more nonsense."

"But it's not nonsense, Mavi. Last night another drummer or piper would have . . ."

Her mother raised her hand in warning, and Menolly bit shut her lips.

"No tuning, Menolly!"

And that was that.

"Now girl, see to the glows before the fleet gets back."

That job took Menolly inexorably to the Harper's room: swept clean of everything that had been personal to Petiron. She was also reminded of the sealed message on the Record room mantel. What if the Masterharper were expecting a message from Petiron about the songmaker? Menolly was so very sure that part of that unopened message was about her. Not that thinking about it did Menolly any good. Even knowing it for a fact would be no help, Menolly decided gloomily. But that didn't stop her from going past Yanus's Record room and peering in at the tempting package on the mantel.

She sighed, turning from the room. By now the Masterharper would have heard of Petiron's death and be sending a new Harper. Maybe the new man would be able to open the message, and maybe, if it was about her, maybe if it said that the songs she'd sent were good ones, Yanus and her mother wouldn't put such restrictions on her about tuning and whistling and everything.

As the winter spun itself out, Menolly found that her sense of loss when she thought of Petiron deepened. He had been the only person in the Sea Hold who had ever encouraged her in anything: and most especially in that one thing that she was now forbidden to do. Melodies don't stop growing in the mind, tapping at fingers, just because they're forbidden. And Menolly didn't stop composing them—which, she felt, was not precisely disobeying.

What seemed to worry Yanus and Mavi most, Menolly reasoned to herself, was the fact that the children, whom she was supposed to teach only the proper Ballads and Sagas, might think Menolly's tunes were Harper-crafted. (If her tunes were that good in her parents' ears, what was the harm of them?) Basically they didn't want her to play her songs aloud where they would be heard and perhaps repeated at awkward times.

Menolly could, therefore, see no harm in writing down new tunes. She played them softly in the empty Little Hall when the children had left, before she began her afternoon chores, carefully hiding her notations among the Harper records in the rack of the Hall. Safe enough, for no one but herself, till the new Harper came, would discover them there.

This mild deviation from the absolute obedience to her father's restriction about tuning did much to ease Menolly's growing frustration and loneliness. What Menolly didn't realize was that her mother had been watching her closely, having recognized the signs of rebellion in her. Mavi didn't want the Hold to be disgraced in any way, and she feared that Menolly, her head turned by Petiron's marked favor, was not mature enough to discipline herself. Sella had warned her mother that Menolly was getting out of hand. Mavi put some of that tale down to sisterly envy. But, when Sella had told Mavi that Menolly had actually started to teach another how to play an instrument, Mavi had been obliged to intervene. Let Yanus get one whisper of Menolly's disobedience and there'd be real trouble in the Hold for the girl.

Spring was coming and with spring, the quieter seas. Perhaps the new Harper would arrive soon.

And then spring did come, a first glorious day. The sweet scents of seabeachplum and marshberry filled the seaward breezes and came in through the opened shutters of the Little Hall. The children were singing loudly, as if shouting got them through the learning faster. True, they were singing one of the longer Sagas, word perfect, but with far more exuberance than was strictly needed. Perhaps it was that exuberance that infected Menolly and reminded her of a tune she'd tried to set down the day before.

She did not consciously disobey. She certainly was unaware that the fleet had returned from an early catch. She was equally unaware that the chords she was strumming were not—officially—of the Harper's craft. And it was doubly unfortunate that this lapse occurred just as the Sea Holder passed the open windows of the Hall.

He was in the Little Hall almost at once, summarily dismissing the youngsters to help unload the heavy catch. Then he silently, which made the anticipation of the punishment worse, removed his wide belt, signaled to Menolly to raise her tunic over her head and to bend over the high harper's stool.

When he had finished, she had fallen to her knees on the hard stone flags, biting her lips to keep back the sobs. He'd never beaten her so hard before. The blood was roaring in her ears so fiercely that she didn't hear Yanus leave the Little Hall. It was a long while before she could ease the tunic over the painful weals on her back. Only when she'd got slowly to her feet did she realize that he'd taken the gitar, too. She knew then that his judgment was irrevocable and harsh.

And unjust! She'd only played the first few bars . . . hummed along . . . and that only because the last chords of the Teaching Ballad had modified into the new tune in her head. Surely that little snitch wouldn't have done any lasting harm! And the children knew all the Teaching Ballads they were supposed to know. She hadn't *meant* to disobey Yanus.

"Menolly?" Her mother came to the classhall door, the carrying thong of an empty skin in her hand. "You dismissed them early? Is that wise . . ." Her mother stopped abruptly and stared at her daughter. An expression of anger and disgust crossed her face. "So you've been the fool after all? With so much at stake, and you had to tune . . ."

"I didn't do it on purpose, Mavi. The song . . . just came into my mind. I'd played no more than a measure . . ."

There wasn't any point in trying to justify the incident to her mother. Not now. The desolation Menolly had felt when she realized her father had taken the gitar intensified in the face of her mother's cold displeasure.

"Take the sack. We need fresh greens," Mavi said in an expressionless voice. "And any of the yellow-veined grass that might be up. There should be some."

Resignedly, Menolly took the sack and, without thinking,

looped the thong over her shoulder. She caught her breath as the unwieldy sack banged against her scored back.

Before Menolly could avoid it, her mother had flipped up the loose tunic. She gave an inarticulate exclamation. "You'll need numbweed on some of those."

Menolly pulled away. "What good's a beating then, if it's numbed away first chance?" And she dashed out of the Hall.

Much Mavi cared if she hurt, anyhow, except that a sound body works harder and longer and faster.

Her thoughts and her misery spurred her out of the Hold, every swinging stride she took jarring her sore back. She didn't slow down because she'd the whole long track in front of the Hold to go. The faster she went, the better, before some auntie wanted to know why the children were out of lessons so soon, or why Menolly was going green-picking instead of Teaching.

Fortunately she encountered no one. Everyone was either down at the Dock Cave, unloading, or making themselves scarce to the Sea Holder's eyes so they wouldn't have to. Menolly charged past the smaller holds, down aways on the marshroad, then up the righthand track, south of the Half-Circle. She'd put as much distance between herself and Sea Hold as she could: all perfectly legitimate, in search of greenery.

As she jogged along the sandy footpath, she kept her eyes open for fresh growth, trying to ignore the occasional rough going when she'd jar her whole body. Her back began to smart. She gritted her teeth and paced on.

Her brother, Alemi, had once said that she could run as well as any boy of the Hold and outdistance the half of them on a long race. If only she had been a boy . . . Then it wouldn't have mattered if Petiron had died and left them Harperless. Nor would Yanus have beaten a boy for being brave enough to sing his own songs.

The first of the low marsh valleys was pink and yellow with blooming seabeachplum and marshberry, slightly blackened here and there: more from the low-flying queens catching the odd Thread that escaped the main wings. Yes, and there was the patch that the flame-thrower had charred: the one Thread infestation that had gotten through. One day, Menolly told herself, she'd just throw open a window's steel shutters and *see* the dragons charring Thread in the sky. What a sight that must be for certain!

Fearful, too, she reckoned, having seen her mother treat men for Threadburn. Why, the mark looked as if someone had drawn a point-deep groove with a red-hot poker on the man's arm, leaving the edges black with singed skin. Torly would always bear that straight scar, puckered and red. Threadscore never healed neatly.

She had to stop running. She'd begun to sweat heavily and her back was stinging. She loosened her tunic belt, flapping the soft runner-beast hide to send cooling draughts up between her shoulder blades.

Past the first marsh valley, up over the rocky hump hill into the next valley. Cautious going here: this was one of the deep, boggy places. No sign of yellow-veined grasses. There had been a stand last summer two humpy hills over.

She heard them first, glancing up with a stab of terror at the unexpected sounds above. Dragons? She glanced wildly about for the telltale gray glitter of skyborne Thread in the east. The greeny blue sky was clear of that dreaded fogging, but not of dragonwings. She heard dragons? It couldn't be! They didn't swarm like that. Dragons always flew in ordered wings, a pattern against the sky. These were darting, dodging, then swooping and climbing. She shaded her eyes. Blue flashes, green, the odd brown and then . . . Of course, sun glinted golden off the leading, dartlike body. A queen! A queen that tiny?

She expelled the breath she'd been holding in her amazement. A fire lizard queen? It had to be. Only fire lizards could be that small and look like dragons. Whers certainly didn't. And whers didn't mate midair. And that's what Menolly was seeing: the mating flight of a fire lizard queen, with her bronzes in close pursuit.

So fire lizards weren't boy talk! Awed, Menolly watched the swift, graceful flight. The queen had led her swarm so high that the smaller ones, the blues and greens and browns, had been forced down. They circled now at a lower altitude, struggling to keep the same direction as the high fliers. They dipped and dashed in mimicry of the queen and bronzes.

They had to be fire lizards! thought Menolly, her heart almost stopping at the beauty and thrill of the sight. Fire lizards! And they *were* like dragons. Only much, much smaller. She didn't know all the Teachings for nothing. A queen dragon was gold: she mated with the bronze who could outfly her. Which was exactly what was happening right now with the fire lizards.

Oh, they were beautiful to behold! The queen had turned sunward and Menolly, for all her eyes were very longsighted, could barely pick out that black mote and trailing cluster.

She walked on, following the main group of fire lizards. She'd bet anything that she'd end up on the coastline near the Dragon Stones. Last fall her brother Alemi had claimed he'd seen fire lizards there at dawn, feeding on fingertails in the shallows. His report had set off another rash of what Petiron had called "lizard-fever." Every lad in the Sea Hold had burned with plans to trap a fire lizard. They'd plagued Alemi to repeat his sighting.

It was just as well that the crags were unapproachable. Not even an experienced boatman would brave those treacherous currents. But, if anyone had been *sure* there were fire lizards there . . . Well no one would know from her.

Even if Petiron had been alive, Menolly decided, she would not have told him. He'd never seen a fire lizard, though he'd admitted to the children that the Records allowed that fire lizards did exist.

"They're seen," Petiron had told her later, "but they can't be captured." He gave a wheezing chuckle. "People've been trying to since the first shell was cracked."

"Why can't they be caught?"

"They don't want to. They're smart. They just disappear . . ."

"They go *between* like dragons?"

"There's no proof of that," said Petiron, a trifle cross, as if she'd been too presumptuous in suggesting a comparison between fire lizards and the great dragons of Pern.

"Where else can you disappear to?" Menolly had wanted to know. "What is *between*?"

"Some place that isn't." Petiron had shuddered. "You're neither here nor there," and he gestured first to one corner of the Hall and then toward the Sea Dock on the other side of the Harbor. "It's cold, and it's nothing. No sight, no sound, no sensations."

"You've ridden dragonback?" Menolly had been impressed.

"Once. Many Turns ago." He shuddered again in remembrance. "Now, since we're touching on the subject, sing me the Riddle Song."

"It's been solved. Why do we have to know it now?"

"Sing it for me so I'll know that you know it, girl," Petiron had said testily. Which was no reason at all.

But Petiron had been very kind to her, Menolly knew, and her throat tightened with remembered regret for his passing. (Had he gone *between?* The way dragons did when they lost their riders or grew too infirm to fly? No, one left nothing behind, going *between.* Petiron had left his body to be slipped into the deeps.) And Petiron had left more behind than his body. He'd left her every song he'd ever known, every lay, every ballad, saga, every fingering, chord and strum, every rhythm. There wasn't any way a stringed instrument could be played that she didn't know, nor any cadence on the drums at which she wasn't time-perfect. She could whistle double-trills as well as any wherry with her tongue or on the reeds. But there had been some things Petiron wouldn't—or perhaps couldn't—tell her about her world. Menolly wondered if this was because she was a girl and there were mysteries that only the male mind could understand.

"Well," as Mavi had once told Menolly and Sella, "there are feminine puzzles that no mere man could sort, so that score is even."

"And one more for the feminine side," said Menolly as she followed the fire lizards. A mere girl had seen what all the boys—and men—of the Sea Hold had only dreamed of seeing, fire lizards at play.

They'd ceased following the queen and her bronzes and now indulged in mock air battles, swooping now and then to the land itself. And seemingly under it. Until Menolly realized that they must be over the beaches. The sand was slipping under her feet. An unwary step could plunge her into the holes and dips. She could hear the sea. She changed her course, keeping to the thicker patches of coarse marsh grasses. The ground would be firmer there, and she'd be less visible to the fire lizards.

She came to a slight rise, before the bluff broke off into a steep dive onto the beaches. The Dragon Stones were beyond in the sea, slightly hidden by a heat haze. She could hear fire lizards chirping and chattering. She crouched in the grasses and then, dropping to her full length, crept to the bluff edge, hoping for another glimpse of the fire lizards.

They were quite visible—delightfully so. The tide was out, and they were exceedingly busy in the shallows, picking rock-mites from the tumbled exposed boulders, or wallowing on the narrow edging of red and white sand, bathing themselves with great enthusiasm in the little pools, spreading their delicate wings to dry. There were several flurries as two fire lizards vied for the same choice morsel. In that alone, she decided, they must differ from dragons; she'd never heard of dragons fighting amongst themselves for anything. She'd heard that dragons feeding among herds of runner-beasts and wherries were something horrible to behold. Dragons didn't eat that frequently, which was as well or not all the resources of Pern could keep the dragons fed.

Did dragons like fish? Menolly giggled, wondering if there were any fish in the sea big enough to satisfy a dragon's appetite. Probably those legendary fish that always eluded the Sea Hold nets. Her Sea Hold sent their tithe of sea produce, salted, pickled or smoked, to Benden Weyr. Occasionally a drag-onrider came asking for fresh fish for a special feasting, like a Hatching. And the women of the Weyr came every spring and fall to berry or cut withies and grasses. Menolly had once served

Manora, the headwoman of Benden Lower Caverns, and a very pleasant gentle woman she'd been, too. Menolly hadn't been allowed to stay in the room long because Mavi shooed her daughters out, saying that she had things to discuss with Manora. But Menolly had seen enough to know she liked her.

The whole flock of lizards suddenly went aloft, startled by the return of the queen and the bronze who had flown her. The pair settled wearily in the warm shallow waters, wings spread as if both were too exhausted to fold them back. The bronze tenderly twined his neck about his queen's and they floated so, while blues excitedly offered the resting pair fingertails and rock mites.

Entranced, Menolly watched from her screen of seagrass. She was utterly engrossed by the small doings of eating, cleaning and resting. By and by, singly or in pairs, the lesser fire lizards winged up to the first of the sea-surrounded bluffs, lost quickly from Menolly's sight as they secreted themselves in tiny creviced weyrs.

With graceful dignity, the queen and her bronze rose from their bathing. How they managed to fly with their glistening wings so close together, Menolly didn't know. As one, they seemed to dart aloft, then glided in a slow spiral down to the Dragon Stones, disappearing on the seaside and out of Menolly's vision.

Only then did she become conscious of discomfort; of the hot sun on her welted back, sand in the waistband of her trousers, seeping into her shoes, dried as sweaty grit on her face and hands.

Cautiously, she wriggled back from the edge of the bluff. If the fire lizards knew they'd been overseen, they might not return to this cove. When she felt she'd crawled far enough, she got to a crouching position and ran for a way.

She felt as rarely privileged as if she'd been asked to Benden Weyr. She kicked up her heels in an excess of joy and then, spotting some thick marsh grass canes in the bog, snicked one off at the waterline. Her father may have taken her gitar away, but there were more materials than strings over a sounding box to make music.

She measured the proper length barrel and cut off the rest. She deftly made six holes top and two bottom, as Petiron had taught her, and in moments, she was playing her reed pipe. A saucy tune, bright and gay because she was happy inside. A tune about a little fire lizard queen, sitting on a rock in the lapping sea, preening herself for her adoring bronze.

She'd a bit of trouble with the obligatory runs and found herself changing keys, but when she'd rehearsed the tune several times, she decided she liked it. It sounded so different from the sort of melody Petiron had taught her, different from the traditional form. Furthermore, it sounded like a fire lizard song: sprightly, cunning, secretive.

She stopped her piping, puzzled. Did the dragons know about fire lizards?

CHAPTER 3

Holder, watch; Holder, learn
Something new in every Turn.
Oldest may be coldest, too.
Sense the right: find the true!

When Menolly finally got back to the Sea Hold, the sky was darkening. The Hall was bustling with the usual end of day activity. The oldsters were setting the dinner tables, tidying the great Hall and chattering away as if they hadn't met for Turns instead of only that morning.

With luck, thought Menolly, she could get her sack down to the water rooms . . .

"Where did you go for those greens, Menolly? Nerat?" Her mother appeared in front of her.

"Almost."

Immediately Menolly saw that her pert words were ill-timed. Mavi roughly grabbed the sack and peered inside critically.

"If you'd not made the trip worth the while . . . Sail's been sighted."

"Sail?"

Mavi closed the sack and shoved it back into Menolly's hands. "Yes, sail. You should have been back hours ago. Whatever possessed you to take off so far with Thread . . ."

"There weren't any greens nearer . . ."

"With Thread due to fall anytime? You're a fool twice over."

"I was safe enough. I saw a dragonrider doing his sweep . . ."

That pleased Mavi. "Thank heavens we're beholden to Benden. They're a proper Weyr." Mavi gave her daughter a shove toward the kitchen level. "Take those, and be sure the girls wash every speck of sand off. Who knows who's sailing in?"

Menolly slipped through the busy kitchen, countering orders flung at her by various other women who saw in her a capable assistant at their own tasks. Menolly merely brandished the sack and proceeded down to the water rooms. There some of the older but still able women were busily sandscouring the best metal plates and trays.

"I must have one basin for the greens, auntie," said Menolly, pushing up to the rank of stone sinks.

"Greens is easier on old skin than sand," said one of the women in a quavering, long-suffering voice and promptly deposited her pile of plates into the sink beside her and pulled her plug.

"More sand in greens than cleaning," another woman remarked in an acid tone.

"Yes, but take it *off* greens," said the obliging one. "Oh, what a lovely mess of yellow-veins, too. Where did you find them this time of year, daughter?"

"Halfway to Nerat." Menolly suppressed her grin at their startled shrieks of dismay. The farthest they'd stir from the Hold was the ledge in front on a sunny day.

"With Thread falling? You naughty girl!" "Did you hear about the sail?" "Who do you suppose?" "The new Harper, who else?" There was a wild chorus of cackling laughs and great wonderings about the appearance of the new Harper.

"They always send a young one here."

"Petiron was old!"

"He got *that* way. Same as we did!"

"How would you remember?"

"Why not? I've lived through more Harpers than you have, my girl."

"You have not! I came here from Red Sands in Ista . . ."

"You were born at Half-Circle, you old fool, and I birthed you!"

"Ha!"

Menolly listened to the four old women arguing back and forth until she heard her mother demanding to know if the greens had been washed. And where were the good plates and how was she to get anything done with all the gossip?

Menolly found a sieve large enough to hold the washed greens and brought them up for her mother's inspection.

"Well, that'll be enough for the head table," Mavi said, poking at the glistening mound with her fork. Then she stared at her daughter. "You *can't* appear like that. Here you, Bardie, take the greens and put the dressing on them. The one in the brown flask on the fourth shelf in the cool room. You, Menolly, have the goodness to get yourself sandfree and decently dressed. You're to attend Old Uncle. The moment he opens his mouth, shove something into it or we'll be hearing him all night long."

Menolly groaned. Old Uncle smelled almost as much as he chattered.

"Sella's much better handling him, Mavi . . ."

"Sella's to attend head table. You do as you're told and be grateful!" Mavi fixed her rebellious daughter with a stern eye, tacitly reminding her of her disgrace. Then Mavi was called away to check a sauce for the baking fish.

Menolly went off to the bathing rooms, trying to convince herself that she was lucky she hadn't been banished completely from the Hall this evening. Though tending Old Uncle came as close as could be to banishment. Honor obliged the Sea Holder to have all his household there to greet the new Harper.

Menolly shucked off the dirty tunic and breeches, and slipped into the warm bathing pool. She swung her shoulders this way and that for the water to wash the sand and sweat as painlessly as possible from her sore back. Her hair was all gritty with sea sand, too, so she washed that. She was quick because she'd have her hands full with Old Uncle. It'd be much better to have him all arranged in his hearth seat before everyone else assembled for dinner.

Draping her dirty clothes around her, Menolly took the calculated risk that few people would be in the High Hold at this hour and charged up the dimly lit steps from the bathing pools to the sleeping level. Every glow in the main corridor was uncovered, which meant that the Harper, if such it were, would have a guided tour of the Hold later. She dashed down to the narrow steps leading to the girls' dormitories, and got into her cubicle without a soul the wiser.

When she got to Old Uncle's room, later, she had to clean his face and hands and slip a clean tunic over his bony shoulders. All the while he was chattering about new blood in the Hold and hee-hee who was the new Harper going to marry? He'd a thing or two to tell the Harper, give him the chance, and why did she have to be so rough? His bones ached. Must be a change in the weather because his old legs never failed to give warning. Hadn't he warned them about the big storm a while back? Two boats had been lost with all crew. If they'd paid attention to his warning, it wouldn't have happened. His own son was the worst one for not listening to what his father said and why was she hurrying him so? He liked to take his time. No, couldn't he have the blue tunic? The one his daughter had made him, matching his eyes, she'd said. And why hadn't Turlon come to see him today as he'd asked and asked and asked, but who paid him any heed anymore?

The old man was so frail that he was no burden to a strong girl like Menolly. She carried him down the steps, he complaining all the way about people who'd been dead before she was born. Old Uncle's notion of time was distorted, that's what Petiron had told her. Brightest in Uncle's memory were his earlier days, when he'd been Sea Holder of Half-Circle, before a tangled trawler line had sliced off his legs below the knee. The great Hall was almost ready for guests when Menolly entered with him.

"They're tacking into Dock," someone was saying as Menolly arranged Old Uncle in his special seat by the fire. She wrapped him well in the softened wherhides and tied the strap that would keep him upright. When he got excited, Old Uncle had a tendency to forget he had no feet.

"Who's tacking into Dock? Who's coming? What's all the hubblebubble about?"

Menolly told him, and he subsided, moments later wanting to know in a querulous tone of voice if anyone was going to feed him or was he supposed to sit here dinnerless?

Sella, in the gown she'd spent all winter making, swirled past Menolly, pressing a small packet into her hand.

"Feed him these if he gets difficult!" And she skimmed away before Menolly could say a word.

Opening the packet, Menolly saw balls of a sweet made from seaweed, flavored with purple grass seed. One could chew these for hours, keeping the mouth fresh and moist. Small wonder Sella'd been able to keep Old Uncle happy. Menolly giggled and then wondered why Sella was being so helpful. It must have pleased Sella no end to learn Menolly had been displaced as Harper. Or would she know? Mavi wouldn't have mentioned it. Ah, but the Harper was here now, anyhow.

Now that she had Old Uncle settled, Menolly's curiosity got the better of her and she slipped over to the windows. There was no sign of the sail in the harbor now, but she could see the cluster of men, glows held high, as they walked around the shore from the Dock to the Hold proper. Keen though her eyes were, Menolly could not pick out the new faces and that was that.

Old Uncle began one of his monologues in a high-pitched voice, so Menolly scooted back to his side before her mother could notice she'd left her post. There was so much bustle, putting food on the tables, pouring the welcoming cups of wine, all the Hold arranging itself to meet the guests, no one noticed what Menolly was or wasn't doing.

Just then, Old Uncle came to himself again, eyes bright and focused on her face. "What's the stir today, girl? Good haul? Someone getting spliced? What's the lay?"

"There's a new Harper coming, everyone thinks, Old Uncle."

"Not another one?" Old Uncle was disgusted. "Harpers ain't what they used to be when I was Sea Holder, not by a long crack. I mind myself of one Harper we had . . ."

His voice fell clearly in the suddenly quiet Hall.

"Menolly!" Her mother's voice was low, but the urgency was unmistakable.

Menolly fumbled in her skirt pocket, found two sweetballs and popped them into old Uncle's mouth. Whatever he'd been about to say was stopped by the necessity of dealing with two large round objects. He mumbled contentedly to himself as he chewed and chewed and chewed.

All the food had been served and everyone seated before Menolly got so much as a glimpse of the new arrivals. There had been a new Harper. She heard his name before she ever saw his face. Elgion, Harper Elgion. She heard that he was young and good-looking and had brought two gitars, two wooden pipes and three drums, each carried separately in its own case of stiffened wherhide. She heard that he'd been very seasick across Keroon Bay and wasn't doing justice to the lavish dinner spread in his honor. With him had come a craftmaster from the Smith-crafthall to do the metal work required on the new ship and other repairs beyond the metalman in the Sea Hold. She heard that there was urgent need at Igen Hold for any salted or smoked fish the Sea Hold might have to spare on the return voyage.

From where Menolly sat with Old Uncle, she could see the backs of heads at the high table and occasionally a profile of one of the visitors. Very frustrating. So was Old Uncle and the other elderly relatives whose old bones rated them a spot near the fire. The aunts were, as usual, squabbling over who had received the choicer portions of fish, and then Old Uncle decided to call them to order, only his mouth was full at that moment and he choked. So the aunts turned on Menolly for trying to stuff him to an early death. Menolly could hear nothing over their babble.

She tried to content herself with the prospect of hearing the Harper sing, as he surely would once the interminable meal was ended. But it was hot so close to the big fire and the heat made Old Uncle smell worse than ever, and she was very tired after the day's exertions.

She was roused from a half doze by a sudden hall-wide thudding of heavy seaboots. She jerked fully awake to see the tall figure of the new Harper rising at the head table. He had his gitar ready and was taking an easy stance, one foot on the stone bench.

"You're sure this Hall isn't rocking?" he asked, strumming a few chords to test the instrument's pitch. He was assured that the Hall had been steady for many, many Turns, never known to rock at all. The Harper affected not to be reassured as he tuned the G-string slightly higher (to Menolly's relief). He made the gitar moan then, like a seasick soul.

As laughter rippled through the eager audience, Menolly strained to see how her father was taking this approach. The Sea Holder had little humor. A Harper's welcome was a serious occasion, and Elgion did not appear to realize this. Petiron had often told Menolly how carefully Harpers were chosen for the Hold they were assigned to. Hadn't anyone warned Elgion about her father's temperament?

Suddenly Old Uncle cut across the gentle strumming with a cackle of laughter. "Ha! A man with humor! That's what we need in this Hold—some laughter. Some music! Been missing it. Let's have some rollicking tunes, some funny songs. Give us a good rib-popping ditty, Harper. You know the ones I like."

Menolly was aghast. She fumbled in her skirt pocket for some of the sweetballs as she shushed Old Uncle. This was exactly the sort of incident that she was supposed to prevent.

Harper Elgion had turned at the imperious order, bowing with good respect to the old gentleman by the hearth.

"I would that I could, Old Uncle," he said most courteously, "but these are serious times," and his fingers plucked deep somber notes, "very serious times and we must put lightness and laughter behind us. Square our backs to the problems that face us . . ." and with that he swung into a new exhortation to obey the Weyr and honor the dragonrider.

The sticky sweetballs had got warmed and stuck to the fabric of her pocket, but Menolly finally got some out and into Old Uncle's mouth. He chewed angrily, fully aware that his mouth was being plugged and resenting it. He chewed as fast as he could, swallowing to clear his mouth for more complaints. Menolly was only just aware that the new tune was forceful, the words stirring. Harper Elgion had a rich tenor voice, strong and sure. Then old Uncle began to hiccup. Noisily, of course. And to complain, or try to, through the hiccups. Menolly hissed at him to hold his breath, but he was furious at not being allowed to talk, at getting hiccups, and he started to pound the arm of his chair. The thumps made an out-of-tempo counterpoint to the Harper's song and brought her furious glances from the head table.

One of the aunts gave her some water for the old man, which he overturned on Menolly. The next thing, Sella was beside her, gesturing that they were to take the old man back to his quarters instantly.

He was still hiccuping as they put him back to bed, and still beating the air with punctuated gestures and half-uttered complaints.

"You'll have to stay with him until he calms down, Menolly, or he'll fall out of bed. Whyever didn't you give him the sweet-balls? They always shut him up," Sella said.

"I did. They're what started him hiccuping."

"You can't do anything right, can you?"

"Please, Sella. You stay with him. You manage him so well. I've had him all evening and not heard a word . . ."

"*You* were told to keep him quiet. *You* didn't. *You* stay." And Sella swept out of the room, leaving Menolly to cope.

That was the end of the first of Menolly's difficult days. It took hours for the old man to calm down and go to sleep. Then, as Menolly wearily got to her cubicle, her mother arrived to berate her soundly for the inattention that had given Uncle a chance to embarrass the entire Hold. Menolly was given no chance to explain.

The next day, Thread fell, sequestering them all within the Hold for hours. When the Fall was over, she had to go with the flame-thrower crews. The leading edge of Thread had tipped the marshes, which meant hours of plodding through sticky marsh mud and slimy sand.

She was tired enough when she returned from that task, but then they all had to help load the big nets and ready the boats for a night trawl. The tide was right then.

She was roused before sunrise the next morning to gut and salt the phenomenal catch. That took all the live-long day and sent her to bed so weary she just stripped off her dirty clothes, and dropped into her sleeping furs.

The next day was devoted to net-mending, normally a pleasant task because the Hold women would chat and sing. But her father was anxious for the nets to be repaired quickly so that he could take the evening tide again for another deep-sea cast. Everyone bent to his work without time for talk or singing while the Sea Holder prowled among them. He seemed to watch Menolly more often than anyone else, and she felt clumsy.

It was then that she began to wonder if perhaps the new Harper had found fault with the way the youngsters had been taught their Ballads and Sagas. Time and again Petiron had told her that there was only one way to teach them and, as she had learned properly from him, she must have passed on the knowledge correctly. Why then did her father seem to be so annoyed with her? Why did he glare at her so much? Was he still angry with her for letting Old Uncle babble?

She worried enough to ask her sister about it that evening when the ships had finally set sail and everyone else could relax a little.

"Angry about Old Uncle?" Sella shrugged. "What on earth are you talking about, girl? Who remembers that? You think entirely too much about yourself, Menolly, that's your biggest problem. Why should Yanus care one way or another about *you?*"

The scorn in Sella's voice reminded Menolly too acutely that she was only a girl, too big for a proper girl, and the youngest of a large family, therefore of least account. It was in no way a consolation to be insignificant, even if her father was, for that reason, less likely to notice her. Or remember her misdeeds. Except that he'd remembered about her singing her own songs to the youngsters. Or had Sella forgotten that? Or did Sella even know that?

Probably, thought Menolly as she tried to find a comfortable spot in the old bed rushes for her weary body. But then, what Sella said about Menolly thinking only of herself applied even more to Sella, who was always thinking about her appearance and her self. Sella was old enough to be married to some advantage to the Hold. Her father had only three fosterlings at the moment, but four of Menolly's six brothers were out at other Sea Holds, learning their trade. Now, with a Harper to speak for them all again, perhaps there'd be some rearrangements.

The next day the Hold women spent in washing clothes. With Threadfall past, and a good clear sunny day, they could count on fast drying. Menolly hoped for a chance to speak to her mother to find out if the Harper had faulted her teaching, but the opportunity never arose. Instead, Menolly came in for another scolding from Mavi for the state of her clothes, unmended; her bed furs, unaired; her hair, her sloppy appearance and her slothfulness in general. That evening Menolly was quite content to take a bowl of soup and disappear into a shadowy corner of the big kitchen rather than be noticed again. She kept wondering why she was being singled out for so much misunderstanding.

Her thoughts kept returning to the sin of having strummed a few bars of her own song. That, and being a girl and the only one who could teach or play in the absence of a real Harper.

Yes, she finally decided, that was the reason for her universal disfavor. No one wanted the Harper to know that the youngsters had been schooled by a girl. But, if she hadn't taught them right, then Petiron had taught her all wrong. That didn't hold water. And, if the old man had really written the Masterharper about her, wouldn't the new Harper have been curious, or sought her out? Maybe her songs hadn't been as good as old

Petiron had thought. Probably Petiron had never sent them to the Masterharper. And that message hadn't said anything about her. At any rate, the packet was now gone from the mantel in the Records room. And, the way things were going, Menolly would never get close enough to Elgion to introduce herself.

Sure as the sun came up, Menolly could guess what she'd have to do the next day—gather new grasses and rushes to repack all the beds in the Hold. It was just the sort of thing her mother would think of for someone so out of favor.

She was wrong. The ships came back to port just after dawn, their holds packed with yellow-stripe and packtails. The entire Hold was turned out to gut, salt and start the smoke-cave.

Of all the fish in the sea, Menolly detested packtails the most. An ugly fish, with sharp spines all over, it oozed an oily slime that ate into the flesh of your hands and made the skin peel off. Packtails were more head and mouth than anything else but hack the front end off and the rounded, blunt tail could be sliced off the backbone. Grilled fresh it was succulent eating: smoked it could be softened later for baking or boiling and be as tasty as the day it was caught. But packtails were the messiest, hardest, toughest, smelliest fish to gut.

Halfway through the morning, Menolly's knife slipped across the fish she was slicing, gashing her left palm wide open. The pain and shock were so great that Menolly just stood, stupidly staring at her hand bones, until Sella realized that she wasn't keeping pace with the others.

"Menolly, just dreaming . . . Oh, for the love of . . . Mavi! Mavi!" Sella could be irritating, but she could keep her wits. As she did now, grabbing Menolly's wrist and stopping the spurt of blood from the severed artery.

As Mavi came and led her past the furiously working hold-ers, Menolly was seized with a sense of guilt. Everyone glared at her as if she'd deliberately wounded herself to get out of work-ing. The humiliation and silent accusations brought tears to her eyes, not the pain nor the sick feeling in her hand.

"I didn't do it on purpose," Menolly blurted out to her mother as they reached the Hold's infirmary.

Her mother stared at her. "Who said that you did?"

"No one! They just looked it!"

"My girl, you think entirely too much about yourself. I assure you that no one was thinking any such thing. Now hold your hand, so, for a moment."

The blood spurted up as Mavi released the pressure on the tendon in Menolly's wrist. For one instant Menolly thought she might faint, but she was determined not to think of herself again. She pretended that she didn't own the hand that Mavi was going to have to fix.

Mavi now deftly fastened a tourniquet and then laved the wound with a pungent herbal lotion. Menolly's hand began to numb, increasing her detachment from the injury. The bleeding ceased, but somehow Menolly couldn't bring herself to look into the wound. Instead she watched the intent expression on her mother's face as she quickly stitched the severed blood ves-sel and closed the long slice. Then she slathered quantities of salve on the cut and bound the hand in soft cloths.

"There! Let's hope I got all that packtail slime out of the wound."

Concern and doubt caused Mavi to frown, and Menolly became fearful. Suddenly she remembered other things: women losing fingers and . . .

"My hand will be all right, won't it?"

"We'll hope so."

Mavi never lied, and the small hard ball of sick fear began to unknot in Menolly's stomach.

"You should have some use of it. Enough for all practical purposes."

"What do you mean? Practical purposes? Won't I be able to play again?"

"Play?" Mavi gave her daughter a long, hard stare, as if she'd mentioned something forbidden. "Your playing days are over, Menolly. You're way past the teaching . . ."

"But the new Harper has new songs . . . the ballad he sang the first night . . . I never heard all of it. I don't know the chording. I want to learn . . ." She broke off, horribly frightened by the closed look on her mother's face, and the shine of pity in her eyes.

"Even if your fingers will work after that slice, you won't be playing again. Content yourself that Yanus was so indulgent while old Petiron was dying . . ."

"But Petiron . . ."

"That's enough *buts*. Here, drink this. I want you in your bed before it puts you to sleep. You've lost a lot of blood, and I can't have you fainting away on me."

Stunned by her mother's words, Menolly barely tasted the bitter wine and weed. She stumbled, even with her mother's help, up the stone steps to her cubicle. She was cold despite the furs, cold in spirit. But the wine and weed had been liberally mixed, and she couldn't fight the effect. Her last conscious thought was of misery, of being cheated of the one thing that had made her life bearable. She knew now what a dragonless rider must feel.

CHAPTER 4

Black, blacker, blackest
And cold beyond frozen things.
Where is between when there is naught
To Life but fragile dragons' wings?

Despite her mother's care in cleaning the wound, Menolly's hand was swollen by evening and she was feverish with pain. One of the old aunts sat with her, placing cool cloths on her head and face, and gently crooning what she thought would be a comforting song. The notion was misplaced since, even in her delirium, Menolly was aware that music had now been forbidden her. She became more irritated and restless. Finally Mavi dosed her liberally with fellis juice and wine, and she fell into a deep slumber.

This proved to be a blessing because the hand had so swollen that it was obvious some of the packtail slime had gotten in the bloodstream. Mavi called in one of the other Hold women deft in such matters. Luckily for Menolly, they decided to release the coarse stitches, to allow better drainage of the infection. They kept Menolly heavily dosed and hourly changed the hot poulticing of her hand and arm.

Packtail infection was pernicious, and Mavi was dreadfully afraid that they might have to remove Menolly's arm to prevent a further spread. She was constantly by her daughter's side, an attention that Menolly would have been surprised, and gratified, to receive, but she remained unconscious. Fortunately the angry red lines faded on the girl's swollen arm on the evening of the fourth day. The swelling receded, and the edges of the terrible gash assumed the healthier color of healing flesh.

Throughout her delirium, Menolly kept begging "them" to let her play just once more, just once again, pleading in such a pitiful tone that it all but broke Mavi's heart to realize that unkind fortune had made that impossible. The hand would always be crippled. Which was as well since some of the new Harper's questions were provoking Yanus. Elgion very much wanted to know who had drilled the youngsters in their Teaching Songs and Ballads. At first, thinking that Menolly had been nowhere near as skilled as everyone had assumed, Yanus had told Elgion that a fosterling had undertaken the task and he'd returned to his own Hold just prior to the Harper's arrival.

"Whoever did has the makings of a good Harper then," Elgion told his new Holder. "Old Petiron was a better teacher than most."

The praise unexpectedly disturbed Yanus. He couldn't retract his words, and he didn't want to admit to Elgion that the person was a girl. So Yanus decided to let matters stand. No girl could be a Harper, any way the road turned. Menolly was too old now to be in any of the classes, and he'd see that she was busy with other things until she came to think of her playing as some childish fancy. At least she hadn't disgraced the Hold.

He was, of course, sorry that the girl had cut herself so badly, and not entirely because she was a good worker. Still it kept her out of the Harper's way until she forgot her silly tuning. Once or twice though, while Menolly was ill, he missed her clear sweet voice in counter-song, the way she and Petiron used to sing. Yet he dismissed the matter from his mind. Women had more to do than sit about singing and playing.

There were exciting doings in the Holds and Weyrs, according to Elgion's private report to him. Troubles, too, deep and worrisome enough to take his mind from the minor matter of a wounded girl.

One of the questions that Harper Elgion often posed concerned the Sea Hold's attitude toward their Weyr, Benden. Elgion was curious as to how often they came in contact with the Oldtimers at Ista Weyr. How did Yanus and his holders feel about dragonriders? About the Weyrleader and Weyrwoman of Benden? If they resented dragonmen going on Search for young boys and girls of the Holds and Crafthalls to become dragonriders? Had Yanus or any of his Hold ever attended a Hatching?

Yanus answered the questions with the fewest possible words, and at first this seemed to satisfy the Harper.

"Half-Circle's always tithed to Benden Weyr, even before Thread fell. We know our duty to our Weyr, and they do theirs by us. Not a single burrow of Thread since the Fall started seven or more Turns ago."

"Oldtimers? Well, with Half-Circle beholden to Benden Weyr, we don't much see any of the other Weyrs, not as the people in Keroon or Nerat might when the Fall overlaps two Weyrs' boundaries. Very glad we were that the Oldtimers would come *between* so many hundreds of Turns to help our time out."

"Dragonmen are welcome any time at Half-Circle. Come spring and fall, the women are here anyway, gathering seabeachplums and marshberries, grasses and the like. Welcome to all they want."

"Never met Weyrwoman Lessa. I see her on her queen Ramoth in the sky after a Fall now and then. Weyrleader F'lar's a fine fellow."

"Search? Do they find any likely lad at Half-Circle, it will be to our honor, and he's our leave to go."

Although the problem had never worried the Sea Holder; no one from Half-Circle had answered a Search. Which was as well, Yanus thought privately. If a lad happened to be chosen, every other lad in the Hold would take to grumbling that he should have been picked. And on the seas of Pern, you had to keep your mind on your work, not on dreams. Bad enough to have those pesky fire lizards appearing now and then by the Dragon Stones. But as no one could get near enough to the stones to catch a fire lizard, no harm was done.

If the new Harper found his Holder an unimaginative man, hardworking and hidebound, he had been well prepared for it by his training. His problem was that he must provoke a change, subtle at first, in what he found; for Masterharper Robinton wanted each of his journeymen to get every Holder and Craftmaster to think beyond the needs of their own lands, Hall and people. Harpers were not simply tellers of tales and singers of songs; they were arbiters of justice, confidants of Holders and Craftmasters, and molders of the young. Now, more than ever, it was necessary to alter hide-bound thinking, to get everyone, starting with the young and working on the old, to consider more of Pern than the land they kept Thread-free or the problems of their particular area. Many old ways needed shaking up, revising. If F'lar of Benden Weyr hadn't done some shaking up, if Lessa hadn't made her fantastic ride back four hundred Turns to bring up the missing five Weyrs of dragonriders, Pern would be writhing under Thread, with nothing green and growing left on the surface. The Weyrs had profited and so had Pern. Similarly the holds and crafts would profit if they only were willing to examine new ideas and ways.

Half-Circle could expand, Elgion thought. The present quarters were becoming cramped. The children had told him that there were more caves in the adjacent bluffs. And the Dock Cavern could accommodate more than the thirty-odd craft now anchored so safely there.

By and large, though, Elgion was rather relieved at his situation, since this was his first post as Harper. He had his own well-furnished apartments in the Hold, enough to eat, though the diet of fish might soon pall on a man accustomed to red meat, and the Seaholders were generally pleasant people, if a little dour.

Only one thing puzzled him: who had drilled the children so perfectly? Old Petiron had sent word to the Harper that there was a likely songmaker at Half-Circle, and he had included two scored melodies that had greatly impressed the Masterharper. Petiron had also said that there'd be some difficulty in the Sea Hold about the songmaker. A new Harper, for Petiron had known that he was dying when he wrote the Masterharper, would have to go carefully. This was a Hold that had kept much to itself and observed all the old ways.

So Elgion had kept his counsel on the matter of the songmaker, certain that the lad would make himself known. Music was hard to deny and, based on the two songs Elgion had been shown, this lad was undeniably musical. However, if the chap were a fosterling and away from the Hold, he'd have to await his return.

Elgion had soon managed to visit all the different smaller holds in the Half-Circle palisade and gotten to know most people by name. The young girls would flirt with him or gaze at him with sorrowful eyes and sighs when he played in the evenings at the Great Hall.

There was really no way in which Elgion would have realized that Menolly was the person he wanted. The children had been told by the Sea Holder that the Harper would not like to know that they'd been drilled by a girl, so they were not to bring disgrace on the Hold by telling him. After Menolly cut her hand so badly, it was rumored that she'd never use it again, so everyone was told that it would be heartless to ask her to sing in the evenings.

When Menolly was well of the infection and her hand healed but obviously stiff, no one was thoughtless enough to remind her of her music. She herself stayed away from the singing in the Great Hall. And since she could not use her hand well and so many occupations in the Hold required two, she was frequently sent away in the day to gather greens and fruits, usually alone.

If Mavi was perplexed by the quietness and passivity of her youngest child, she put it down to the long and painful recovery, not to loss of her music. Mavi knew that all manner of pain and trouble could be forgotten in time, and so she did her best to keep her daughter occupied. Mavi was a very busy woman, and Menolly kept out of her way.

Gathering greens and fruit suited Menolly perfectly. It kept her out in the open and away from the Hold, away from people. She would have her morning drink, bread and fish quietly in the great kitchen when everyone was dashing around to feed the men of the Hold, either going out to fish or coming back in from a night's sailing. Then Menolly would wrap up a fishroll and take one of the nets or skin slings. She'd tell the old aunt in charge of the pantry that she was going out for whatever it was, and since the old aunt had a memory like a seine net, she wouldn't remember that Menolly had done the same thing the day before or realize that she would do the same the day after.

When spring was fully warming the air and making the marshes brilliant with green and blossom color, spider-claws began to walk in from the sea to lay their eggs in the shallower cove waters. As these plump shellfish were a delicacy in themselves, besides adding flavor to every dish when dried or smoked, the young people of the Hold—Menolly with them— were sent off with traps, spades and nets. Within four days the nearby coves were picked clear of spiderclaws and the young harvesters had to go farther along the coast to find more. With Thread due to fall anytime, it was unwise to stray too far from the Hold, so they were told to be very careful.

There was another danger that concerned the Sea Holder considerably: tides had been running unusually high and full this Turn. Much higher water in the harbor and they'd not get the two big sloops in or out of the Cavern unless they unstepped the masts. Due notice was taken of the high-tide lines, and there was much shaking of heads when it was observed that the line was two full hands higher than ever before recorded.

The lower caverns of the Hold were checked against possible seepage. Bags of sand were filled and placed along the lower portions of the seawalls around the harbor.

A good storm and the causeways would be awash. Yanus was concerned enough to have a long chat with Old Uncle to see if he remembered anything from his earlier and clearer days of Sea Holding. Old Uncle was delighted to talk and ranted on about the influence of the stars, but when Yanus, Elgion and two of the other older shipmasters had sifted through what he'd said, it was not to any great increase in knowledge. Everyone knew that the two moons affected the tides, not the three bright stars in the sky.

They did, however, send a message about these curious tides to Igen Hold to be forwarded with all possible speed to the main Seacraft Hold at Fort. Yanus didn't want to have his biggest boats caught out in the open, so he kept careful check on the tides, determined to leave them within the Dock Cavern if the tide rose another hand higher.

When the youngsters went out to gather spiderclaws, they were told to keep their eyes open and report back anything unusual, especially new high-water marks on the coves. Only Thread deterred the more adventurous lads from using this as an excuse for ranging far down the coast. Menolly, who preferred to explore the more distant places alone, mentioned Thread to them as often as possible.

Then, after the next Threadfall, when everyone was sent out for spiderclaws, Menolly made certain that she got a headstart on the boys, making good use of her long legs.

It was fine to run like this, Menolly thought, putting yet another rise between her and her nearest pursuers. She altered her stride for uneven ground. It wouldn't do to break an ankle now. Running was something even a girl with a crippled hand could do well.

Menolly closed her mind to that thought. She'd learned the trick of not thinking about anything: she counted. Right now she counted her strides. She ran on, her eyes sweeping ahead of her to save her feet. The boys would never catch her now, but she was running for the sheer joy of the physical effort, chanting a number to each stride. She ran until she got a stitch in her side and her thighs felt the strain.

She slowed, turning her face into the cool breeze blowing offshore, inhaling deeply of its freshness and sea odors. She was somewhat surprised to see how far she had come down the coast. The Dragon Stones were visible in the clear air, and it was only then that she recalled the little queen. Unfortunately, she also remembered the tune she'd made up that day: the last day, Menolly now realized, of her trusting childhood.

She walked on, following the line of the bluffs, peering down to see if she could spot new high-water marks on the stone escarpments. Tide was halfway in now, Menolly decided. And yes, she could see the lines of sea debris from the last tide, in some places right up against the cliff face. And this had been a cove with a deep beach.

A movement above, a sudden blotting of the sun, made her gaze upward. A sweep rider. Knowing perfectly well that he couldn't see her, she waved vigorously anyhow, watching the graceful glide as the pair dwindled into the distance.

Sella had told her one evening when they were preparing for bed that Elgion had flown on dragons several times. Sella had given a quiver of delighted terror, vowing that she wouldn't have the courage to ride a dragon.

Privately Menolly thought that Sella wouldn't likely have the opportunity. Most of Sella's comments, and probably thoughts, were centered on the new Harper. Sella was not the only one, Menolly knew. If Menolly could think how silly all the Hold girls were being about Harper Elgion, it didn't hurt so much to think about harpers in general.

Again she heard the fire lizards before she saw them. Their excited chirpings and squeals indicated something was upsetting them. She dropped to a crouch and crept to the edge of the bluff, overlooking the little beach. Only there wasn't much beach left, and the fire lizards were hovering over a spot on the small margin of sand, almost directly below her.

She inched up to the edge, peering down. She could see the queen darting at the incoming waves as if she could stop them with her violently beating wings. Then she'd streak back, out of Menolly's line of sight, while the rest of the creatures kept milling and swooping, rather like frightened herdbeasts running about aimlessly when wild wherries circled their herd. The queen was shrieking at the top of her shrill little voice, obviously trying to get them to do something. Unable to imagine what the emergency could be, Menolly leaned just a little farther over the edge. The whole lip of the cliff gave way.

Clutching wildly at sea grasses, Menolly tried to prevent her fall. But the sea grass slipped cuttingly through her hand and she slid over the edge and down. She hit the beach with a force that sent a shock through her body. But the wet sand absorbed a good deal of the impact. She lay where she'd fallen for a few minutes, trying to get her breath into her lungs and out again. Then she scrambled to her feet and crawled away from an incoming wave.

She looked up the side of the bluff, rather daunted by the fact that she'd fallen a dragon length or more. And how was she going to climb back up? But, as she examined the cliff face, she could see that it was not so unscalable as she'd first thought. Almost straight up, yes, but pocked by ledges and holds, some fairly large. If she could find enough foot and hand holds, she'd be able to make it. She dusted the sand from her hands and started to walk toward one end of the little cove, to begin a systematic search for the easiest way up.

She'd gone only a few paces when something dove at her, screeching in fury. Her hands went up to protect her face as the little queen came diving down at her. Now Menolly recalled the curious behavior of the fire lizards. The little queen acted as if she were protecting something from Menolly as well as the encroaching sea, and she looked about her. She was within handspans of stepping into a fire lizard clutch.

"Oh, I'm sorry. I'm sorry. I wasn't looking! Don't be mad at me," Menolly cried as the little fire lizard came at her again. "Please! Stop! I won't hurt them!"

To prove her sincerity, Menolly backtracked to the far end of the beach. There she had to duck under a small overhang. When she looked around, there wasn't a sign of the little queen. Menolly's relief was short-lived, for how was she to find a way up the cliff if the little firelizard kept attacking her every time she approached the eggs. Menolly hunched down, trying to get comfortable in her cramped refuge.

Maybe if she kept away from the eggs? Menolly peered up the cliff directly above her. There were some likely looking holds. She eased herself out the far side, keeping one eye on the clutch, basking in the hot sun, and reached for the first ledge.

Immediately the fire lizard came at her.

"Oh, leave me alone! Ow! Go away. I'm trying to."

The fire lizard's talons had raked her cheek.

"Please! I won't hurt your eggs!"

The little queen's next pass just missed Menolly, who ducked back under the ledge.

Blood oozed from the long scratch, and Menolly dabbed at it with the edge of her tunic.

"Haven't you got any sense?" Menolly demanded of her now invisible attacker. "What would I want with your silly eggs? Keep 'em. I just want to get home. Can't you understand? I just want to go home."

Maybe if I sit very still, she'll forget about me, Menolly thought and pulled her knees up under the chin, but her toes and elbows protruded from under the overhang.

Suddenly a bronze fire lizard materialized above the clutch, squeaking worriedly. Menolly saw the queen swooping to join him, so the queen must have been on the top of the ledge, waiting, just waiting for Menolly to break cover.

And to think I made up a pretty tune about you, Menolly thought as she watched the two lizards hovering over the eggs. The last tune I ever made up. You're ungrateful, that's what you are!

Despite her discomfort, Menolly had to laugh. What an impossible situation! Held under a cramped ledge by a creature no bigger than her forearm.

At the sound of her laughter, the two fire lizards disappeared. Frightened, were they? Of laughter?

"A smile wins more than a frown," Mavi was fond of saying.

Maybe if I keep laughing, they'll know I'm friendly? Or get scared away long enough for me to climb up? Saved by a laugh?

Menolly began to chuckle in earnest, for she had also seen

that the tide was coming in rather quickly. She eased out of her shelter, flung the carry-sack over her shoulder, and started to climb. But it proved impossible to chuckle and climb. She needed breath for both.

Abruptly both the little queen and the bronze were back to harry her, flying at her head and face. The fragile-looking wings were dangerous when used as a weapon.

No longer laughing, Menolly ducked back under her ledge, wondering what to do next.

If laughter had startled them, what about a song? Maybe if she gave that pair a chorus of her tune, they'd let her go. It was the first time she'd sung since she'd seen the lizards, so her voice sounded rough and uncertain. Well, the lizards would *know* what she meant, she hoped, so she sang the saucy little song. To no one.

"Well, so much for that notion," Menolly muttered under her breath. "Which makes the lack of interest in your singing absolutely unanimous."

No audience? Not a fire lizard's whisker in sight?

As fast as she could, Menolly slipped from her shelter and came face to face, for a split second, with two fire lizard faces. She ducked down, and they evidently disappeared because when she cautiously peered again, the ledge where they'd been perched was empty.

She had the distinct impression that their expressions had registered curiosity and interest.

"Look, if wherever you are, you can hear me . . . will you stay there and let me go? Once I'm on the top of the cliff, I'll serenade you till the sun goes down. Just let me get up there!"

She started to sing, a dutiful dragon song as she once again emerged from her refuge. She was about five steps upward when the queen fire lizard emerged, with help. With squeaks and squeals she was driven back down. She could even hear claws scraping on the rock above her. She must have quite an audience by now. When she didn't need one!

Cautiously she looked up, met the fascinated whirling of ten pairs of eyes.

"Look, a bargain! One long song and then let me up the cliff? Is that agreed?"

Fire lizard's eyes whirled.

Menolly took it that the bargain was made and sang. Her voice started a flutter of surprised and excited chirpings, and she wondered if by any possible freak they actually understood that she was singing about grateful holds honoring dragon-riders. By the last verse she eased out into the open, awed by the sight of a queen fire lizard and nine bronzes entranced by her performance.

"Can I go now?" she asked and put one hand on the ledge.

The queen dived for her hand, and Menolly snatched it back.

"I thought we'd struck a bargain."

The queen chirped piteously, and Menolly realized that there had been no menace in the queen's action. She simply wasn't allowed to climb.

"You don't want me to go?" Menolly asked.

The queen's eyes seemed to glow more brightly.

"But I have to go. If I stay, the water will come up and drown me." And Menolly accompanied her words with explanatory gestures.

Suddenly the queen let out a shrill cry, seemed to hold her-self midair for a moment and then, her bronzes in close pursuit, she glided down the sandy beach to her clutch. She hovered over the eggs, making the most urgent and excited sounds.

If the tide was coming in fast enough to endanger Menolly, it was also frighteningly close to swamping the nest. The little bronzes began to take up the queen's plaint and several, greatly daring, flew about Menolly's head and then circled back to the clutch.

"I can come there now? You won't attack me?" Menolly took a few steps forward.

The tone of the cries changed, and Menolly quickened her step. As she reached the nest, the little queen secured one egg from the clutch. With a great laboring of her wings, she bore it upward. That the effort was great was obvious. The bronzes hovered anxiously, squeaking their concern but, being much smaller, they were unable to assist the queen.

Now Menolly saw that the base of the cliff at this point was littered with broken shells and the pitiful bodies of tiny fire lizards, their wings half-extended and glistening with egg fluid. The little queen now had raised the egg to a ledge, which Menolly had not previously noticed, about a half-dragon length up the cliff-face. Menolly could see the little queen deposit the egg on the ledge and roll it with her forelegs toward what must be a hole in the cliff. It was a long moment before the queen reappeared again. Then she dove toward the sea, hovering over the foamy crest of a wave that rolled in precariously close to the endangered clutch. With a blurred movement, the queen was hovering in front of Menolly and scolding like an old aunt.

Although Menolly couldn't help grinning at the thought, she was filled with a sense of pity and admiration for the courage of the little queen, single-handedly trying to rescue her clutch. If the dead fire lizards were that fully formed, the clutch was near to hatching. No wonder the queen could barely move the eggs.

"You want me to help you move the eggs, right? Well, we'll see what I can do!"

Ready to jump back if she had mistaken the little queen's imperious command, Menolly very carefully picked up an egg. It was warm to the touch and hard. Dragon eggs, she knew, were soft when first laid but hardened slowly on the hot sands of the Hatching Grounds in the Weyrs. These definitely must be close to hatching.

Closing the fingers of her damaged hand carefully around the egg, Menolly searched for and found foot and hand holds, and reached the queen's ledge. She carefully deposited the egg. The little queen appeared, one front talon resting proprietarily on the egg, and then she leaned forward, toward Menolly's face, so close that the fantastic motion of the many-faceted eyes were clearly visible. The queen gave a sort of sweet chirp and then, in a very businesslike manner, began to scold Menolly as she rolled her egg to safety.

Menolly managed three eggs in her hand the next time. But it was obvious that between the onrushing tide and the startling number of eggs in the clutch, there'd be quite a race.

"If the hole were bigger," she told the little queen as she deposited three eggs, "some of the bronzes could help you roll."

The queen paid her no attention, busy pushing the three eggs, one at a time, to safety.

Menolly peered into the opening, but the fire lizard's body obscured any view. If the hole was bigger and the ledge consequently broader, Menolly could bring the rest of the eggs up in her carry-sack.

Hoping that she wouldn't pull down the cliffside and bury the queen, clutch and all, Menolly prodded cautiously at the mouth of the opening. Loose sand came showering down.

The queen took to scolding frantically as Menolly brushed the rubble from the ledge. Then she felt around the opening. There seemed to be solid stone just beyond. Menolly yanked away at the looser rock, until she had a nice tunnel exposed with a slightly wider opening.

Ignoring the little queen's furious complaints, Menolly climbed down, unslinging her sack when she reached the ground. When the little queen saw Menolly putting the eggs in the sack, she began to have hysterics, beating at Menolly's head and hands.

"Now, look here," Menolly said sternly, "I am not stealing your eggs. I am trying to get them all to safety in jig time. I can do it with the sack but not by the handful."

Menolly waited a moment, glaring at the little queen who hovered at eye level.

"Did you understand me?" Menolly pointed to the waves, more vigorously dashing up the small beach. "The tide is coming in. Dragons couldn't stop it now." Menolly put another egg carefully in the sack. As it was she'd have to make two, maybe three trips or risk breaking the eggs. "I take this," and she gestured up the ledge, "up there. Do you understand, you silly beast?"

Evidently, the little creature did because, crooning anxiously, she took her position on the ledge, her wings half-extended and twitching as she watched Menolly's progress up to her.

Menolly could climb faster with two hands. And she could, carefully, roll the eggs from the mouth of the sack well down the tunnelway.

"You'd better get the bronzes to help you now, or we'll have the ledge stacked too high."

It took Menolly three trips in all, and as she made the last climb, the water was a foot's width from the clutch. The little queen had organized her bronzes to help, and Menolly could hear her scolding tones echoing in what must be a fair-sized cave beyond the tunnel. Not surprising since these bluffs were supposed to be riddled with caverns and passages.

Menolly gave a last look at the beach, water at least ankle deep on both ends of the little cove. She glanced upward, past the ledge. She was a good halfway up the cliff now, and she thought she could see enough hand and foot holds ahead.

"Good-bye!" She was answered by a trill of chirps, and she chuckled as she imagined the scene: the queen marshaling her bronzes to position her eggs just right.

Menolly did not make the cliff top without a few anxious moments. She was exhausted when she finally flopped on the sea grasses at the summit, and her left hand ached from unaccustomed gripping and effort. She lay there for some time, until her heart stopped thudding in her ribs and her breath came more easily. An inshore breeze dried her face, cooling her; but that reminded her of the emptiness of her stomach. Her exertions had reduced the rolls in her pouch to crumby fragments, which she gobbled as fast as she could find them.

All at once the enormity of her adventure struck her, and she was torn between laughter and awe. To prove to herself that she'd actually done what she remembered, she crept cautiously to the bluff edge. The beach was completely underwater. The sandy wallow where the fire lizard eggs had baked was being tideswept smooth. The rubble that had gone over the edge with her had been absorbed or washed away. When the tide retreated, all evidence of her energies to save herself and the clutch would be obliterated. She could see the protuberance of rock down which the queen had rolled her eggs but not a sign of a fire lizard. The waves crashed with firm intent against the Dragon Stones when she gazed out to sea, but no bright motes of color flitted against the somber crags.

Menolly felt her cheek. The fire lizard's scratch was crusted with dried blood and sand.

"So it did happen!"

However did the little queen know I could help her? No one had ever suggested that fire lizards were stupid. Certainly they'd been smart enough for endless Turns to evade every trap and snare laid to catch them. The creatures were so clever, indeed, that there was a good deal of doubt about their existence, except as figures of overactive imaginations. However, enough trustworthy men had actually seen the creatures, at a distance, like her brother Alemi when he'd spotted some about the Dragon Stones, that most people did accept their existence as fact.

Menolly could have sworn that the little queen had understood her. How else could Menolly have helped her? That proved how smart the little beast was. Smart enough certainly to avoid the boys who tried to capture them . . . Menolly was appalled. Capture a fire lizard? Pen it up? Not, Menolly supposed with relief, that the creature would stay caught long. It only had to pop *between*.

Now why hadn't the little queen just gone *between* with her eggs, instead of arduously transporting them one by one? Oh, yes, *between* was the coldest place known. And cold would do the eggs harm. At least it did dragon eggs harm. Would the clutch be all right now in the cold cavern? Hmmm. Menolly peered below. Well, if the queen had as much sense as she'd already shown, she'd get all her followers to come lie on the eggs and keep them warm until they did hatch.

Menolly turned her pouch inside out, hoping for some crumbs. She was still hungry. She'd find enough early fruits and some of the succulent reeds to eat, but she was curiously loath to leave the bluff. Though, it was unlikely that the queen, now her need was past, would reappear.

Menolly rose finally and found herself stiff from the unaccustomed exercise. Her hand ached in a dull way, and the long scar was red and slightly swollen. But, as Menolly flexed her fingers, it seemed that the hand opened more easily. Yes, it did. She could almost extend the fingers completely. It hurt, but it was a stretchy-hurt. Could she open her hand enough to play again? She folded her fingers as if to chord. That hurt, but again, it was a stretchy-hurt. Maybe if she worked her hand a lot more . . . She had been favoring it until today when she hadn't given it a thought. She'd used it to climb and carry and everything.

"Well, you did me a favor, too, little queen," Menolly called, speaking into the breeze and waving her hands high. "See? My hand is better."

There was no answering chirp or sound, but the soft whistle of the seaborne breeze and the lapping of the waves against the bluff. Yet Menolly liked to think that her words had been heard. She turned inland, feeling considerably relieved and rather pleased with the morning's work.

She'd have to scoot now and gather what she could of greens and early berries. No point in trying for spiderclaws with the tide so high.

CHAPTER 5

Oh, Tongue, give sound to joy and sing
Of hope and promise on dragonwing.

No one, as usual, noticed Menolly when she got back to the Hold. Dutifully she saw the harbormaster and told him about the tides.

"Don't you go so far, girl," he told her kindly. "Thread's due any day now, you know. How's the hand?"

She mumbled something, which he didn't hear anyway, as a shipmaster shouted for his attention.

The evening meal was hurried since all the masters were going off to the Dock Cavern to check tide, masts and ships. In the bustle Menolly could keep to herself.

And she did—seeking the cubicle and the safety of her bed as soon as possible. There she hugged to herself the incredible experience of the morning. She was certain that the queen had understood her. Just like the dragons, fire lizards knew what was in the mind and heart of a person. That's why they disappeared so easily when boys tried to trap them. They'd liked her singing, too.

Menolly gave herself a squeeze, ignoring the spasm of pain in her now stiff hand. Then she tensed, remembering that the bronzes had been waiting to see what the queen would do. She was the clever one, the audacious one. What was it Petiron was always quoting? "Necessity breeds solution."

Did fire lizards really understand people, even when they kept away from them, then, Menolly puzzled again. Of course, dragons understood what their riders were thinking, but dragons Impressed at Hatching to their riders. The link was never broken, and the dragon would only hear that one person, or so Petiron had said. So *how* had the little queen understood her?

"Necessity?"

Poor queen! She must have been frantic when she realized that the tide was going to cover her eggs! Probably she'd been depositing her clutches in that cove for who knows how long? How long did fire lizards live? Dragons lasted the life of their rider. Sometimes that wasn't so long, now that Thread was dropping. Quite a few riders had been so badly scored they'd died and so had their dragons. Would the little fire lizards have a longer life, being smaller and not in so much danger? Questions darted through Menolly's mind, like fire lizards' flashing, she thought, as she cuddled into the warmth of her sleeping fur. She'd try to go back tomorrow, maybe, with food. She rather thought fire lizards would like spiderclaws, too, and maybe then she'd get the queen's trust. Or maybe it would be better if she didn't go back tomorrow? She should stay away for a few days. Then, too, with Thread falling so often, it was dangerous to go so far from the safety of the Hold.

What would happen when the fire lizard eggs hatched? What a sight that would be! Ha! All the lads in the Sea Hold talking about catching fire lizards and she, Menolly, had not only seen but talked to them and handled their eggs! And if she were lucky, she might even see them hatching, too. Why, that would be as marvelous as going to a dragon Hatching at one of the Weyrs! And no one, not even Yanus, had been to a Hatching!

Considering her exciting thoughts, it was a wonder that Menolly was able to sleep.

The next morning her hand ached and throbbed, and she was stiff from the fall and the climbing. Her half-formed notion of going back to the Dragon Stones' cove was thwarted by the weather, of all things. A storm had blown in from the sea that night, lashing the harbor with pounding waves. Even the Dock Cavern waters were turbulent, and a wind whipped with such whimsical force that walking from Hold to Cavern was dangerous.

The men gathered in the Great Hall in the morning, mending gear and yarning. Mavi organized her women for an exhaustive cleaning of some of the inner Hold rooms. Menolly and Sella were sent down to the glow storage so often that Sella vowed she didn't need light to show her the way anymore.

Menolly worked willingly enough, checking glows in every single room in the Hold. It was better to work than to think. That evening she couldn't escape the Great Hall. Since everyone had been in all day, everyone needed entertainment and was going. The Harper would surely play. Menolly shuddered. Well, there was no help for it. She had to hear music sometime. She couldn't avoid it forever. And at least she could sing along with the others. But she soon found she couldn't even have that pleasure. Mavi gestured to her when the Harper began to tune his gitar. And when the Harper beckoned for everyone to join in the choruses, Mavi pinched Menolly so hard that she gasped.

"Don't roar. You may sing softly as befits a girl your age," Mavi said. "Or don't sing at all."

Across the Hall, Sella was singing, not at all accurately and loud enough to be heard in Benden Hold; but when Menolly opened her mouth to protest, she got another pinch.

So she didn't sing at all but sat there by her mother's side, numb and hurt, not even able to enjoy the music and very conscious that her mother was being monstrously unfair.

Wasn't it bad enough she couldn't play anymore—yet—but not to be allowed to sing? Why, everyone had encouraged her to sing when old Petiron had been alive. And been glad to hear her. Asked her to sing, time and again.

Then Menolly saw her father watching her, his face stern, one hand tapping not so much to the time of the music but to some inner agitation. It was her father who didn't want her to sing! It wasn't fair! It just wasn't fair! Obviously they knew and were glad she hadn't come before. They didn't want her here.

She wrenched herself free from her mother's grip and, ignoring Mavi's hiss to come back and behave herself, she crept from the Hall. Those who saw her leave thought sadly that it was such a pity she'd hurt her hand and didn't even want to sing anymore.

Wanted or not, creeping out like that would send Mavi looking for her when there was a pause in the evening's singing. So Menolly took her sleeping furs and a glow and went to one of the unused inner rooms where no one would find her. She brought her clothes, too. If the storm cleared, she'd be away in the morning to the fire lizards. *They* liked her singing. They liked *her*!

Before anyone else was up, she had risen. She gulped down a cold klah and ate some bread, stuffed more in her pouch and was almost away. Her heart beat fast while she struggled with the big metal doors of the Hold entrance. She'd never opened them before and hadn't appreciated how very solid they were. She couldn't, of course, bar them again, but there was scarcely any need.

Sea mist was curling up from the quiet harbor waters, the entrances to the dock Cavern visible as darker masses in the gray. But the sun was beginning to burn through the fog, and Menolly's weather-sense told her that it would soon be clear.

As she strode down the broad holdway, mist swirled up and away from her steps. It pleased Menolly to see something give way before her, even something as nebulous as fog. Visibility was limited, but she knew her path by the shape of the stones along the road and was soon climbing through the caressing mists to the bluff.

She struck somewhat inland, toward the first of the marshes. One cup of klah and a hunk of bread was not enough food, and she remembered some unstripped marshberry bushes. She was over the first humpy hill and suddenly the mist had left the land, the brightness of the spring sun almost an ache to the eyes.

She found her patch of marshberry and picked one handful for her face, then one for the pouch.

Now that she could see where she was going, she jogged down the coast and finally dropped into a cove. The tide was just right to catch spiderclaws. These should be a pleasant offering to the fire lizard queen she thought as she filled her bag. Or could fire lizards hunt in fog?

When Menolly had carried her loaded sack through several long valleys and over humpy hills, she was beginning to wish she'd waited a while to do her netting. She was hot and tired. Now that the excitement of her unorthodox behavior had waned, she was also depressed. Of course, it was quite likely that no one had noticed she'd left. No one would realize it was she who had left the Hold doors unbarred, a terrible offense against the Hold safety rules. Menolly wasn't sure why—because who'd want to enter the Sea Hold unless he had business there? Come all that dangerous way across the marshes? For what? There were quite a few precautions scrupulously observed in the Sea Hold that didn't make much sense to Menolly: like the Hold doors being barred every night, and unshielded glows never being left in an unused room, although it was all right in corridors. Glows wouldn't burn anything, and think of all the barked shins that would be saved by leaving a few room glows unshielded.

No, no one was likely to notice that she was gone until there was some unpleasant or tedious job for a one-handed girl to do. So they wouldn't assume that *she'd* opened the Hold door. And since Menolly was apt to disappear during the day, no one would think anything about her until evening. Then someone might just wonder where Menolly was.

That was when she realized that she didn't plan to return to the Hold. And the sheer audacity of that thought was enough to make her halt in her tracks. Not return to the Hold? Not go back to the endless round of tedious tasks? Of gutting, smoking, salting, pickling fish? Mending nets, sails, clothes? Cleaning dishes, clothes, rooms? Gathering greens, berries, grasses, spider-claws? Not return to tend old uncles and aunts, fires, pots, looms, glowbaskets? To be able to sing or shout or roar or play if she so chose? To sleep . . . ah, now where would she sleep? And where would she go when there was Thread in the skies?

Menolly trudged on more slowly up the sand dunes; her mind churning with these revolutionary ideas. Why, everyone had to return to the Hold at night! The Hold, any hold or cot or weyr. Seven Turns had Thread been dropping from the skies, and no one traveled far from shelter. She remembered vaguely from her child-hood that there used to be caravans of traders coming through the marshlands in the spring and the summer and early fall. There'd been gay times, with lots of singing and feasting. The Hold doors had not been barred then. She sighed, those had been happier times . . . the good old days that Old Uncle and the aunties were always droning on about. But once Thread started falling, everything had changed . . . for the worse . . . at least that was the overall impression she had from the adults in the Hold.

Some stillness in the air, some vague unease caused Menolly to glance about her apprehensively. There was certainly no one else about at this early hour. She scanned the skies. The mist banking the coast was rapidly dispersing. She could see it retreating across the water to the north and west. Toward the east the sky was brilliant with sunrise, except for what were probably some traces of early morning fog in the northeast. Yet something disturbed Menolly. She felt she should know what it was.

She was nearly to the Dragonsong Stones now, in the last marsh before the contour of the land swept gently up toward the seaside bluff. It was as she traversed the marsh that she identified the odd quality: it was the stillness. Not of wind, for that was steady seaward, blowing away the fog, but a stillness of marsh life. All the little insects and flies and small wrigglers, the occasional flights of wild wherries who nested in the heavier bushes were silent. Their myriad activities and small noises began as soon as the sun was up and didn't cease until just before dawn, because the nocturnal insects were as noisy as the daytime ones.

It was this quiet, as if every living thing was holding its breath, that was disturbing Menolly. Unconsciously she began to walk faster and she had a strong urge to glance over her right shoulder, toward the northeast—where a smudge of gray clouded the horizon . . .

A smudge of gray? Or silver?

Menolly began to tremble with rising fear, with the dawning knowledge that she was too far from the safety of the Hold to reach it before Thread reached her. The heavy metal doors, which she had so negligently left ajar, would soon be closed and barred against her, and Thread. And, even if she were missed, no one would come for her.

She began to run, and some instinct directed her toward the cliff edge before she consciously remembered the queen's ledge. It wasn't big enough, really. Or she could go into the sea? Thread drowned in the sea. So would she, for she couldn't keep under the water for the time it would take Thread to pass. How long would it take the leading edge of a Fall to pass over? She'd no idea.

She was at the edge now, looking down at the beach. She could see her ledge off to the right. There was the lip of the cliff that had broken off under her weight. That was the quick way down, to be sure, but she couldn't risk it again, and didn't want to.

She glanced over her shoulder. The grayness was spreading across the horizon. Now she could see flashes against that gray. Flashes? Dragons! She was seeing dragons fighting Thread, their fiery breath charring the dreaded stuff midair. They were so far away that the winking lights were more like lost stars than dragons fighting for the life of Pern.

Maybe the leading edge wouldn't reach this far? Maybe she was safe. "Maybes seldom are" as her mother would say.

In the stillness of the air, a new sound made itself heard: a soft rhythmic thrumming, something like the tuneless humming of small children. Only different. The noise seemed to come from the ground.

She dropped, pressing one ear to a patch of bare stone. The sound was coming from within.

Of course! The bluff was hollow . . . that's why the queen lizard . . .

On hands and knees, Menolly scooted to the cliff edge, looking for that halfway ledge of the queen's.

Menolly had enlarged the entry once. There was every chance she could make it big enough to squirm through. The little queen would certainly be hospitable to someone who had saved her clutch!

And Menolly didn't come empty-handed as a guest! She swung the heavy sack of spiderclaws around to her back. Grabbing handfuls of the grasses on the lip of the cliff, she began to let herself slowly down. Her feet fumbled for support; she found one toehold and dug half that foot in, the other foot prodding for another place.

She slithered badly once, but a rock protrusion caught her in the crotch before she'd slipped far. She laid her face against the cliff, gulping to get back her breath and courage. She could feel the thrumming through the stone, and oddly, that gave her heart. There was something intensely exciting and stimulating about that sound.

Sheer luck guided her foot to the queen's ledge. She'd risked only a few glances beneath her—the aspect was almost enough to make her lose her balance completely. She was trembling so much with her exertions that she had to rest then. Definitely the humming came from the queen's cavern.

She could get her head into the original opening. No more. She began to tear at the sides with her bare hands until she thought of her belt knife. The blade loosened a whole section all at once, showering her with sand and bits of rock. She had to clean her eyes and mouth of grit before she could continue. Then she realized that she'd gotten to sheer rock.

She could get herself into the shelter only up to her shoulders. No matter how she turned and twisted, there was an outcropping that she could not pass. Once again she wished she were as small as a girl ought to be. Sella would have had no trouble crawling through that hole. Resolutely, Menolly began to chip at the rock with her knife, the blows jarring her hand to the shoulder, and making no impression at all on the rock.

She wondered frantically how long it had taken her to get down the cliff. How long did she have before Thread would be raining down on her unprotected body?

Body? She might not get past the bobble in the wall with her shoulders . . . but . . . She reversed her position, and feet, legs, hips, all right up to the shoulders passed into the safety of solid rock. Her head was covered, but only just, by the cliff overhang.

Did Thread *see* where it was going when it fell? Would it notice her, crowded into this hole as it flashed by? Then she saw the thong of the carry-sack where she'd looped it over the ledge to keep it handy but out of her way. If Thread got into the spiderclaws . . .

She pulled herself far enough out of the hole to cast an eye above. No silver yet! No sound but the steadily increasing thrumming. That wouldn't have anything to do with Thread, would it?

The carry-sack thong had bitten into the ledge and she had a job freeing it, having to yank rather hard. The next thing she knew the sack came free, the force of her pull threw her backward, cracking her head on the roof of her tunnel, and then the surface beneath her buttocks started to slide, out and down. Menolly clawed her way into the tunnel, as the ledge slowly detached itself from the face of the cliff and tumbled down onto the beach.

Menolly scrambled back quickly, afraid more of the entrance would go, and suddenly she was in a cave, wide, high, deep, clutching the carry-sack and staring at the greatly widened mouth.

The thrumming was behind her and, startled at what she could only consider to be an additional threat, she whirled.

Fire lizards were perched around the walls, clinging to rock spur and ledge. Every eye glinted at the mound of eggs in the sandy center of the cave. The thrumming came from the throats of all the little fire lizards, and they were far too intent on what was happening to the eggs to give any heed to her abrupt appearance.

Just as Menolly realized that she was witnessing a Hatching, the first egg began to rock and cracks appeared in its shell.

It rocked itself off the mound of the clutch and, in hitting the ground, split. From the two parts emerged a tiny creature, not much bigger than Menolly's hand, glistening brown and creeling with hunger, swaying its head back and forth and tottering forward a few awkward steps. The transparent brown wings unfolded, flapping weakly to dry, and the creature's balance improved. The creel turned to a hiss of displeasure, and the little brown peered about defensively.

The other fire lizards crooned, encouraging it to some action. With a tiny shriek of anger, the little brown launched itself toward the cave opening, passing so close to Menolly she could have touched it.

The brown fire lizard lurched off the eroded lip of the cave, pumping its wings frantically to achieve flight. Menolly gasped as the creature dropped, and then sighed with relief as it came into sight briefly, airborne, and flew off, across the sea.

More creeling brought her attention back to the clutch. Other fire lizards had begun to hatch in that brief period, each one shaking its wings and then, encouraged by the weyrmates, flopping and weaving toward the cave mouth, defiantly independent and hungry.

Several greens and blues, a little bronze and two more browns hatched and passed Menolly. And then, as she watched a little blue launch itself, Menolly screamed. No sooner had the blue emerged from the safety of the cliff than she saw the thin, writhing silver of Thread descending. In a moment, the blue was covered with the deadly filaments. It uttered one hideous shriek and disappeared. Dead? Or *between?* Certainly badly scored.

Two more little fire lizards passed Menolly, and she reacted now.

"No! No! You can't! You'll be killed." She flung herself across their path.

The angry fire lizards pecked at her unprotected face and while she covered herself, made their escape. She cried aloud when she heard their screams.

"Don't let them go!" She pleaded with the watching fire lizards. "You're older. You know about Thread. Tell them to stop!" She half-crawled, half-ran to the rock where the golden queen was perched.

"Tell them not to go! There's Thread out there! They're being killed!"

The queen looked at her, the many-faceted eyes whirling

violently. The queen chuckled and chirped at her, and then crooned as yet another fledgling spread its wings and began to totter toward sure death.

"Please, little queen! Do something! Stop them!"

The thrill of being the witness to a Hatching of fire lizards gave way to horror. Dragons had to be protected because they protected Pern. In Menolly's fear and confusion, the little fire lizards were linked to their giant counterparts.

She turned to the other lizards now, begging them to do something. At least until the Threadfall was over. Desperately she plunged back to the cave mouth and tried to turn the little fire lizards back with her hands, blocking their progress with her body. She was overwhelmed with pangs of hunger, belly-knotting, gut-twisting hunger. It took her only a moment to realize that the driving force in these fire lizards was that sort of hunger: that was what was sending them senselessly forth. They had to eat. She remembered that dragons had to eat, too, when they first Hatched, fed by the boys they Impressed.

Menolly wildly grabbed for her carry-sack. With one hand she snatched a fire lizard back from the entrance, and with the other, a spiderclaw from the sack. The little bronze screeched once and then bit the spiderclaw behind the eye, neatly killing it. Wings beating, the bronze lifted itself free of Menolly's grasp and with more strength than Menolly would have thought the newborn creature could possess flew its prey to a corner and began tearing it apart.

Menolly reached out randomly now and, with some surprise, found herself holding the one queen in the clutch. She snagged two spiderclaws from the sack in her other hand, and deposited them and the queen in another corner. Finally realizing she couldn't handfeed the whole clutch, she upended the sack, spilling the shellfish out.

Newly hatched fire lizards swarmed over and after the spiderclaws. Menolly caught two more lizards before they could reach the cave mouth and put them squarely in the center of their first meal. She was busy trying to make sure that each new fire lizard had a shellfish when she felt something pricking her shoulder. Surprised, she looked up to find the little bronze clinging to her tunic. His round eyes were whirling and he was still hungry. She gave him an unclaimed spiderclaw and put him back in his corner. She tossed the little queen another and snared several other spiderclaws for her "specials."

Not many more of the newly hatched got out, not with a source of food so nearby. She'd had a fair haul in the sack, but it didn't take long for the hungry fire lizards to devour every last morsel. The poor things were still sounding starved as they creeled about, tipping over claws and body shells, trying to find any scraps overlooked. But they stayed in the cave and now the older fire lizards joined them, nuzzling or stroking, making affectionate noises.

Utterly exhausted, Menolly leaned back against the wall, watching their antics. At least they'd not all died. She glanced apprehensively at the entrance and saw no more writhing lengths of Thread falling past. She peered further. There wasn't even a trace of the menacing gray fog on the horizon. Threadfall must be over.

And not a moment too soon. Now she was experiencing hunger thoughts from all the fire lizards. Rather overpoweringly, in fact. Because she realized how hungry she herself was.

The little queen, the old queen, began to hover in the cave, squeaking an imperious command to her followers. Then she darted out and the old clutch began to follow her. The fledglings, moving awkwardly, made their virgin flight, and within moments, the cave was empty of all but Menolly, her torn sack, and a pile of empty spiderclaw and fire lizard shells.

With their exit, some of Menolly's hunger eased and she remembered the bread she'd tucked in her pocket. Feeling a bit guilty at this belated discovery, she gratefully ate every crumb.

Then she made herself a hollow in the sand, pulled the torn carry-sack over her shoulders, and went to sleep.

CHAPTER 6

Lord of the Hold, your charge is sure
In thick walls, metal doors, and no verdure.

Threadfall was well past, the flame-thrower crews safely back in Half-Circle Hold before anyone missed Menolly. Sella did because she didn't want to have to tend Old Uncle. He had had another seizure, and someone had to stay by his bedside.

"That's about all she's good for now anyway," Sella told Mavi and then hastily demurred at her mother's stern look. "Well, all she does is drag about, cradling that hand of hers as if it were precious. She gets off all the *real* work . . ." Sella let out a heavy sigh.

"We've enough trouble this morning what with someone leaving the Hold doors unfastened and Thread falling . . ." Mavi shuddered at the thought of that brace of horrors; the mere notion of Thread cascading down, able to wriggle within the Hold, turned her stomach. "Go find Menolly and see that she knows what to do in case the old man has another fit."

It took Sella the better part of an hour to realize that Menolly was neither in the Hold nor among those baiting long-lines. She hadn't been among the flame-thrower crews. In fact, no one could remember having seen or spoken to her all day.

"She couldn't have been out hunting greens like she usually does," said an old auntie thoughtfully, pursing her lips. "Threadfall was on directly we'd our morning klah. Didn't see her in the kitchen then, either. And she's usually so good about helping, one-handed and all that she is, poor dear."

At first Sella was just annoyed. So like Menolly to be absent when needed. Mavi was a good deal too lenient with the child. Well, if she'd not been in the Hold in the morning, she'd been caught out in the Thread. And that served her right.

Then Sella wasn't so sure. She began to feel the first vestige of fright. If Menolly had been out during Threadfall, surely there'd be . . . something . . . left that Thread couldn't eat.

Gulping back nausea at that thought, she sought out her brother, Alemi, who was in charge of the flame-throwers.

"Alemi, you didn't see anything . . . unusual . . . when you were ground checking?"

"What do you mean by 'unusual'?"

"You know, traces . . ."

"Of what? I've no time now for riddles, Sella."

"I mean, if someone were caught out during Threadfall, how would you know?"

"Whatever are you tacking around?"

"Menolly's nowhere in the Hold, or the Dock, or anywhere. She wasn't on any of the teams . . ."

Alemi frowned. "No, she wasn't, but I thought Mavi needed her in the Hold for something."

". . . There! And none of the aunties remember seeing her this morning. *And* the Hold doors were unbarred!"

"You think Menolly left the Hold early?" Alemi realized that a strong, tall girl like Menolly could very easily have managed the door bars.

"You know how she's been since she hurt her hand: creeping away every chance she gets."

Alemi did know, for he was fond of his gawky sister, and he particularly missed her singing. He didn't share Yanus's reservations about Menolly's ability. And he didn't honestly agree with Yanus's decision to keep knowledge of it from the Harper, especially now that there was a Harper in the Hold to keep her in line.

"Well?" Sella's prompting irritated him out of his thoughts.

"I saw nothing unusual."

"Would there *be* something? If Thread did get her?"

Alemi gave Sella a long hard look. She sounded as if she'd be glad if Menolly did get Threaded.

"There'd be nothing left if she'd been caught by Thread. But no Thread got through the Benden wings."

With that he turned on his heel and left his sister, mouth agape. His reassurance was curiously no consolation to Sella. However, since Menolly was so obviously missing, Sella could take some pleasure in informing Mavi of this fact, adding her theory that Menolly had committed the enormous crime of leaving the Hold doors unbarred.

"Menolly?" Mavi was handing out sea salt and spiceroot to the head cook when Sella imparted her news. "Menolly?"

"Yes, Menolly. She's gone. Not been seen, and she's the one left the Hold doors unbarred. With Thread falling!"

"Thread wasn't falling when Yanus discovered the doors open." Mavi corrected Sella mechanically. She shuddered at the thought of anyone, even a recalcitrant daughter, caught out in the silvery rain of Thread.

"Alemi said no Thread got through the dragons, but how can he be sure?"

Mavi said nothing as she locked up the condiment press and

spun the rollers. "I'll inform Yanus. And I'll have a word with Alemi, too. You'd better take care of Old Uncle."

"Me?"

"Not that that's real work, but it is suited to your temperament and ability."

Yanus was silent for a long moment when he heard of Menolly's disappearance. He didn't like untoward things happening, such as the Hold doors being left unbarred. He'd worried about that all during the Fall and the fishing after the Fall. It wasn't good for a Sea Holder to have his mind diverted from the task at hand. He felt some relief that the mystery had been solved, and a keen annoyance and anxiety about the girl. Foolish thing for her to have done—leave the Hold that early. She'd been sulking ever since that beating. Mavi hadn't kept her busy enough to make her forget the nonsense of tuning.

"I've heard that there're plenty of caves in the cliffs along the coast," Elgion said. "The girl probably took shelter in one."

"She probably did," said Mavi briskly, grateful to the Harper for such a sensible suggestion. "Menolly knows the coast very well. She must know every crevice by now."

"She'll be back then," Yanus said. "Give her time to get over the fright of being out during Threadfall. She'll be back." Yanus found relief in this theory and turned to less distressing business.

"It *is* spring," said Mavi, more to herself than to the others. Only the Harper caught the anxious note in her voice.

Two days later Menolly had not returned, and the entire Sea Hold was alerted to her disappearance. No one remembered seeing her on the day of Threadfall. No one had seen her since. Children sent out for berries or spiderclaws had encountered no trace of her, nor had she been in any of the caves they knew.

"Not much point in sending out a search," said one of the shipmasters, mindful that there was more surety of catching fish than finding any trace of a foolish girl. Particularly one with a crippled hand. "Either she's safe and doesn't choose to come back, or . . ."

"She could be hurt . . . Threadscored, a broken leg or arm . . ." said Alemi, "unable to make her way back."

"Shouldn't've been out anyway without letting someone know where she'd gone." The shipmaster's eyes moved toward Mavi, who did not catch this implied negligence on her part.

"She was used to going out for greens first thing in the morning," Alemi said. If no one else would defend Menolly, he would speak up.

"Did she carry a belt knife? Or a metal buckle?" asked Elgion. "Thread doesn't touch metal."

"Aye. We'd find that much of her," said Yanus.

"If Thread got her," said the shipmaster darkly. He rather favored the notion that she'd fallen into a crevice or over the edge of the bluff, in terror at finding herself out during Threadfall. "Her body'd wash up around the Dragon Stones. Current throws up a lot of sea trash down that way."

Mavi caught her breath in a sound very like a sob.

"I don't know the girl," Elgion said quickly, seeing Mavi's distress. "But if she did, as you say, stay out a good deal of the time, she'd know the land too well to go over the edge of a cliff."

"Threadfall's enough to rattle anyone's wits . . ." said the ship-master.

"Menolly is not stupid," said Alemi with such feeling that everyone looked at him in surprise. "And she knew her Teaching well enough to know what to do if she were caught out."

"Right enough, Alemi," said Yanus sharply and rose to his feet. "If she were able and of a mind to return, she'd have done so. Everyone who is abroad is to keep a sharp eye for any trace of her. That includes sea as well as land. As Sea Holder, I cannot in conscience do more than that, under the circumstances. And the tide is making. To the boats now."

While Elgion did not actually expect the Sea Holder to institute an intensive search for a lost girl, he was surprised at the decision. Mavi, even, accepted it, almost as if she were glad of an excuse, as if the girl were an embarrassment. The shipmaster was obviously pleased by his Sea Holder's impartiality. Only Alemi betrayed resentment. The Harper motioned to the young man to hang back as the others filed out.

"I've some time. Where would you suggest I look?"

Hope flashed in Alemi's eyes, then as suddenly wariness clouded them.

"I'd say it's better if Menolly remains where she is . . ."

"Dead or hurt?"

"Aye." Alemi sighed deeply. "And I wish her luck and long life."

"Then you think she's alive and chooses to be without Hold?"

Alemi regarded the Harper quietly. "I think she's alive and better off wherever she is than she would be in Half-Circle." Then the young Sea Man strode after the others, leaving the Harper with some interesting reflections.

He was not unhappy at Half-Circle Hold. But the Masterharper had been correct in thinking that Elgion would have to make quite a few adjustments to life in this Sea Hold. It would be a challenge, Robinson had told Elgion, to try to broaden the narrow outlook and straitened thinking of the isolated group. At the moment Elgion wondered if the Masterharper had not vastly overrated his abilities when he was unable to get the Sea Holder, or his family, to even try to rescue a blood relation.

Then, shifting through the tones of voices, rather than the words spoken, Elgion came to realize that this Menolly posed some sort of problem to her Hold beyond the crippled hand. For the life of him, Elgion couldn't remember seeing the girl, though he thought he could recognize every member of the Hold. He'd spent considerable time now with every family unit, with the children in the Little Hall, with the active fishermen, with the honorably retired old people.

He tried to recall when he'd seen a girl with an injured hand and had only the fleetingest recollection of a tall, gawky figure hurrying out of the Hall one evening when he'd been playing. He hadn't seen the girl's face, but he'd recall her slumping figure if he saw it again.

It was regrettable that Half-Circle Hold was so isolated that there was no way to send a drum-message. He could signal the next dragonrider he saw, as an alternative, and get word to Benden Weyr. The sweep riders could keep their eyes open for the girl, and alert any Holds beyond the marshes and down the coast. How she could have gotten that far with Thread falling, Elgion didn't know, but he'd feel better taking some measures to find her.

He had also made no headway in discovering the identity of the songmaker. And Masterharper had charged him to have that lad in the Harpercrafthall for training as soon as possible. Gifted songmakers were a rare commodity. Something to be sought and cherished.

By this time Elgion understood why the old Harper had been so cautious about identifying the lad. Yanus thought only of the sea, of fishing, of how to use every man, woman and child of his Sea Hold to the Hold's best advantage. He had them all well-trained. Yanus would certainly have looked askance at any able-bodied lad who spent too much time tuning. There was, in fact, no one to help Elgion with the evening task of entertainment. One likely lad had a fair sense of rhythm, and Elgion had already started him on the drum, but the majority of his students were thick-fingered. Oh, they knew their Teachings, spot-on, but they were passive musically. No wonder Petiron had been so effusive about the one really talented child among so many deadheads. Too bad the old man had died before he received Robinton's message. That way the boy would have known that he was more than acceptable as a candidate to the Harpercrafthall.

Elgion watched the fishing fleet out of the harbor and then rounded up several lads, got meatrolls from an auntie in the Hold kitchen, and set off on, ostensibly, a food gathering mission.

As Harper he was acquainted with them; but mindful that he was the Harper, the boys regarded him with respect and kept him at a distance. The moment he told them that they should keep their eyes open for Menolly, for her belt knife, if they knew it, or belt buckle, the distance widened inexplicably. They all seemed to know, though Elgion doubted that the adults had told them, that Menolly had been missing from the Hold for some days. They all seemed equally reluctant to look for her, or to suggest to him possible areas in which to search. It was as if, Elgion told himself with frustrated anger, they were *afraid* the Harper would find her. So he tried to regain their confidence by telling them that Yanus had suggested that everyone who went outside the Hold should keep their eyes open for the lost girl.

He came back with his charges to the Hold, with sacksful of berries, greens and some spiderclaws. The only information the boys had volunteered about Menolly during the entire morning was that she could catch more spiderclaws than anyone.

As it turned out, Elgion didn't have to signal for a dragonrider. The next day a bronze wingleader came circling down to the beach at Half-Circle, greeting Yanus affably and asking if he might have a few words with the Harper.

"You'll be Elgion," said the young man, raising his hand in greeting. "I'm N'ton, rider of Lioth. I heard you were settling in."

"What can I do for you, N'ton?" and Elgion tactfully walked the bronze rider out of Yanus's earshot.

"You've heard of fire lizards?"

Elgion stared at N'ton in surprise for a moment before he laughed. "That old myth!"

"Not really a myth, friend," said N'ton. Despite the laughing mischief in his eyes, he was speaking in earnest.

"Not a myth?"

"Not at all. Would you know if the lads here have spotted any along the coast? They tend to leave their clutches in beach sands. It's the eggs we want."

"Really? Actually it isn't the lads who've seen them, but the Sea Holder's son, not the fanciful sort, although I didn't really credit . . . he saw some around some rock crags known as the Dragon Stones. Down the coast some ways." Elgion pointed the direction.

"I'll go have a look myself. But this is what has happened. F'nor, brown Canth's rider, has been injured." N'ton paused.

"He's been convalescing at Southern Hold. He found, and Impressed," and again N'ton paused significantly to emphasize his last word, "a fire lizard queen . . ."

"Impressed? I thought only dragons . . ."

"Fire lizards are much like dragons, only smaller."

"But this would mean . . ." And Elgion was lost in the wonder of that meaning.

"Yes, precisely, Harper," said N'ton with a wide grin. "And now everyone wants a fire lizard. I can't imagine Yanus Sea Holder wasting the time and energy of his men looking for fire lizard clutches. But if fire lizards have been seen, any cove with warm sand might just hide a clutch."

"The high tides this spring have been flooding most of the coves."

"Too bad. See if you can't organize the Hold youngsters to search. I don't think you'd have much resistance . . ."

"None at all." And Elgion realized that N'ton, dragonrider though he now was, must have been susceptible to the same boyhood designs on fire lizards that Elgion had once planned. "When we find a clutch, what do we do?"

"*If* you find one," N'ton said, "fly the signal banner and the sweep rider will report. If the tide is threatening, put the clutch in either warm sand or warmed hides."

"If they should hatch, you did mention they can be Impressed . . ."

"I hope you're that lucky, Harper. Feed the fledglings. Stuff their faces with as much as they can eat, talking all the time. That's how you Impress. But then, you've been to a Hatching, haven't you? So, you know how to go about it. Same principle involved."

"Fire lizards." Elgion was enchanted with the prospect.

"Don't Impress them all, Harper. I'd like one of the little beasties myself."

"Greedy?"

"No, they're engaging little pets. Nothing as intelligent as my Lioth there," and N'ton grinned indulgently at his bronze who was scrubbing one cheek in the sand. As he turned back to Elgion, N'ton noticed the line of awed children, lining the sea-wall, all eyes on Lioth's action. "You'll have no lack of help, I suspect."

"Speaking of help, Wingleader, a young girl of the Sea Hold is missing. She went out the morning of the last Fall and hasn't been seen since."

N'ton whistled softly and nodded sympathetically. "I'll tell the sweep riders. She probably took shelter, if she'd any sense. Those palisades are riddled with caves. How far have you searched?"

"That's it. No one has bothered to."

N'ton scowled and glanced toward the Sea Holder. "How old a girl?"

"Come to think of it, I don't know. His youngest daughter, I believe."

N'ton snorted. "There are other things in life than fish."

"So I used to believe."

"Don't be so sour so young, Elgion. I'll see you come to the next Hatching at Benden."

"I'd appreciate that."

"I suspect so." With a farewell wave, N'ton strode back to his bronze dragon, leaving Elgion with an easier conscience and the prospect of some relief from the monotony of the Sea Hold.

CHAPTER 7

Who wills,
Can.
Who tries,
Does.
Who loves,
Lives.

It took Menolly four days to find the right sort of rocks to spark a fire. She'd had plenty of time before that to dry seaweeds and gather dead marshberry bushes for fuel, and to build a little hearth in the side of the big cavern where a natural chimney took the smoke up. She'd gathered a generous pile of sweet marsh grasses for bedding and picked out the seam of the carry-sack to make herself a rug. It wasn't quite long enough unless she curled up under it, but the fire lizards insisted on sleeping about and around her and their bodies made up the lack. In fact, she was quite comfortable at night.

With fire, she was very comfortable. She found a stand of young klahbark trees, and though the resultant brew was harsh, it woke her up very well. She went to the clay deposits that Half-Circle Hold used and got sufficient clay to make herself several cups, plates and rude containers for storage, which she hardened in the ashes of her fire. And she filled in the holes of a dishlike porous rock in which she could boil water. With all the fish she needed in the sea in front of her, she ate as well as, if not better than, she would have in the Hold. Although, she did miss bread.

She even made herself a sort of path down the cliff face. She carved out footrests and staked in some handholds, to make both ascent and descent safer.

And she had company. Nine fire lizards were constantly in attendance.

The morning after her hectic adventure, Menolly had been absolutely stunned to wake with the unaccustomed weight of warm bodies about her. Scared, too, until the little creatures roused, with strong thoughts of renewed hunger and love and affection for her. Driven by their need, she had climbed down the treacherous rock face to the sea and gathered fingertails, trapped in the shallow tidal pools. She wasn't quite able to dig rockmites, but when she showed her charges where they could get them out with their long, agile tongues, the creatures found their instinct adequate for the job. Having fed her friends, Menolly was too tired to go in search of sparking rocks and had eaten a flat fish raw. Then she and the fire lizards had crept back into the cavern and slept again.

As the days went by their appetite drove Menolly to lengths she wouldn't have attempted for her own comfort. The result was that she was kept entirely too busy to feel either sorry for or apprehensive about herself. Her friends had to be fed, comforted and amused. She also had to supply her own needs—as far as she was able—and she was able to do a lot more than she'd suspected she could. In fact, she began to wonder about a lot of things the Hold took for granted.

She had automatically assumed, as she supposed everyone

did, that to be caught without shelter during Threadfall was tantamount to dying. No one had ever correlated the fact that the dragonriders cleared most of the Thread from the skies before it fell—that was the whole point of having dragons—with the idea that as a result there was very little Thread to fall on the unsheltered. Hold thinking had hardened into an inflexible rule—to have no shelter during Threadfall was to experience death.

In spite of her increasing independence, however, had Menolly been alone, she might have regretted her foolishness and crept back to the Sea Hold. But the company and wonder of the fire lizards gave her all the diversion she needed. And they loved her music.

It was no great trick at all to make one reed pipe, and a lot more fun to put five together so she could play a counter-tune. The fire lizards adored the sounds and would sit listening, their dainty heads rocking in time with the music she played. When she sang, they'd croon, at first off-key; but gradually, she thought, their "ear" improved, and she had a soft chorus. Menolly sang, in amused duty, all the Teaching Ballads, particularly the ones about dragons. The fire lizards might understand less than a child three Turns old, but they responded with small cries and flapping wings to any of the dragon songs, as if they appreciated the fact that she was singing about their kin.

There was no doubt in Menolly's mind that these lovely creatures were related to the huge dragons. How, she didn't know and didn't really care. But if you treated them the way weyrmen treated their dragons, the fire lizards responded. She, in turn, began to understand their moods and needs, and insofar as she was able, supplied them.

They grew quickly, those first days. So quickly that she was hard pressed to keep their mouths full. Menolly didn't see too much of the other hatchlings, the ones she hadn't fed or had fed only casually. She saw them now and again, smaller creatures, as the entire weyr fed on the rockmites at low tide. The little queen and her bronze mate would often hover, watching Menolly and her small group. The queen sometimes scolded Menolly or perhaps berated the fire lizard Menolly was holding. Menolly wasn't sure which. And occasionally the queen would even fly at one of the fledglings, beating it soundly with her wings. For what reason, Menolly could never figure out, but the little ones meekly submitted to her discipline.

Occasionally Menolly offered food to one of the others, but they'd never take it if she remained near. Nor would any of the older fire lizards, including the queen. Menolly concluded that that was as well, otherwise she'd have to spend every single waking moment feeding lazy fire lizards. The nine she'd Impressed were quite enough to keep sated.

When she saw the first skin lesion on the little queen, Menolly wondered where she would find oil. They'd all need it. Cracks in the skin would be deadly for the young fire lizards if they had to go *between*. And with natural enemies around, like wherries and eager boys from nearby Holds, *between* was a needed refuge.

The closest source of oil swam in the sea. But she'd no boat to catch the deep-sea oily fishes, so she searched the coast for dead fish and found a packtail washed up during the night. She slit the carcass, carefully, always working the knife blade away from her, and squeezed the oil from the skin into a cup. Not the most pleasant of jobs; and by the time she'd finished, she had a bare cupful of unpleasantly fishy yellow oil. Yet it did work. The queen might not smell very pleasant, but the oil did coat the crack. For good measure, she smeared all her friends.

The stench in the cavern that night was almost more than she could endure, and she fell asleep trying to think of alternatives. By morning the possibilities had narrowed down to one: sweetening the fish oil with certain marsh grasses. She couldn't get the pure sweet oil they used in the Hold because that was traded from Nerat; it was pressed from the flesh of a hot-climate fruit that grew abundantly in the rain forests there. The oily seed pod that grew from a sea bush would not be available until fall; and while she could get some oil from black marshberries, it would take immense quantities, which she'd prefer to eat.

With her fire lizards as winged escort, she made her way south and inland, toward country little penetrated by the Sea Holders as being too far, these days, from shelter.

Menolly set out as soon as the sun was up and varied her pace between a striding walk and an easy jog. She decided to go on as far as she could until the sun was mid-heaven; she couldn't risk being too far from her cave when night fell.

The fire lizards were excited, darting about until she scolded them for wasting their energy. They took enough feeding without all that flying and all they could count on in this flat marsh area were berries and a few early sour plums. They took turns clinging to her shoulders and hair then, until the little brown pulled at her once too often, and she shooed them all off.

She was soon past any familiar terrain and began to proceed more slowly. It wouldn't do to be bogged down. Midday found her deep in the marshes, gathering berries for herself, her friends and her basket. She'd managed to harvest some of the aromatic grasses she wanted, but not enough for her purpose. She had decided to sweep in a wide circle back toward her cliff cave when she heard distant cries.

The little queen heard them, too, landing on Menolly's shoulder and adding her agitated comments.

Menolly told her to be quiet so she could hear, and to her surprise, the little queen instantly obeyed. The others subsided, and all seemed to wait expectantly. Without diversion Menolly recognized the distinctive and frantic noise of a distressed wherry.

Following the sound, Menolly crossed the slight rise into the next bog valley and saw the creature, wings flapping, head jerking but its legs and body firmly captured by treacherous sinking sands.

Oblivious to the excitement of the fire lizards who recognized the wherry as an enemy, Menolly ran forward, drawing her knife. The bird had been eating berries from the bushes edging the boggy sands and stupidly stepped into the mire. Menolly approached the sands cautiously, making certain that she was stepping on firm land. She got close enough—the frightened bird not even aware of her proximity—and plunged her knife into its back, at the base of the neck.

One more frightened squawk and the thing was dead, limp wings settling on the surface and rapidly submerging.

Menolly unbuckled her belt to make a loop of the buckle end. Grabbing the tough branches of a berry bush, she leaned out just far enough to snap the loop around the head of the bird. She tightened the loop and slowly began to pull.

Not only was there wherry meat here to feed herself and the fire lizards, but the layer of fat under its tough hide would provide her with the best possible grease for her friends' fragile skins.

Again, to Menolly's surprise, the fire lizard queen appeared to understand the situation. She sank her tiny talons into a wherry wing and pulled the tip out of the mud. She squeaked shrilly at the others, and before Menolly realized it, all of them had seized some tenable part of the wherry and were exerting their efforts to pull it from the bogsand.

It took a lot of pulling and shrill fire lizard orders, but they managed to get the wherry out of the sands and onto firm ground.

The rest of her day was spent in sawing through the tough outer hide to disembowel and dress the carcass. The fire lizards made an enthusiastic meal of the entrails and the blood that flowed from the wherry's neck. The sight somewhat nauseated Menolly, but she set her jaw and tried to ignore the voracity with which her otherwise gentle companions attacked the unexpected delicacy.

She hoped the taste of hot raw meat wouldn't change their temperaments, but she reckoned that dragons didn't become savage from their diet of live meat so it was fair to assume that the fire lizards wouldn't. At least, they were well fed for the day.

The wherry had been a good-sized bird, doubtless feeding somewhere in the lower reaches of Nerat for its fatty layer was juicy. It couldn't be a northern bird. Menolly skinned it, stopping twice to hone her knife sharp. She carved the meat from the bones, stuffing it into the hide to carry home. When she had finished, she had a hefty burden, and the bones were by no means stripped clean. Too bad she couldn't tell the old queen where they were.

She was rigging a forehead sling of her belt and the leg skin when suddenly the air was alive with fire lizards. With creels of shrill delight, the old queen and her bronzes settled on the bones. Menolly backed hastily away before the fire lizards decided to attack her for the meat she carried.

She had plenty of time on her long and tiring march back to the sea cave to wonder about their appearance. She could easily believe that the little queen could understand what she was thinking, and the others she had been taking care of. But had the young queen told the others? Or had Menolly some tenuous contact with the old queen, too?

Her special group showed no inclination to remain with the others, but kept her company, sometimes disappearing or making lazy figures in the sky. Sometimes the little queen sat on her shoulder for a few dragon lengths, chirruping sweetly.

It was fully dark long before Menolly reached her refuge. Only the moonlight and familiarity with the access route helped her down the cliff face. Her hearth fire was sullen embers, which she wearily coaxed into a cheery blaze. She was too tired to do more than wrap a piece of wherry meat in a few leaves of seaweed and stick it in the heated sands by the fire to cook for the morning. Then she wrapped herself up in her carry-sack and fell asleep.

She rendered the fat over the next several days, wishing time and again for one decent cooking pot. She heaped aromatic herbs into the hot fat and poured the mixture into clay pots for cooling. The wherry meat had a slightly fishy taste, which suggested that the stupid bird had been of a seaside flock rather than an inland or mountain group. But the cooled grease smelled of the herbs. Not, Menolly supposed, that the fire lizards minded how they smelled so long as their itching skin was soothed.

They loved to be oiled, lying on their backs, their wings

spread for balance, curling around her hand as she spread oil on their softer belly hide. They hummed with delight at the attention, and when she had finished each one, the creature would stroke her cheek with its small triangular head, the glistening eyes sparkling with brilliant colors.

She was beginning to find individual traits among her nine charges. The little queen was exactly as she should be: into everything, bossing everyone else, as imperious and demanding as a Sea Holder. She'd listen, however, very quietly to Menolly. And she'd listen to the old queen, too. But she paid no heed to any of the others, although they were expected to obey anything she said. She'd peck them fast enough if they disobeyed her.

There were two bronzes, three browns, a blue and two greens. Menolly felt a little sorry for the blue. He seemed to be left out or picked upon by the others. The two greens were always scolding him. She named him Uncle, and the greens became Auntie One and Auntie Two. Two was slightly smaller than One. Because one of the bronzes preferred to hunt for rockmites while the other was deft at diving into pools for fingertails, they became Rocky and Diver. The browns were so much alike that for a long time they remained nameless, but gradually she found that the largest of the trio usually fell asleep, given any opportunity to do so, so she called him Lazybones. The second was Mimic because he always did what he saw the other doing; and the third was Brownie for lack of any other distinguishing feature.

The little queen was Beauty because she was and because she took such elaborate pains with her grooming and required much more attention and oiling than the others. She was forever digging at her talons with her teeth, spreading them to clean between the toes, or licking any specks of dust from her tail, burnishing her neck ridges in the sand or grass.

At first Menolly talked to her creatures to hear the sound of her own voice. Later she spoke with them because they seemed to understand what she was saying. They certainly gave every indication of intelligent listening, humming, or crooning an encouraging response when she paused. And they never seemed to get enough of her singing to them, or playing her pipes. She couldn't exactly say that they harmonized with her, but they did hum softly in tune as she played.

CHAPTER 8

Wheel and turn
Or bleed and burn.
Fly between,
Blue and green.
Soar, dive down,
Bronze and brown.
Dragonmen must fly
When Threads are in the sky.

As it turned out, Alemi sailed Elgion to the Dragon Stones to search there for the elusive fire lizards. One windy day, not long after the visit of N'ton, the young Sea Man broke a leg bone when the rough seas tossed him against the pilot house of his ship. They were coming into harbor and the high tide made for heavier waters there than he'd expected. Yanus grumbled a good deal about Alemi being too experienced a seaman to get injured, but his grumbling subsided when Mavi pointed out that here was a chance to see if Alemi's first mate would be capable of assuming command of the ship being finished in the building Cavern.

Alemi tried to take the injury in good part, but after four days in bed, with the swelling eased, he was heartily bored and restless. He plagued Mavi so constantly that she handed him the crutch she had not meant to give him for a full sevenday more, and suggested that if he broke his neck, too, he would have only himself to blame.

Alemi had more sense than that and navigated the inner stairways, narrow and dark, slowly and carefully; he kept to the wider outer stairs and the Sea Hold's main rooms and the hold-way whenever possible.

While he had some mobility, he didn't have much activity if the fishing fleet was out, so he was soon attracted by the sound of the children learning a new ballad from the Harper. He caught Elgion's eye and received a courteous wave to enter the Little Hall. If the children were startled to hear a baritone suddenly take up the learning, they had too much respect for the Harper to do more than hazard a quick peek and the class progressed.

To Alemi's pleasure he found himself as quick to memorize the new words and tune as the youngsters, and he thoroughly enjoyed the session; he was almost sorry when Elgion excused them.

"How's the leg, Alemi?" the Harper asked when the room had emptied.

"I'll have a weather-wise ache now for sure."

"Is that why you did it?" Elgion said with a broad grin. "I'd heard you wanted to be sure Tilsit got a chance at command."

Alemi let out a snort of laughter. "Nonsense. I haven't had a rest since the last five-day gale. That's a fine ballad you're teaching."

"That's a fine voice you were singing it with, too. Why don't you sound out more often? I was beginning to think the sea wind snatches the voice of everyone at about twelve Turns."

"You should have heard my sis . . ." and Alemi stopped, flushed, and clamped his lips tight.

"Which reminds me: I took the liberty of asking N'ton, Lioth's rider, to spread the word at Benden Weyr that she's missing. She may still be alive, you know."

Alemi nodded slowly.

"You Sea Holders are full of surprises," said Elgion, thinking to switch to a less painful topic. He went to the racks of wax tablets and removed the two he sought. "These must have been done by that fosterling who took over when Petiron died. The other slates are all in the older script notations, which the old Harper used. But these . . . A lad who can do this sort of work is needed in the Harper's craft. You don't know where the boy is now, do you?"

Alemi was torn between duty to the Hold and love of his sister. But she wasn't in the Hold anymore, and commonsense told Alemi that she must be dead if, in this length of time, with dragonriders looking for her, she hadn't been found. Menolly was only a girl, so what good did it do that her songs found favor with the Harper? Alemi was also reluctant to put the lie to his father. So, despite the fact that Elgion was impressed by the songs, since the songmaker was beyond them, Alemi answered truthfully that he didn't know where "he" was.

Elgion wrapped the waxed slates carefully, and with a noticeable sigh of regret. "I'll send them on to the Harper Crafthall anyway. Robinton will want to use them."

"Use them? They're that good?" Alemi was startled and regretted the lies still more.

"They're cracking good. Maybe if the lad hears them, he'll come forward on his own." Elgion gave Alemi a rueful smile. "Since it's obvious there's some reason you can't name him." He chuckled at the Sea Man's reaction. "Come now, man, the lad was sent away in some sort of disgrace, wasn't he? That happens, as any harper worth his salt knows—and understands. Hold honor and all that. I won't tease you anymore. He'll surface to the sound of his own music."

They talked of other things then, until the fishing fleet returned—two men of the same age but different background: one with an inquisitive interest in the world beyond his Sea Hold, and the other quite willing to satisfy it. Elgion was, in fact, delighted to find none of Yanus's denseness and inflexibility in Alemi, and the Harper began to feel that after all he might be able to follow Master Robinton's ambitious plan of broadening understanding beyond the limits of this Sea Hold.

Alemi was back the following day after the children had been dismissed, with more questions. He stopped midsentence finally, apologizing profusely for taking so much of Elgion's time.

"I tell you what, Alemi, I'll teach you what you'd like to know if you'll teach me how to sail."

"Teach you to sail?"

Elgion grinned. "Yes, teach me to sail. The smallest child in my class knows more about that than I do, and my professional standing is in jeopardy. After all, a Harper is supposed to know everything.

"I may be wrong but I can't imagine that you need both legs to sail one of those little skiffs the children use."

Alemi's face lit up, and he pounded the Harper on the back with enthusiasm.

"Of course I can. By the First Shell, man, I'd be glad to do it. Glad."

And nothing would satisfy Alemi but to take the Harper down to the Dock Cavern immediately and give him the fundamentals of seamanship. In his own subject, Alemi was as good an instructor as the Harper; and Elgion was able to tack across the Harbor by himself by the end of the first lesson. Of course, as Alemi remarked, the wind was from the right quarter and the sea calm, ideal sailing conditions.

"Which rarely prevail?" asked Elgion; and he was rewarded by Alemi's tolerant chuckle. "Well, practice makes perfect, and I'd better learn the practical."

"And the theory."

So their friendship was cemented by mutual exchanges of knowledge and long visits together. Although their conversation touched many subjects, Elgion hesitated to bring up the subject of fire lizards, or the fact that the Weyr had asked him to search for traces of the elusive little creatures. He had, however, searched as much of the accessible coastline as he could on foot. There were some beaches that should be checked now from the seaside. With Alemi teaching him how to handle the skiff, he hoped he'd soon be able to do it himself. Elgion knew with certainty that Yanus would be completely scornful of any search for fire lizards, and the Harper didn't want to implicate Alemi in any plan that would bring Yanus's anger down on his head. Alemi was in bad enough straits over breaking his leg.

One clear bright morning, Elgion decided to put his solution to the test. He dismissed the children early, then sought out Alemi and suggested that today was not only a fine day but the sea was rough enough to test his ability. Alemi laughed, cast a wise eye at the clouds, and said that it would be mild as a bathing pool by afternoon but that the practice now would be useful to Elgion's progress.

Elgion wheedled a large package of fish rolls and spicecakes from a kitchen auntie, and the two men set off. Alemi was agile enough now with his crutch and splint-bound leg on land, but he was glad of any excuse to be on the sea.

Once beyond the protecting arms of the Half-Circle cliffs, the sea was choppy with crosscurrent and wind; Elgion's skill would be well tested. Alemi, disregarding an occasional wetting as the skiff plunged in and out of the wave troughs, played silent passenger while the Harper fought tiller and sheet to keep them on the course Alemi had set down the coast. The Sea Man became aware of the windshift some moments before Elgion, but it was the mark of his abilities as a teacher that Elgion was quick enough to notice the change.

"Wind's slacking off."

Alemi nodded, adjusting his cap slightly for the wind's new direction. They sailed on, the wind slackening to a gentle pressure against the sail, the skiff's speed aided more by the deep current than the wind.

"I'm hungry," Alemi announced as he and Elgion saw the stumpy violet crags of the Dragon Stones to leeward.

Elgion released the sheet line, and Alemi pulled the sail down, furling it with absent skill against the boom. At his direction, Elgion lashed the tiller so that the current carried them idly downcoast.

"Don't know why," Alemi said through a mouthful of fishroll, "food always tastes better on the sea."

Elgion contented himself to a nod since his mouth was full. He also had a good appetite; not, he qualified to himself, that he had been working overhard, just hanging on to the tiller and adjusting the sail sheet now and then.

"Come to think, don't often have time to eat on the sea,"

Alemi added. He gestured to include their leisurely bobbing, the skiff itself and the informal meal. "Haven't been this lazy on a sail since I was old enough to haul a net." He stretched and then adjusted his splinted leg slightly, grimacing against the awkwardness and discomfort. Suddenly he leaned away from the bulwark, to reach into the small locker fitted against the curve of the hull. "Thought so." Grinning, he held up fishline, hook and dry worm.

"Can't you leave off?"

"What? And have Yanus give out about unproductive hands?" Alemi deftly threaded line to hook and baited it. "Here. You might as well try hook line and bait. Or does the Masterharper object to cross-crafting?"

"The more crafts the better, says Master Robinton."

Alemi nodded, his eyes on the current. "Aye, sending lads away to other Sea Holds for fostering doesn't quite answer, does it?" Deftly he threw the line from him, watched the cast carry it well away from the drifting skiff and sink.

Elgion gave a fair imitation of that cast and settled himself, as Alemi had, to wait for results.

"What would we be catching out here?"

Alemi drew his mouth up in a grimace of indifference. "Probably nothing. Tide's full, current's strong, midday. Fish feed at dawn, unless there's Thread."

"Is that why you use the dry worm? Because it resembles Thread?" Elgion couldn't suppress the shudder that went down his spine at the thought of loose Thread.

"You're right."

The silence that often grips fishermen settled comfortably in the boat.

"Yellow-stripe, if anything," Alemi finally said in answer to the question that Elgion had almost forgotten he'd asked. "Yellow-stripe or a very hungry packtail. They'll eat anything."

"Packtail? That's good eating."

"Line'll break. Packtail's too heavy for this."

"Oh."

The current was inexorably drawing them closer to the Dragon Stones. But, although he wanted to get Alemi talking about them, Elgion couldn't find the proper opening. At about the point where Elgion felt he'd better speak or they'd be pulled by the current into the Stones, Alemi casually glanced around. They were only several dragon lengths from the most seaward of the great crags. The water now lapped peacefully against the base, exposing occasionally the jagged points of submerged rock, eddying around others. Alemi unfurled the sail and hauled on the sheet line.

"We need more sea room near those. Dangerous with sunken rock. When the tide's making, current can pull you right in. If you sail this way by yourself, and you'll soon be able to, make sure you keep your distance."

"The lads say you saw fire lizards there once." Elgion found the words out of his mouth before he could censor them.

Alemi shot him a long amused look. "Let's say I can't think what else it could've been. They weren't wherries: too fast, too small, and wherries can't maneuver that way. But fire lizards?" He laughed and shrugged his shoulders, indicating his own skepticism.

"What if I told you that there are such things? That F'nor, Canth's rider, Impressed one in Southern and so did five or six other riders? That the Weyrs are looking for more fire lizard clutches, and I've been asked to search the beaches?"

Alemi stared at the Harper. Then the skiff rocked in the subtle cross currents. "Mind now, pull the tiller hard aport. No, to your left, man!"

They had the looming Dragon Stone comfortably abaft before further conversation.

"You can Impress fire lizards?" If Alemi's voice was incredulous, an eager light sparkled in his eyes, and Elgion knew he'd made an ally; he told as much as he, himself, knew.

"Well, that would explain why you rarely see grown ones, and why they evade capture so cleverly. They *hear* you coming." Alemi laughed, shaking his head. "When I think of the times . . ."

"Me, too." Elgion grinned broadly, remembering his boyhood attempts to rig a successful trap.

"We're to look on beaches?"

"That's what N'ton suggested. Sandy beaches, sheltered places, preferably hard for small active boys to find. There's plenty of places where a fire lizard queen could hide a clutch around here."

"Not with the tides so high this season."

"There must be some beaches deep enough." Elgion felt impatient with Alemi's arguments.

The Sea Man motioned Elgion out of the tiller seat, and deftly tacked about.

"I saw fire lizards about the Dragon Stones. And those crags'd be right good weyrs. Not that I think we'd have a chance of seeing them today. They feed at dawn: that's when I saw them. Only," and Alemi chuckled, "I thought my eyes were deceiving me since it was the end of a long watch and a man's eyes can play tricks with him at dawn."

Alemi sailed the little skiff far closer to the Dragon Stones than Elgion would have dared. In fact the Harper found himself gripping the weatherboard very hard and edging his body away from the towering crags as the skiff breezed lightly by. There was no doubt that the crags were riddled with holes, likely weyrs for fire lizards.

"I wouldn't try this tack except when the tide is full, Elgion," said Alemi as they sailed between the innermost crag and the tide-washed land. "There's a right mess of bottom-reaming rocks here even at half-tide."

It was quiet, too, with the waves softly caressing the narrow verge of sand between sea and cliff. Quiet enough for the unmistakable sound of piping to carry across the water to Elgion.

"Did you hear that?" Elgion grabbed Alemi's arm.

"Hear what?"

"The music!"

"What music?" Alemi wondered briefly if the sun were strong enough to give the Harper a stroke. But he sharpened his ears for any unusual sound, following the line of Elgion's stare to the cliffs. His heart leaped for a moment, but he said, "Music? Nonsense! Those cliffs are riddled with caves and holes. All you hear is the wind . . ."

"There isn't any wind now . . ."

Alemi had to admit that because he'd let the boom out and was even beginning to wonder if they had enough wind to come about on a tack that would clear the northern side of the stones.

"And look," said Elgion, "there's a hole in the cliff face. Big enough for a person to get into, I'd wager. Alemi, can't we go inshore?"

"Not unless we walk home, or wait for high tide again."

"Alemi! That's music! Not wind over blow holes! That's someone playing pipes."

An unhappy furtive thought crossed Alemi's face so plainly that Elgion jumped to a conclusion. All at once, all the pieces fell into place.

"Your sister, the one who's missing. *She* wrote those songs. She taught the children, not that conveniently dismissed fosterling!"

"Menolly's not playing any pipes, Elgion. She sliced her left hand, gutting packtail, and she can't open or close her fingers."

Elgion sank back to the deck, stunned but still hearing the clear tone of pipes. Pipes? You'd need two whole hands to play multiple pipes. The music ceased and the wind, rising as they tacked past the Dragon Stones, covered his memory of that illusive melody. It could have been the land breeze, sweeping down over the cliffs, sounding into holes.

"Menolly did teach the children, didn't she?"

Slowly Alemi nodded. "Yanus believed the Sea Hold disgraced to have a girl taking the place of a Harper."

"Disgraced?" Once again Elgion was appalled at the obtuseness of the Sea Holder. "When she taught so well? When she can turn a tune like the ones I've seen?"

"She can play no more, Elgion. It would be cruel to ask now. She wouldn't even sing in the evenings. She'd leave as soon as you started to play."

So he'd been right, thought Elgion, the tall girl had been Menolly.

"If she's alive, she's happier away from the Hold! If she's dead . . ." Alemi didn't continue.

In silence they sailed on, the Dragon Stones falling away, back into violet indefiniteness as each man avoided the other's gaze.

Now Elgion could understand many things about Menolly's disappearance and the general reluctance at the Hold to discuss her or find her. There was no doubt in his mind that her disappearance was deliberate. Anyone sensitive enough to compose such melodies must have found life in the Sea Hold intolerable: doubly so with Yanus as Sea Holder and father. And then to be considered a disgrace! Elgion cursed Petiron for not making the matter plain. If only he had told Robinton that the promising musician were a girl, she might have been at the Harperhall before that knife had a chance to slip.

"There'd be no clutches on the Dragon Stones' cove," Alemi said, breaking into Elgion's rueful thoughts. "Water's right up to the bluff at high tide. There is one place . . . I'll take you there after the next Threadfall is past. A good long day's sail down the coast. You *can* Impress a fire lizard, you say?"

"I'll set the signal for N'ton to talk to you after Fall." Elgion was happy enough to use any subject to break the restraint that had fallen between them. "Evidently you or I can Impress, though lowly Harpers and young Sea Men may be far down on the list for available eggs."

"By the dawn star, when I think of the hours I spent as a small fellow . . ."

"Who hasn't?" Elgion grinned back, eager too for the chance.

This time their silence was companionable, and when they exchanged glances, it was for remembered boyish fancies of capturing the elusive and much desired fire lizard.

As they tacked into the Dock Cavern late that afternoon, Alemi had a final word for Elgion.

"You understand why you're not to know it was Menolly who did the teaching?"

"The Sea Hold is not disgraced." Elgion felt Alemi's hand tighten on his arm so he nodded. "But I would never betray that confidence."

If his solemn response reassured the Sea Man, it reinforced Elgion's determination to find out who had made that pipe music. Was it possible to play multiple pipes with one hand? He was convinced that he'd heard music, not wind over blowholes. Somehow, whether on the pretext of searching for fire lizards or not, he must get close enough to examine that cave in the Dragon Stones' cove.

The next day was rainy, a thin soft drizzle that did not deter the fishermen but that made both Elgion and Alemi unwilling to take a long and possibly fruitless journey in an open boat.

That same evening Yanus asked Elgion to excuse the children from lessons the following morning as they'd be needed to gather seaweed for the smoke-cave. Elgion granted considered permission, masterfully suppressing a desire to thank the Sea Holder for a free day, and determined to rise early and be off to seek the answer to the music mystery. He was up as soon as the sun, first in the Great Hall, so that he had to unbar the metal doors, little realizing as he did so that he would be following an unnerving precedent. With fish rolls and dried fruit in his pouch, his own pipe slung across his back, a stout rope about his middle (for he rather thought he might need it climbing down that cliff face), Elgion was away.

CHAPTER 9

Oh, Tongue, give sound to joy and sing
Of hope and promise on dragonwing.

The hunger of the fire lizards roused Menolly from sleep. There was nothing in the cave to eat because the previous day had been wet enough to keep them all inside. She saw that the tide was well out, and the day was clear.

"If we scramble, we can get down coast and pick us up a nice lot of spiderclaws. They'll be gone soon," she told her friends. "Or we can look for rockmites. So come along, Beauty." The little queen hummed from her warm nest in the rushes, and the others began to stir. Menolly reached down and tickled Lazy's neck where he lay by her feet. He slapped at her, rousing enough to let out a huge yawn. His eyelids peeled back and his eyes sparkled faintly red.

"Now, don't you all start in on me. I got you up so we could be off. You won't be hungry long if we all stir smartly."

As she descended agilely to the beach, her friends swooping gracefully from the cave, some of the other fire lizards were feeding in the shallows. Menolly called out a greeting to them. She wondered, as she often did, if the other fire lizards, with the notable exception of the queen, were at all aware of her. She felt it rude not to acknowledge their presence whether they responded or not. Maybe one day they would have grown so used to her, that they'd answer.

She slipped on the wet rocks at the far end of the cove, wincing as a sharp edge made itself painfully felt through the thinning soles of her boots. *That* was a matter she'd have to attend to soon, new boot soles. With such rough surfaces, she couldn't go barefoot. And she certainly couldn't climb barefooted, not if she had toes like a watchwher. She'd have to get another wherry, tan its leg hide to a proper toughness. But how could she sew the new leather to her old bootsole? She looked down at her feet, placing them carefully, as much to save the leather as her feet.

She took her band to the farthest cove they'd yet explored, far enough down the coast for the Dragon Stones to be knobs on the horizon. But the long walk was worth the effort for spiderclaws scurried wildly up and down the wide, gently curving beach. The bluff had dwindled to a height just above her head in some places, and at the far end of the crescent sands, a stream fed into the sea.

Beauty and the others were soon playing havoc with the spiderclaws, diving down on their intended prey, then darting up to the cliffs to eat. When her net was full, Menolly searched for enough sea wreckage to start a fire. That was how she found the clutch, covered as it was and almost level with the beach surface. But she saw the faint outline of a mound, suspiciously circular. She brushed away enough sand to expose the mottled shell of a hardening fire lizard egg. She glanced around carefully, wondering if the queen was anywhere about; but she saw only her own nine. She put a gentle finger on the exposed egg: it was softish. Quickly she patted the sand back into place and hurried from the clutch. The high-tide mark on this beach was a long way from threatening the eggs. It pleased her to realize that this beach was a long way from any Hold so these fire lizard eggs were safe.

She gathered sufficient wood, made a rude hearth, started her fire, killed the spiderclaws deftly and laid them on a conveniently flat stone and went exploring while they baked.

The stream flowed broad into the sea; sand banks had formed and reformed to judge by the myriad channels. Menolly followed the stream inland, looking for the sweet cresses that often grew where the water freshened. Submarine bodies moved upstream, too, and she wondered if she could catch one of the big specklers. Alemi often boasted that he could tickle them into his grasp as they fought the current. Thinking of the spiderclaws roasting on her fire, Menolly decided to leave that exercise until another day. She did want some greens; succulent cresses with their odd tangy aftertaste would make a good addition to spiderclaws.

She found the greens well above the tidewater, where the stream was fed by tiny trickles from the flat marshy lands through which it looped. She was greedily stuffing a handful of greens into her mouth before she really took in her surroundings. In the distance, low on the horizon, were lightning flashes against a gray sky.

Thread! Fear rooted her to the ground; she nearly choked on the half-chewed mouthful of greens. She tried to talk herself out of terror by counting the flashes of dragon fire that made a pattern across the sky: a wide, long pattern. If the dragonriders were already at work, the Thread wouldn't get as far as here. She was a long way from it.

But how far away was safe? She'd just made it to the cave before that other Fall. She was too far away, run as fast as ever she could, to reach the cave's safety now. She'd the sea behind her. Water! She'd the stream beside her. Thread drowned in water. But how deep did it fall before it drowned?

She told herself firmly that now was not the time to panic. She forced herself to swallow the last of the cress juices. Then she had no control over her legs; they took off with her and she was running, toward the sea and toward the rock safety of her cave.

Beauty appeared above her head, swooping and chittering as she caught Menolly's fear. Rocky and Diver arrived with Mimic popping in a half-breath later. They experienced her alarm, circling around her head as she ran, calling out with the piercingly sweet tenor bugle of challenge. Then they all disappeared. Which made running easier for Menolly. She could concentrate on where she was putting her feet.

She made diagonally for the beaches, wondering briefly if it wouldn't be smarter to go along the shoreline. She'd be that much nearer the dubious safety of the water. She hurdled a ditch; managed to keep her balance as her left foot twisted on landing; staggered a few paces before she found her stride again. No, there'd be more rocks on the shore, cutting down her speed and increasing the danger of a badly twisted ankle.

Two queens gleamed golden in the air above her, and Rocky and Diver were back, with Lazybones, Mimic and Brownie. The two queens chittered angrily, and the males, to Menolly's surprise, flew ahead of her now, and high enough not to be a nuisance. She ran on.

She came to a height, and the incline robbed her of breath so that she staggered to the summit and had to drop to a walk, clutching her right side against the nagging stitch, but somehow moving forward. Ahead of her the Dragon Stones were more than knobs but too distant to reassure. One look over her shoulder at the sky bursts of dragon fire told her that the Thread was gaining on her.

She broke into a run again, the two queens gliding right over her head, and she felt oddly protected. She had her second wind now, and her stride, and felt as if she could run forever. If she could only run fast enough to stay beyond the reach of Thread . . . She kept her eyes on the Dragon Stones, refusing to look over her shoulder: that unnerving sight caught the breath she needed for running.

She ran as close to the bluff edge as she dared. She'd slithered down one cliff without desperate damage to herself: she'd risk it again to get into the water if she had to.

She ran, one eye on the Dragon Stones, one for the ground ahead of her feet.

She heard the whoosh, heard the fire lizards' startled chirrups, saw the shadow and fell to the ground covering her head instinctively with her hands, her body taut for the first feel of flesh-scoring Thread. She smelled fire-stone, and felt the air heavy against her body.

"Get on your feet, you silly fool! And hurry. Leading edge is nearly on us!"

Incredulous, Menolly looked up, right into the whirling eyes of a brown dragon. He cocked his head and hummed urgently.

"Get up!" said his rider.

Menolly wasted no time after a frantic look at the fire blossoms and the sight of a line of dragons swooping and disappearing. She scrambled to her feet, dove for the brown rider's extended hand and one of the fighting strap ends, and got herself firmly astride the brown's neck behind his rider.

"Hang on to me tightly. And don't be afraid. I'm to take you *between* to Benden. It'll be cold and dark, but I'll be with you."

The relief of being rescued when she was fearing injury or death was too overwhelming for speech. The brown dragon half-ran to the bluff edge, dropped down briefly to get wing room, and then surged up. Menolly felt herself pressed against the soft warm flesh and burrowed into the hide-clad back of her rescuer, struggling for a lungful of air to ease her tight chest. She had one brief glimpse of her little fire lizards trying vainly to follow when the dragon winked into *between*.

Sweat froze on her forehead and cheeks, down her back, on her calves, her wet and ragged boots and her sore feet. There was no air to breathe and she felt she would suffocate. She tightened her hands convulsively on the dragonrider, but she couldn't feel him or the dragon she knew she was riding.

Now, she thought with that part of her mind that wasn't frozen in panic, she fully understood that Teaching Song. In terror, she fully understood it.

Abruptly, sight, sound, feeling, and breath returned. They were spiraling down at a dizzying height above Benden Weyr. As big as Half-Circle was, this place of dragons and dragonmen was bigger by half again as much. Why, the immense harbor of Half-Circle would have fitted with dragon lengths to spare in the Bowl of the Weyr.

As the dragon circled, she saw the giant Star Stones, and the Eye Rock, which told when the Red Star would make its fateful Passes. She saw the watch dragon beside the Stones, heard him trumpet a greeting to the brown she rode. Between her legs she felt the rumble of response in the brown's throat. As they glided down, she saw several dragons on the Bowl floor, with people gathered about them; saw the steps leading to the queen's weyr, and the yawning maw of the Hatching Ground. Benden was vaster than she'd imagined.

The brown landed near the other dragons, and Menolly now realized that the dragons had been Thread-scored and were being treated. The brown dragon half-folded his wings, craning his neck around to the two on his back.

"You can relax your death hold, lad," said the brown rider with tolerant amusement as he unfastened the fighting straps from his belt.

Menolly jerked her hands free with a muttered apology. "I can't thank you enough for finding me. I thought Thread would get me."

"Whoever let you out of your Hold so near to Threadfall?"

"I was catching spiderclaws. Went out early."

He accepted that hurried explanation, but now Menolly wondered how she could make it plausible. She couldn't remember the name of the nearest Hold on the Nerat side of Half-Circle.

"Down you go, lad, I've got to rejoin my wing to mop up."

That was the second time he'd called her "lad."

"You've a fine pace on you. Ever think of going for a hold runner?"

The brown rider swung her forward so she could slide down the brown's shoulders. The moment her feet touched the ground, she thought she'd faint with the pain. She grabbed frantically at the brown's foreleg. He nuzzled her sympathetically, humming to his rider.

"Branth says you're hurt?" The man slid down quickly beside her.

"My feet!" She'd run the boots to uppers without knowing

it, and her lacerated feet were bloody from toe to heel.

"I'll tell the world. Here we go!"

He grabbed her by the wrist, gave a practiced yank and laid her over his shoulder. As he made for the entrance to the lower Caverns, he called out for someone to bring a pot of numbweed.

She was uprighted into a chair, the blood singing in her ears. Someone was propping her damaged feet onto a stool while women converged on her from several sides.

"Hey, Manora, Felena," yelled the brown rider urgently.

"Just look at his feet! He's run them raw!"

"T'gran, wherever . . ."

"Saw him trying to outrun Thread down Nerat way. Bloody near did!"

"Bloody's quite accurate. Manora, could you spare a moment, please?"

"Should we wash the feet first or . . ."

"No, a cup of weed first," was T'gran's suggestion. "You'll have to cut the boots off . . ."

Someone was holding a cup against her lips, bidding her drink it all down. On a stomach empty of anything but a few blades of cress, the fellis juice acted so quickly that the circle of faces about her became a confused blur.

"Good heavens, the holders have gone mad, going out in Threadfall." Menolly thought the speaker sounded like Manora. "This is the second one we've rescued today."

After that, voices became indistinguishable mumbles. Menolly was unable to focus her eyes. She seemed to be floating a few handspans off the ground. Which suited her because she didn't want to use her feet anyway.

Seated at a table on the other side of the kitchen cavern,

Elgion at first thought the boy had fainted with relief at being rescued. He could appreciate the feeling certainly, having been sighted by a dragonrider as he was pelting back toward Half-Circle, fully winded and despairing of life. Now, with his stomach full of good weyr stew, his wits and breath restored, he was forced to face his folly in going outside the Hold so close to a Fall. And, more daunting to contemplate, the reception on his return to Half-Circle. Talk about disgracing the Sea Hold! And his explanation that he was searching for fire lizard eggs would not go down well with Yanus. Even Alemi, what would he think? Elgion sighed and watched as several weyrwomen carried the boy off toward the living caverns. He half-rose, wondering if he should have volunteered to help. Then he saw his first fire lizard and forgot everything else.

It was a little golden queen, swooping into the cavern, calling piteously. She seemed to hover motionless in midair, then winked out of sight. A moment later, she was diving into the kitchen cavern again, less agitated but looking for something or someone.

A girl emerged from the living cavern, saw the fire lizard and held up her arm. The little queen delicately landed, stroking the girl's face with her tiny head while the girl evidently reassured her. The two walked out into the Bowl.

"You've never seen one, Harper?" asked an amused voice, and Elgion came out of his trance to attend the weyrwoman who'd been serving him food.

"No, I hadn't."

She laughed at the wistfulness in his voice. "That's Grall, F'nor's little queen," Felena told him. Then abruptly she asked Elgion if he'd like more stew.

He politely declined because he'd already had two platefuls:

food being the weyr's way of reassuring those they rescued.

"I really should be finding out if I can get back to Half-Circle Sea Hold. They'll have discovered my absence and . . ."

"Don't worry on that account, Harper, for word was passed back through the fighting wings. They'll let Half-Circle know you're safely here."

Elgion expressed proper gratitude, but he couldn't help fretting over Yanus's displeasure. He would simply have to make it clear that he'd been following Weyr orders, and Yanus was nothing if not obedient to his Weyr. Nonetheless, Elgion did not relish his return to the Sea Hold. He also couldn't politely insist on going when he chose because the dragons were tired as they returned to their Weyr, Thread successfully obliterated on this Fall.

Some of the young Harper's worst apprehensions were relieved by T'gellan, the bronze wingleader in charge of that Fall.

"I myself told them you were safe, and a good thing, too. They were all ready to mount a search. Which, for old Yanus, is a remarkable concession."

Elgion grimaced. "I suppose it wouldn't look well to lose two Harpers in a short time."

"Nonsense. Already Yanus prizes you above fish! Or so Alemi said."

"Was he angry?"

"Who? Yanus?"

"No, Alemi."

"Why? I'd say he was better pleased than Yanus to hear you were safe and scoreless at Benden. More important, *did* you see any signs of fire lizard clutches?"

"No."

T'gellan sighed, stripping off his wide riding belt and opening the heavy wherhide jacket. "How we need the silly creatures."

"Are they that useful?"

T'gellan gave him a long look. "Possibly not. Lessa thinks them a real nuisance; but they look, and act, like dragons. And they give those narrow-minded, hidebound, insensitive Lord Holders just that necessary glimpse of what it is to ride a dragon. *That* is going to make life ... and progress ... easier for us in the Weyrs."

Elgion rather hoped that this had been made plain to Yanus; and he was going to tactfully suggest that he was ready to go back to the Sea Hold when the bronze rider was called away to check a dragon's wing injury.

Elgion found the additional delay instructive. He decided he would put his observations to good use in getting back into Yanus's favor—for he had an opportunity to see Weyr life as unsung in Saga and Ballad. An injured dragon cried as piteously as a child until his wounds were salved with numbweed. A dragon also cried distressingly if his rider was injured. Elgion watched the touching sight of a green dragon, crooning anxiously at her rider as he leaned against her forearm, while the weyrwomen dressed his Threadscored arm. Elgion saw the weyrlings bathing and oiling their young beasts, the Weyr's several fire lizards assisting. He saw the youngsters of the Weyr refilling firestone sacks for the next Fall, and couldn't fail to notice that they made less work of the onerous chore than Sea Hold lads would have done. He even ventured to peer into the Hatching Ground where golden Ramoth lay curled protectively around her eggs. He ducked out of sight, hoping she hadn't seen him.

Time passed so quickly that Elgion was surprised to hear the kitchen women calling everyone in to eat. He hovered at the entrance, wondering what to do when T'gellan grabbed him by the arm and propelled him to an empty table.

"G'sel, come over here with that bronze nuisance of yours. I want the Half-Circle Harper to see him. G'sel has one of the original clutch F'nor discovered in Southern," T'gellan said in an undertone as they watched the stocky young man weaving his way through the tables toward them, balancing a bronze fire lizard on his forearm.

"This is Rill, Harper," G'sel said, extending his arm to Elgion. "Rill, be courteous; he's a Harper."

With great dignity the fire lizard extended his wings, executing what Elgion construed to be a bow, while the jeweled eyes regarded him intently. Not knowing how one saluted a fire lizard, Elgion tentatively extended his hand.

"Scratch his eye ridges," G'sel suggested. "They all love that."

To Elgion's delight and amazement, the fire lizard accepted the caress, and as Elgion's stroking eased an itch, Rill's eyelids began to close in sensuous pleasure.

"He's another convert," said T'gellan, laughing and pulling out his chair. The noise roused the fire lizard from somnolence and he hissed softly at T'gellan. "They're bold creatures, too, you'll notice, Harper, with no respect for degree."

This was evidently an old jibe, for G'sel, seating himself, paid it no heed, but coaxed Rill to step onto a padded shoulder rest so he could eat the dinner now being served.

"How much do they understand?" Elgion asked, taking the chair opposite G'sel so he could see Rill better.

"To hear Mirrim talk about her three, everything."

T'gellan snorted with good-natured derision.

"I can ask Rill to carry a message to any place he's already been. No, to a *person* he knows at another Hold or Weyr I've taken him to. He follows me no matter where I go. Even during Threadfall." At T'gellan's snort, G'sel added, "I told you to watch today, T'gellan. Rill was with us."

"Yes, so tell Elgion how long it takes Rill to come back from delivering a message."

"All right, all right," said G'sel with a laugh as he stroked Rill affectionately. "And when you've one of your own, T'gellan . . ."

"Possibly, possibly," the bronze rider said easily. "Unless Elgion here finds us another clutch, we'll just have to stay jealous of you."

T'gellan changed the subject then to ask about Half-Circle Hold, general questions that did not embarrass or compromise Elgion. T'gellan evidently knew Yanus's reputation.

"If you feel too isolated there, Harper, don't fail to fly the signal and we'll pop you up for an evening here."

"Hatching's soon," G'sel suggested, grinning and giving Elgion a wink.

"He'll be here for that certainly," T'gellan agreed.

Then Rill creeled for a bite to eat while the bronze rider chided G'sel for turning the lizard into an importunate beggar. Elgion noticed T'gellan, himself, finding a titbit for the little bronze, however, and he, too, offered Rill some meat, which the creature daintily accepted from the knife.

By the end of the meal Elgion was ready to brave Yanus's worst displeasure and wrath to find a fire lizard clutch and Impress a fire lizard of his own. That prospect made his inevitable return easier.

"I'd better do you the honors, Elgion," T'gellan said, rising at last from the table. "And I'd also better get you back early. No sense aggravating Yanus more than necessary."

Elgion wasn't certain how to take that remark or the wink that accompanied it, particularly as it was now full dark and for all he knew, the Hold doors were already barred for the night. Too late now to wish he'd gone back as soon as the dragonriders had returned from the Fall. But then he wouldn't have met Rill.

They were aloft, Elgion reveling in the experience, craning his head to see as much as possible in the clear night air. He had only a glimpse of the Higher Benden Range hills before T'gellan asked Monarth to take them *between*.

Suddenly, it was no longer full dark: the sun was a handspan above the glowing sea as they burst into the air above Half-Circle Harbor.

"Told you I'd get you back early," T'gellan said, turning to grin at the Harper's startled exclamation. "We're not supposed to time it, but all in a good cause."

Monarth circled down lazily so that everyone in the Sea Hold was gathered on the holdway when they landed. Yanus strode a few paces ahead of the others while Elgion searched the faces for Alemi's.

T'gellan leaped from the bronze's shoulder and made a show of assisting Elgion as the entire Hold cheered loudly for their Harper's safe return.

"I'm neither crippled or old," Elgion muttered under his breath, aware of Yanus's approach. "Don't overdo it."

T'gellan laid his arm across Elgion's shoulders in a comradely fashion, beaming at the oncoming Sea Holder. "Not at all," he said out of the corner of his mouth. "The Weyr approves!"

"Sea Holder, I am profoundly embarrassed at the inconvenience . . ."

"No, Harper Elgion," T'gellan interrupted him, "any apologies are the Weyr's. You were adamant in wishing to return to Half-Circle immediately. But Lessa needed to have his report, Yanus, so we had to wait."

Whatever Yanus had been about to say to his erring Harper was neatly blocked by T'gellan's obvious approval. The Sea Holder rocked a bit on his feet, blinking as he reorganized his thoughts.

"Any fire lizard sign you discover must be made known to the Weyr as soon as possible," T'gellan continued blithely.

"Then that tale is true?" Yanus asked in a grumble of disbelief. "Those . . . those creatures do exist?"

"They do indeed, sir," Elgion replied warmly. "I have seen, touched and fed a bronze fire lizard; his name is Rill. He's about as big as my forearm . . ."

"You did? He is?" Alemi had pushed through the crowd, breathless from excitement and the exercise of hobbling as fast as he could down the holdway. "Then you did find something in the cave?"

"The cave?" Elgion had forgotten all about his original destination that morning.

"What cave?" demanded T'gellan.

"The cave . . ." and Elgion gulped and then boldly embroidered on the lie T'gellan had begun, "I told Lessa about. Surely you were in the room then."

"What cave?" demanded Yanus, stepping close to the younger men, his voice half-angry because he was being excluded from the conversation.

"The cave that Alemi and I spotted on the shore near the Dragon Stones," Elgion said, trying to give the proper cues. "Alemi," Elgion had to address T'gellan now, "is the Sea Man who saw the fire lizards last spring near the Dragon Stones. Two-three days back, we sailed down the coast and saw the cave. That's where I think it's likely we'll find fire lizard eggs."

"Well, then, since you're now safely in your Hold, Harper Elgion, I will leave you." T'gellan couldn't wait to get back to Monarth. And the cave.

"You'll let us know if you find anything, won't you?" Elgion called after him and received only a wild arm gesture before the bronze rider swung himself up to Monarth's back.

"We offered him no hospitality for his trouble in returning you," Yanus said, worried and somewhat aggrieved by the bronze rider's precipitous departure.

"He'd just eaten," Elgion replied, as the bronze dragon beat his way upward above the sunset-lit waters of the harbor.

"So early."

"Ah, he'd been fighting Thread. And he's wingleader, so he must be back at the Weyr."

That did impress Yanus.

Rider and dragon winked out, drawing a startled exclamation of delight from everyone. Alemi caught Elgion's eye, and the Harper had to suppress his grin: he'd share the full jest with Alemi later. Only would the joke be on himself if after all the half-truths T'gellan found fire lizard eggs . . . or a piper . . . in the cave?

"Harper Elgion," said Yanus firmly, waving the rest of the holders away from them as he pointed to the Hold door. "Harper Elgion, I'd be grateful for a few words of explanation."

"Indeed, sir, and I've much to report to you of happenings in the Weyr." Elgion respectfully followed the Sea Holder. He knew now how to deal with Yanus with no further recourse to evasions or lies.

CHAPTER 10

Then my feet took off and my legs went, too,
So my body was obliged to follow
Me with my hands and my mouth full of cress
And my throat too dry to swallow.

When Menolly roused, she was in a quiet dark place and some-thing crooned comfortingly in her ear. She knew it was Beauty, but she wondered how she could be so warm all over. She moved, and her feet felt big, stuffed and very sore.

She must have made some sound because she heard a soft movement and then the glow in the corner of the room was half-unshielded.

"Are you comfortable? Are your feet painful?"

The warmth beside Menolly's ear disappeared. Clever Beauty, Menolly thought with approval after an instant's fear of discovery.

Someone was bending over Menolly now, securing the sleeping furs about her shoulders; someone whose hands were gentle, soothing, who smelled of clean herbs and faintly of numbweed.

"They only hurt a little," Menolly replied untruthfully because her feet had taken to throbbing so hard she was afraid the woman could hear them.

Her soft murmur and her gentle hands denied Menolly's sto-icism.

"You must surely be hungry. You've slept all day."

"I have?"

"We gave you fellis juice. You'd run your feet to ribbons . . ." There was a slight hesitation in the woman's voice. "They'll be fine in a sevenday. No serious cuts." The quiet voice held a ripple of amusement. "T'gran is convinced you're the fastest . . . runner in Pern."

"I'm not a runner. I'm just a girl."

"Not 'just' a girl. I'll get you something to eat. And then it's best if you sleep again."

Alone, Menolly tried not to think of her throbbing feet and a body which felt stone-heavy, immobile. She worried for fear Beauty or some of the others would come and be discovered by the weyrwoman, and what would happen to Lazy with no one to make him hunt for himself and . . .

"I'm Manora," the woman said as she returned with a bowl of steaming stew and a mug. "You realize that you're at Benden Weyr? Good. You may stay here, you know, as long as you wish."

"I can?" A relief as intense as the pain in her feet flooded Menolly.

"Yes, you can," and the firmness of that reply made that right inalienable.

"Menolly is my name . . ." She hesitated because Manora was nodding. "How did you know?"

Manora motioned for her to continue eating. "I've seen you at Half-Circle, you know, and the Harper asked the wingleader to keep search for you . . . after you disappeared. We won't discuss that now, Menolly, but I do assure you that you can stay at Benden."

"Please don't *tell* them . . ."

"As you wish. Finish your stew and take all the drink. You must sleep to heal."

She left as noiselessly as she'd come, but Menolly was reassured. Manora was headwoman at Benden Weyr, and what she said was so.

The stew was delicious, thick with meat chunks and satisfying with herb flavors. She'd almost finished it when she heard a faint rustle and Beauty returned, piteously broadcasting hunger. With a sigh, Menolly pushed the bowl under the little queen's nose. Beauty licked it dry, then hummed softly and rubbed her face against Menolly's cheek.

"Where are the others?" Menolly asked, worriedly.

The little queen gave another hum and began to curl herself up in a ball by Menolly's shoulder. She wouldn't have been so relaxed if the others were in trouble, Menolly thought, as she sipped the fellis juice.

"Beauty," Menolly whispered, nudging the queen, "if anyone comes, you go. You mustn't be seen here. Do you understand?"

The queen rustled her wings irritably.

"Beauty, you mustn't be seen." Menolly spoke as sternly as she could, and the queen opened one eye, which whirled slowly. "Oh dear, won't you understand?" The queen gave a soft reassuring croon and then closed both lids.

The fellis juice was already melting Menolly's limbs into weightlessness. The dreadful throb of her feet eased. As her eyes relentlessly closed, Menolly had one last thought: how had Beauty known where she was?

When Menolly woke, it was to hear faint sounds of children

laughing, an infectious laughter that made her grin and wonder what caused such happiness. Beauty was gone but the space where she'd lain by Menolly's head was warm to the touch. The curtain across the cubicle parted and a figure was silhouetted against the light beyond.

"What's the matter with you all of a sudden, Reppa?" the girl said softly to someone Menolly couldn't see. "Oh, all right. I'm well rid of you for now." She turned and saw Menolly looking at her. "How do you feel today?" As she adjusted the glow for full light, Menolly saw a girl about her own age, dark hair tied primly back from a face that was sad, tired and oddly mature. Then she smiled, and the impression of maturity dissolved. "Did you really run across Nerat?"

"I really didn't, although my feet feel as if *they* had."

"Imagine it! And you holdbred and out during a Fall!" There was a grudging respect in her voice.

"I was running for shelter," Menolly felt obliged to say.

"Speaking of running, Manora couldn't come to see you herself right now so you're in my charge. She's told me exactly what to do," and the girl grimaced with such feeling that Menolly had a swift vision of Manora delivering her precise and careful instructions, "and I've had a lot of experience . . ." An expression of pain and anxiety crossed her face.

"Are you Manora's fosterling?" asked Menolly politely.

The expression deepened for a moment, and then the girl erased all expression from her face, drawing her shoulders up with pride. "No, I'm Brekke's. My name is Mirrim. I used to be in the Southern Weyr."

She made the statement as if that should make all plain to Menolly.

"You mean, in the Southern Continent?"

"Yes," and Mirrim sounded irritated.

"I didn't know anyone lived there." The words were no sooner out of her mouth than Menolly remembered some snippet of information overheard in conversations between Petiron and her father.

"Where have you *been* all your life?" demanded Mirrim, exasperated.

"In Half-Circle Sea Hold," Menolly replied meekly because she didn't wish to offend the girl.

Mirrim stared at her.

"Haven't you ever heard of it?" It was Menolly's turn to be condescending. "We have the biggest dock cavern on Pern."

Mirrim caught her eye, and then both girls began to laugh, the moment in which their friendship began.

"Look, let me help you to the necessary, you must be bursting . . ." and Mirrim briskly threw back the sleeping fur. "You just lean on me."

Menolly had to because her feet were incredibly sore, even with Mirrim supporting most of her weight. Fortunately the necessary was no more than a few steps beyond the sleeping cubicle. By the time Menolly crawled back into her bed, she was shaking all over.

"Stay on your stomach, Menolly; it'll be easier to change your bandages," Mirrim said. "I haven't had to do many feet, it's true; but if you don't have to see what's going on, that makes it easier. Everyone at Southern said my hands are gentle, and I'll drown your feet in numbweed. Or would you want some more fellis juice? Manora said you could."

Menolly shook her head.

"Brekke . . ." and here Mirrim's voice faltered briefly, "Brekke taught me how to change sticky bandages because I . . . Oh, dearie me, your feet look just like raw meat. Ooops, that's not the right thing to say, but they do. They *will* be all right, Manora said," and there was such confidence in that statement that Menolly preferred to believe it, too. "Now Threadscore . . . that's nasty. You've just lost all the skin on your feet, that's all, but I expect you feel that's quite enough. Sorry. Caught you there. Anyway, you'll not even have scars once the new skin grows, and it's really amazing how quickly skin does grow. Or so I've observed. Now Threadscore, that's nasty for healing. Never quite fades. Lucky for you T'gran's Branth spotted you running. Dragons are very longsighted, you know. There, now, this should help . . ."

Menolly gasped involuntarily as Mirrim slathered cool numbweed on her right foot. She'd been biting her lips against the pain while Mirrim, with very gentle hands indeed, had removed the blood-caked bandages but the relief from pain was almost a shock. If she'd only lost the skin from her feet, why did they hurt so much more than her hand had?

"Now, we've only the left foot to go. The numbweed does help, doesn't it? Did you ever have to boil it?" Mirrim asked with a groan and, as usual, didn't wait for an answer. "For three days I just grit my teeth and close my nose and firmly remind myself that it would be so *much* worse if we *didn't* have numbweed. I suppose that's the bad with the good Manora's always saying we have to have. But you'll be relieved to know that there's no sign of infection . . ."

"Infection?" Menolly jerked herself up on her elbows, craning her head about.

"Will you keep still?" Mirrim glared so authoritatively that Menolly forced herself to relax. All she could see of her feet were salve-smeared heels. "And you're very, very lucky there isn't any infection. After all, you'd been running shoeless over sand, dirt and goodness knows what. It took us forever to wash the grit off." Mirrim made a sympathetic sound. "Just as well we'd dosed you good."

"You're sure there's no infection this time?"

"This time? You haven't done this before, have you?" Mirrim's voice was shocked.

"No, not my feet. My hand," and Menolly turned on her side, holding out her scarred hand. She was considerably gratified by the concerned pity in Mirrim's face as she examined the wound.

"However did you do that?"

"I was gutting packtail, and the knife slipped."

"You were lucky to miss the tendons."

"Miss?"

"Well, you are using those fingers. A bit drawn that scar, though." Mirrim clucked her tongue with professional dismay. "Don't think much of your Hold's nursing if that's any sample."

"Packtail slime is difficult, as bad as Threadscore in its own way," Menolly muttered, perversely defending her Hold.

"Be that as it may," and Mirrim gave the foot bandage a final twitch, "*we'll* see you don't have any such trouble with your feet. Now, I'll bring you something to eat. You must be starved . . ."

Now that the worst of the dressing was over and the numb-weed had deadened the pain in her feet, Menolly was definitely aware of the emptiness in her stomach.

"So I'll be right back, Menolly, and if you need anything after that, just shout for Sanra. She's below on the Floor, minding the little ones, and she knows she's to listen for you."

As Menolly worked her way through the generous meal Mirrim brought, she reflected on some harsh truths. Definitely Mavi had given her the distinct impression that she'd never be able to use her hand again. Yet Mavi was too skilled a healer not to have known that the knife had missed the finger tendons. She had deliberately let the hand heal with drawn flesh. It was painfully clear to Menolly that Mavi, as well as Yanus, had not wanted her to be able to play again.

Grimly Menolly vowed that she'd never, never return to Half-Circle. Her reflections made her doubt Manora's assurance that she could stay at Benden Weyr. No matter, she could run away again. Run she could, and live holdless. And that's what she'd do. Why, she'd run across all Pern . . . And why not? Menolly became pleased with the notion. Indeed, there was nothing to stop her running right to the Masterharperhall in Fort Hold. Maybe Petiron *had* sent her songs to Masterharper Robinton. Maybe they were more than just twiddles. Maybe . . . but there was no maybe about returning to Half-Circle Hold! That she would not do.

The issue did not arise over the next few days while her feet itched—Mirrim said that was a good sign of healing—and she found herself beginning to fret with impatience at her disability.

She also worried about her fire lizards now she wasn't able to forage for them. But the first evening when Beauty reappeared, her little eyes darting about the chamber to be sure Menolly was alone, there was nothing of hunger in her manner. She daintily accepted the morsels that Menolly had carefully saved from her supper. Rocky and Diver appeared just as she was drifting off to sleep. However, they promptly curled themselves up to sleep against the small of her back, which they wouldn't have done if they'd been hungry.

They were gone the next morning, but Beauty lingered, stroking her head against Menolly's cheek until she heard footsteps in the corridor. Menolly shooed her away, telling her to stay with the others.

"I know it's boring to stay abed," Mirrim agreed the third morning with a weary sigh that told Menolly Mirrim would gladly have swapped places, "but it's kept you out of Lessa's way. Since the . . . well," and Mirrim censored what she'd been about to say. "With Ramoth broody over those eggs, we're all treading hot sands until they Hatch, so it's better you're here."

"There must be something I can do, now that I'm better. I'm good with my hands . . ." and then Menolly, too, halted uncertainly.

"You could help Sanra with the little ones if you would. Can you tell any stories?"

"Yes, I . . ." and Menolly all but blurted out what she'd done at the Sea Hold, ". . . can at least keep them amused."

Weyrbred children were not like Hold children, Menolly discovered: they were more active physically, possessed of insatiable curiosity for every detail she cared to tell them about fishing and sailing. It was only when she taught them to fashion tiny boats of sticks and wide root leaves and sent them off to sail the skiffs in the Weyr lake that she had any rest the first morning.

In the afternoon, she amused the younger ones by recounting how T'gran had rescued her. Thread was not as automatically horrifying to Weyr children as it would be to Holders, and they were far more interested in her running and rescue than in what she was running from. Unconsciously she fell into a rhyming pattern and caught herself up sharply just before she'd conceived a tune. The children didn't seem to notice fortunately, and then it was time to peel tubers for the evening meal.

It was difficult to subdue that little tune as she worked. Really it had exactly the cadence of her running stride . . .

"Oh!"

"Did you cut yourself?" asked Sanra from the other side of the table.

"No," replied Menolly, and she grinned with great good humor. She had just realized something very important. She wasn't in the Sea Hold any longer. And no one here knew about her harpering. Likewise no one would know if it were her own songs she hummed when she felt like humming. So she began to hum her running song, and was doubly pleased with herself because the tune matched her paring strokes, too.

"It's a relief to hear someone happy," remarked Sanra, smiling encouragingly at Menolly.

Menolly realized then that she'd been vaguely aware all day of the fact that the atmosphere in the living cavern reminded her of those times when the fishing fleet was overdue in a storm and everyone was "waiting." Mirrim was very worried about Brekke but she wouldn't say why, and Menolly was reluctant to broach the girl's sad reserve.

"I'm happy because my feet are healing," she told Sanra and then hurried on, "but I wish someone would tell me what's wrong with Brekke. I know Mirrim's worried sick about her . . ."

Sanra stared at Menolly for a moment. "You mean, you

haven't heard about . . ." she lowered her voice and glanced about to make sure they weren't overheard, ". . . about the queens?"

"No. No one tells girls anything in the Sea Hold."

Sanra looked surprised but accepted the explanation. "Well, Brekke used to be at Southern, you did know that? Good. And when F'lar banished all the rebellious Oldtimers to Southern, the Southerners had to go somewhere. T'bor became Weyrleader at Fort Hold, Kylara . . ." and Sanra's usually gentle voice became hard, "Kylara was Weyrwoman for Prideth, with Brekke and Wirenth . . ." Sanra was having enough trouble telling the tale so Menolly was very glad she hadn't asked Mirrim. "Wirenth rose to mate, but Kylara . . ." and the name was spoken with intense hatred, "Kylara hadn't taken Prideth far enough away. She was close to mating, too, and when Wirenth flew the bronzes, she rose, and . . ."

There were tears in Sanra's eyes, and she shook her head, unable to continue.

"Both queens . . . died?"

Sanra nodded.

"Brekke's alive, though . . . Isn't she?"

"Kylara lost her mind, and we're desperately afraid that Brekke will lose hers . . ." Sanra mopped the tears from her face, sniffing back her sorrow.

"Poor Mirrim. And she's been so good to me!"

Sanra sniffed again, this time from pique.

"Mirrim likes to think she's got the cares of the Weyr on her shoulders."

"Well, I've a lot more respect for her the way she keeps on going when she's worried sick than if she crept off someplace and just felt sorry for herself."

Sanra stared at Menolly. "No need to bristle at me, girl, and if you keep on stabbing your knife that way, you will cut yourself."

"Will Brekke be all right?" asked Menolly after a few minutes' strict attention to her peeling.

"We hope so," but Sanra didn't sound confident. "No, we do. You see, Ramoth's clutch is about to hatch, and Lessa is certain that Brekke could Impress the queen. You see, she can speak to any of the dragons, the way Lessa can, and Grall and Berd are always with her . . . Here comes Mirrim."

Menolly had to admit that Mirrim, who only numbered the same Turns as she did, did assume an officious manner. She could understand that an older woman like Sanra might not take kindly to it. Yet Menolly had no fault to find with Mirrim's ministrations. And she let the girl bustle her off to her cubicle to change the bandages.

"You've been on them all day, and I want to be sure no dirt's in the scabs," she said, briskly.

Menolly obediently lay on her stomach in the bed and then tentatively suggested that perhaps tomorrow she could change her own bandages and save Mirrim some work.

"Don't be silly. Feet are very awkward, but *you're* not. You should just hear C'tarel complain. He got Threadscored during the last Fall. You'd think he was the only one ever in the world scored. And besides, Manora *said* I was to take care of you. You're easy, you don't moan, groan, complain, *and* swear like C'tarel. Now, these *are* healing nicely. In spite of the way it might feel to you. Manora says that feet hurt worse than any part of your body, but hands. That's why it seems much worse to you, I expect."

Menolly had no argument and breathed a sigh of relief that the painful session was now over.

"*You* taught the weyrlings how to make those little boats, didn't you?"

Menolly flipped over, startled, and wondering if she'd done wrong, but Mirrim was grinning.

"You should have *seen* the dragons snorting them about the lake." Mirrim giggled. "Having the grandest time. I haven't laughed so much in weeks. There you are!" And Mirrim bustled away on some other errand.

The following day Mirrim hovering beside her, Menolly walked slowly and not too painfully through the living cavern and into the main kitchen cavern for the first time.

"Ramoth's eggs are just about to Hatch," Mirrim told her as she placed Menolly at one of the worktables along the back side of the huge cave. "There's nothing wrong with your hands, and we'll need all the help we can get for the feast . . ."

"And maybe your Brekke will be better?"

"Oh, she's got to be, Menolly, she's got to be." Mirrim scrubbed her hands together anxiously. "If she isn't, I don't know what will become of her and F'nor. He cares so much. Manora's as worried about him as she is about Brekke . . ."

"It'll all come right, Mirrim. I'm sure it will," Menolly said, putting all the confidence she could muster into her voice.

"Oh, do you really think so?" Mirrim dropped her pose of bustling efficiency and was briefly a young, bewildered girl in need of reassurance.

"I most certainly do!" And Menolly was angry with Sanra's unkind statements of the day before. "Why, when I thought I'd be scored to death, T'gran appeared. And when I thought they'd all be Threaded . . ." Menolly hastily shut her mouth, frantically trying to think of something to fill that gap. She'd almost told Mirrim about saving the fire lizards.

"They must belong to somebody," a man said in a loud, frustrated tone of voice.

Two dragonriders entered the kitchen cavern, slapping dusty gloves against sandy boots and loosening their riding belts.

"They could be attracted by the ones we have, T'gellan."

"Considering how badly we need the creatures . . ."

"In the egg . . ."

"It's a raking nuisance to have a whole flaming fair that no one will claim!"

The next thing Menolly knew, Beauty appeared over her head, gave a terrified squawk and landed on Menolly's thinly clad shoulder. Beauty wrapped her tail, choking tight, about Menolly's neck and buried her face into her hair. Rocky and Diver seized the cloth of her shirt in their claws, struggling to burrow into her arms. The air was full of frightened fire lizards, diving at her; and Mirrim, who made no attempt to defend herself, stared with utter amazement at Menolly.

"Mirrim? Do they belong to you after all?" cried T'gellan as he strode toward their table.

"No, they're not mine." Mirrim pointed to Menolly. "They're hers."

Menolly was speechless, but she managed to contain Rocky and Diver. The others took refuge on ledges above her, broadcasting fear and uncertainty. She was just as confused as the fire lizards, because why were they in the Weyr? And the Weyr seemed to know about fire lizards, and . . .

"We'll soon know whose they are," said a woman's angry

voice, carrying clearly in the pause. A small, slim woman in riding gear came striding purposefully into the main section of the kitchen cavern. "I asked Ramoth to speak to them . . ."

She was followed by another rider.

"Over here, Lessa," T'gellan said, beckoning, but his gaze did not leave Menolly's.

At the sound of that name, she struggled out of the chair, with the fire lizards squawking and trying to retain their balance and hold on her. All Menolly could think of was to keep out of Lessa's way, but she got tangled up in the chairs about the table and painfully stubbed her toes. Mirrim grabbed her arm, trying to make her sit down, and there seemed to be more fire lizards than Menolly could claim circling over her head and chittering wildly.

"Will someone quiet this lot?" demanded the small, dark woman, confronting Menolly, her fists on her riding belts, her eyes snapping with anger. "Ramoth! if you would . . ."

Abruptly, complete silence reigned in the huge kitchen cavern. Menolly felt Beauty trembling more violently than ever against her neck, and the talons of the two bronzes dug into her arms and sides.

"That's better," said Lessa, her eyes brilliant. "And who are you? Are these all yours?"

"My name is Menolly, please and," Menolly glanced up nervously at all the fire lizards perched silently with whirling eyes on ledges and hanging from the ceiling, "not all of these are mine."

"Menolly?" Some of Lessa's anger abated in her perplexity. "Menolly?" She was trying to place the name.

"Manora told you about her, Lessa," said Mirrim, which Menolly thought greatly daring and very much appreciated.

"T'gran rescued her from Threadfall. She'd run her feet raw."

"Ah, yes. So, Menolly, how many fire lizards do look to you?"

Menolly was trying to figure out whether Lessa was annoyed or pleased, and if she had too many fire lizards would she be sent back to Half-Circle. She felt Mirrim prod her in the ribs.

"These," Menolly indicated the three clinging to her and felt Mirrim dig her again, "and only six of those up there."

"Only six of those up there?"

Menolly saw Lessa's fingers drumming on her wide riding belt; she heard one of the dragonriders muffling a sound; and glancing up saw that he had his hand over his mouth. But his eyes were dancing with laughter. Then she dared look at Lessa's face and saw the slight smile on the Weyrwoman's face.

"That makes nine, I think," Lessa said. "Just how did you contrive to impress nine fire lizards, Menolly?"

"I didn't contrive. I was in the cave when they hatched, and they were hungry, you see. I'd a sackful of spiderclaws so I fed them . . ."

"Cave? Where?" Lessa's words were crisp but not unkind.

"On the coast. Above Nerat, by the Dragon Stones."

T'gellan uttered an exclamation. "You were living in that cave? I found jars and pots . . . no sign of fire lizard shells."

"I didn't think fire lizards clutched in caves," Lessa remarked.

"It was only because the tide was high and the clutch would have been washed away. I helped the queen put them into the cave."

Lessa regarded Menolly steadily for a long moment. "You helped the fire lizard?"

"Yes, you see I'd fallen over the cliff, and they—the queen and her bronzes, from the old clutch, not these here," and

Menolly jerked her chin at Beauty, Rocky and Diver, "they wouldn't let me get off the beach until I helped them."

T'gellan was staring at her, but the other two riders were grinning broadly. Then Menolly saw that Mirrim, too, was smiling with delight. More unbelievable to Menolly in her confusion, was the fact that a little brown fire lizard was perched on Mirrim's shoulder, intently staring at Beauty who wouldn't take her head out of Menolly's hair.

"I'd like to hear the whole story, in sequence, one day," Lessa said. "Right now, will you please keep your lot under control and with you? They're upsetting Ramoth and all the others. Nine, eh?" And Lessa sighed, turning away. "When I think where I could use nine eggs to good purpose . . ."

"Please . . . do you need more fire lizard eggs?"

Lessa whirled so fast that Menolly took an involuntarily backward step.

"Of course we need fire lizard eggs! Where have you been that you don't know?" She turned on T'gellan. "You're wingleader. Didn't you inform all the sea holds?"

"Yes, I did, Lessa," and T'gellan looked straight at Menolly now, "just about the time Menolly first disappeared from her hold. Right, Menolly? The sweep riders have been on the lookout for her ever since, but she was holed up snug as you please in that cave, with nine fire lizards."

Menolly hung her head in despair.

"Please, Weyrwoman, don't send me back to Half-Circle Hold!"

"A girl who can impress nine fire lizards," said Lessa in a sharp rippling tone that made Menolly look up, "does not belong in a Sea Hold. T'gellan, find out from Menolly where that clutch is and secure it for us immediately. Let us fervently hope it hasn't hatched." To Menolly's intense relief, Lessa actually smiled at her, obviously in a much improved temper. "Remember to keep those pesky creatures away from Ramoth. Mirrim can help you train them. Hers are quite useful now."

She swept away, leaving the entire cavern breathless. Activity suddenly picked up on all sides of the kitchen. Menolly felt Mirrim pressing her into a chair; she sank weakly down. She found a cup of klah in her hands and heard T'gellan urging her to take a few sips.

"One's first encounter with Lessa is apt to be unnerving."

"She's . . . she's so small," Menolly said dazedly.

"Size is irrelevant."

Menolly turned anxiously to Mirrim. "Did she really mean it? I can stay, Mirrim?"

"If you can impress nine fire lizards, you belong here. But why didn't you tell me about them? Didn't you see mine? I've only the three . . ."

T'gellan clicked his tongue at Mirrim, who stuck hers out at him.

"I told mine to stay in the cave . . ."

"And here we've been wracking our brains," Mirrim went on, "accusing riders of hoarding eggs . . ."

"I didn't *know* you people needed fire lizards . . ."

"Mirrim, stop teasing her; she's unnerved. Menolly, drink your klah and relax," T'gellan told her.

Menolly obediently sipped her klah, but she felt obliged to explain about the boys in her Sea Hold who could think of nothing but snaring fire lizards; and she felt so strongly that that was wrong that she hadn't even mentioned seeing them mating.

"Under the circumstances, you did just as you should, Menolly," said T'gellan. "But let's get to that clutch and rescue it. Where did you see it? How close do you think it is to Hatching?"

"The eggs were still pretty soft when I found them the day T'gran rescued me. And it's about a half-morning's walk from the Dragon Stones."

"A few minutes' glide by dragonback; but south? north? Where?"

"Well, south, where a stream feeds into the sea."

T'gellan raised his eyes in exasperation. "That describes too many places. You'd better come with me."

"T'gellan," Mirrim sounded shocked. "Menolly's feet are in shreds . . ."

"So is Lessa's temper. We'll wrap her feet in hides, but we must get those eggs. And you're not headwoman yet, my girl," T'gellan said, waggling a finger at Mirrim.

It didn't take long to outfit Menolly. Mirrim, as if to make up for her officiousness, brought her own wherhide riding jacket and headgear and a pair of vastly oversized boots. They were eased over Menolly's sore and bandaged feet and fastened tightly around her legs with leather strips.

Rocky and Diver were reassured by tidbits of meat, but Beauty refused to unwrap her tail from Menolly's neck. She chattered angrily at T'gellan when he half-carried Menolly to Monarth, waiting patiently just outside the kitchen cavern.

T'gellan threw Menolly up the dragon's shoulder. She hauled herself up to his neck ridges by the fighting straps, giving her feet one or two painful knocks.

T'gellan started to settle himself in front of Menolly, but

Beauty came alive, hissing menacingly and lashing out at the dragonrider with one foreleg, talons unsheathed.

"She's never been so bad mannered," Menolly said apologetically.

"Monarth, will you speak to her?" asked T'gellan good-naturedly.

The next instant, Beauty stopped mid-hiss, chirped experimentally, her eyes whirling less frantically, and her tail relaxed from its choke hold on Menolly's throat.

"That's a sight better. She does have a baleful stare!"

"Oh dear!"

"I'm teasing you, Menolly. Now, look, I shall have Monarth tell your fair of fire lizards exactly what we're going to do so they don't go mad when we take off."

"Oh, would you?"

"I would, and I . . ." T'gellan paused, "I have. We're away!"

This time Menolly could enjoy the sensations of flying. She couldn't imagine why Petiron had found the experience so horrible. She didn't even fear the lack of all sensation as they went *between*. She did feel the bitter, bitter cold in the soles of her half-healed feet, but the pain lasted such a fleeting second. Abruptly, they were low over the Dragon Stones, coming in from the sea. The sheer thrill of the flight took Menolly's breath away.

"There is a chance that the first queen might lay another clutch in that cave," T'gellan said over his shoulder. "But it should be cleared of your things."

So they landed on the beach with Monarth peering rather disapprovingly at the little cove while the water lapped gently on his feet.

Her group arrived, caroling in wild delight at coming home. A single fire lizard appeared above and to one side of them.

"Look, T'gellan, that's the old queen!"

But she'd gone when T'gellan looked up.

"I'm sort of sorry she saw us here. I was hoping . . . Where was the clutch when you rescued it?"

"We're standing on the place."

Monarth moved to one side.

"Does he hear what I'm telling you?" Menolly whispered anxiously in T'gellan's ear.

"Yes, so be careful how you speak of him. He's very sensitive."

"I haven't said anything, have I, that would hurt his feelings?"

"Menolly!" T'gellan looked back at her, grinning, "I was teasing you."

"Oh!"

"Hmmm. Yes. Well, so you managed to climb that cliff face?"

"It wasn't so hard. If you'll look, you'll see there're plenty of hand and foot holds, even before I made a regular path."

"A regular path? Hmmm. Yes. Monarth, can you get us a bit closer, please?"

Monarth obligingly angled against the cliff face and raised himself to his haunches; Menolly was amazed to see that they could step off his shoulders right into the cave.

Her nine came arrowing into the opening, trumpeting and squealing, their bugles abruptly amplified by the vaulting height of the inner cavern. Just as she and T'gellan reached it, the light was suddenly blocked. Turning, she saw Monarth's head in the opening, his great eyes whirling idly.

"Monarth, get your great, bloody, big head out of the light, will you?" asked T'gellan.

Monarth blinked, gave a little wistful rumble, but removed his great head.

"Why didn't anyone find you on Search, young lady?" T'gellan asked, and she saw that he'd been watching her intently.

"No one's ever been Searched at Half-Circle Sea Hold."

"That shouldn't surprise me. Now, where did the old queen have her clutch?"

"Right where you're standing."

T'gellan jumped sideways, giving her a second admonitory look, which she couldn't interpret. He knelt, running his fingers through the sand, making pleased noises in his throat.

"You tossed out the old shells?"

"Yes. Was that wrong?"

"I don't think so."

"Would she come back here again?"

"She might. If the cove waters remain high the next time she mates. D'you happen to remember when you saw her mating flight?"

"Yes, I do. Because we had Threadfall just after. The one when the leading edge hit the marshes halfway to Nerat."

"Good girl!" T'gellan tipped his head back, pressing his lips together, and Menolly thought he was doing some rapid mental calculations. Alemi had a similar habit when he was charting a course. "Yes. And when did these hatch?"

"I lost track of my sevendays, but they hatched five Falls ago."

"That's great. She may mate before high summer, if fire lizards follow the same sort of cycle the dragons do during a Pass." He glanced around him at the bits and pieces with which she had made the cave livable. "D'you want any of these things?"

"Not many," Menolly said and dove for her sleeping rug. Her pipes were still there, so he hadn't seen them in his first visit to the cave. She bundled the rug round the pipes again. "My oil . . ." she said, grabbing up the pot. "I'll need that."

"Not really," said T'gellan with a grin, "but bring it along. Manora's always interested in such things."

She took her dried herbs, too, and made a neat package, which she could tie on her back. Ruthlessly then she began to chuck her homemade crockery out of the cave entrance.

"Oh!" Aghast, she rushed to the mouth, looking about for Monarth.

"You missed him! He's got more sense than to stay around when there's a cleaning." With that T'gellan launched her boiling pot into the air.

"That's everything, I think," she said.

"Let's go!"

At the entrance, Menolly turned for one last look at the cave and smiled to herself. She'd never thought to leave it, certainly not to step to the shoulders of a dragon. But then, she'd never thought she'd live in a cave like this at all, much less ride a dragon. Nothing now marked that anyone had ever sheltered in this cave. Even the dry sand was falling back into the depressions their feet had made. T'gellan held out his hand to help her to Monarth's back, and then they were away to find the fire lizard's clutch.

CHAPTER 11

The little queen, all golden
Flew hissing at the sea.
To keep it back,
To turn it back
She flew forth bravely.

Menolly and T'gellan brought the thirty-one eggs of the clutch safely to Benden Weyr without so much as cracking a shell in the double, furred sack that had been provided for the journey *between*. Their return caused a flurry of excitement, the weyrfolk crowding around to examine the eggs. Duly informed, Lessa arrived, imperiously ordering a basket of warm sand from the Hatching Ground; directing it to be placed by the small sauce hearth and scrupulously turned at intervals to distribute the heat evenly. She judged that the eggs were a good sevenday from hatching hardness.

"As well," she said in her dry fashion. "One hatching at a time is enough. Better still, we can present the worthies with their eggs at the Impression." She seemed inordinately pleased with that solution and smiled on Menolly. "Manora says that your feet aren't healed yet, so you're in charge of the clutch. And, Felena, get this child out of those ridiculous boots and into some decent clothes. Surely we have something in stores that'll make her look less disreputable."

Lessa departed, leaving Menolly the object of intense scrutiny. Felena, a tall, willowy woman with very beautiful, curved black eyebrows and green eyes, gave her a long appraisal, sent one helper off for clothing from a special press, another to get the tanner to take Menolly's measure for footwear, a child for her shears because Menolly's hair must be trimmed. Who had hacked it off? They must have used a knife. And such pretty hair, too. Was Menolly hungry? T'gellan had snatched her out of the cavern without a nay-yea or maybe. Bring that chair here and push that small table over! Don't stand there gawking, get the girl something to eat.

"How many Turns do you have?" Felena asked on the end of that long series of orders.

"I've fifteen, please," answered Menolly, dazed and trying very hard not to cry. Her throat ached and her chest was tight and she couldn't believe what was happening to her: people fussing over how she looked and what she wore. Above all, Lessa had smiled at her because she was so pleased about the clutch. And it seemed as if she didn't have to worry about being sent back to Half-Circle. Not if the weyrfolk were ordering her shoes and giving her clothes. . . .

"Fifteen? Well, you wouldn't need much more fostering, would you?" Felena sounded disappointed. "We'll see what Manora has in mind for you. I'd like you as mine."

Menolly burst into tears. That provoked more confusion because her fire lizards began swooping dangerously close to people's faces. Beauty pecked at Felena, who was only trying to offer comfort.

"Let us have some order here," said a fresh, authoritative voice. Everyone, except the fire lizards, obediently subsided, and room was made for Manora. "And you be quiet, too," she said to squealing Beauty. "Go on," and she waved at the others, "go sit quietly somewhere. Now, why is Menolly crying?"

"She just burst into tears, Manora," said Felena, as perplexed as everyone else.

"I'm happy, I'm happy, I'm happy," Menolly managed to blurt out, each repetition punctuated by a heaving sob.

"Of course you are," said Manora understandingly, and made gestures to one of the women. "It's been a very exciting and tiring day. Now you just drink this." The woman had returned with a mug. "Now, everyone will go about their duties and let you catch your breath. There, that's better."

Menolly obediently sipped the drink. It wasn't fellis juice, but there was a slightly bitter taste. Manora urged her to drink deeply, and gradually Menolly felt her chest loosen, her throat stop aching and she began to relax.

She looked up to see that Manora was the only one at the little table, sitting with her hands folded serenely in her lap, her aura of calm patience very soothing.

"Feel more like yourself? Now, you just sit quietly and eat. We don't take in many new people, so there's bound to be a fuss about you. Soon enough to do everything else. How many fire lizard eggs did you find in that clutch?"

Menolly found it easy to talk to Manora, and soon she was showing the headwoman the oil and explaining how she'd made it.

"I think you did wonderfully well all on your own, Menolly, not what I'd expect of someone Mavi has trained."

Menolly's ease disappeared at the sound of her mother's name. Involuntarily she clenched her left hand, feeling the scar tissue pull painfully from the intensity of her grip.

"You wouldn't like me to send a message to Half-Circle?" asked Manora. "To say that you're safely here?"

"I don't want you to, please! I'm no use to them there." She held up her scarred hand. "And . . ." she halted, she'd been about to add "a disgrace." "I seem to be useful here," she said quickly, pointing to the basket of fire lizard eggs.

"So you are, Menolly, so you are." Manora rose. "Now eat your meat, and we'll talk again later."

When she had finished her food, Menolly felt much better. She was content to sit in her hearth corner, watching the industry of others. And in a little while, Felena came over with her shears and trimmed Menolly's hair. Then someone watched the fire lizard eggs while Menolly changed into the first brand-new garments she'd ever had, being the youngest in a large family. The tanner came and not only measured her feet for proper boots but by evening he'd also made up some soft hide slippers that fit loosely over her bandaged feet.

She was so changed in appearance that Mirrim, passing her table just before the evening meal, almost failed to recognize her. Menolly had been worrying that Mirrim was deliberately avoiding her because Menolly had Impressed nine fire lizards, but there was no restraint in Mirrim's manner. Flopping into a chair across the table, she heartily approved the hair trim, the clothing and the slippers.

"I heard all about the clutch, but I've been so busy, up, down, in, out, running errands for Manora that I simply haven't had a moment."

Menolly suppressed a grin. Mirrim sounded exactly like Felena.

Then Mirrim cocked her head at Menolly. "You know, you

look so much nicer in proper clothes that I didn't recognize you. Now, if we can only get you to smile once in a while . . ."

Just then a little brown lizard glided in to land on Mirrim's shoulder, snuggling affectionately up to her neck, and peering at Menolly from under her chin.

"Is he yours?"

"Yes, this is Tolly, and I have two greens, Reppa and Lok. And I'll make it very plain that three is quite enough for me. How ever did you manage to feed nine? They're so ravenous all the time!"

The last of Menolly's awkwardness with her friend disappeared as she recounted how she had coped with her fair of fire lizards.

The evening meal was then ready, and Mirrim, ignoring Menolly's protests that she was able to fetch her own, served them both. T'gellan joined their table and managed to coax Beauty, much to Menolly's amazement, to accept some food from his knife.

"Don't be surprised," Mirrim told Menolly with just a touch of condescension. "These greedy guts will eat what's offered from anyone. But that doesn't mean that they'll *look* to whoever feeds them. Besides, with nine . . ." She rolled her eyes so expressively that T'gellan chuckled.

"She's jealous, so she is, Menolly."

"I am not. Three's quite enough, though . . . I would've liked a queen. Let's see if Beauty will come to me. Grall does."

Mirrim concentrated on coaxing Beauty to accept a piece of meat while T'gellan teased her, rather unfairly Menolly thought; but Mirrim returned his jibes with a few tart remarks of her own in a way that Menolly would never have dared address an older man, much less a dragonrider.

She was very tired, but it was pleasant to sit in the big kitchen cavern, listening to T'gellan, watching Mirrim coax Beauty, though it was Lazybones who finally ate from her hand. There were other small groups, chatting late over their evening meal, the women pairing with dragonriders. Menolly noticed wine-skins being passed. She was surprised, at first, because the Sea Hold served wine only on very special occasions. T'gellan sent one of the weyrboys to get him cups and a skin and insisted that Menolly, as well as Mirrim, have a cup.

"Good Benden wine is not to be refused," he told her, filling her cup. "There, now, isn't that the best you've ever tasted?"

Menolly forebore to mention that, barring wine laced with fellis juice, it was the first. Living was certainly conducted on different rules in the Weyr.

When the Weyr's Harper began to play softly, more for his own pleasure than to entertain anyone in the cavern, Menolly did not restrain her fingers from tapping the rhythm. It was a song she liked, though she felt his chords were dull, which was why she began to hum her harmony when it did not discord with his. She wasn't even aware of what she was doing until Mirrim looked up with a smile on her face.

"That was just lovely, Menolly. Oharan? Come over here; Menolly has a new harmony for that one."

"No, no, I couldn't."

"Why not?" demanded T'gellan, and poured a bit more wine in her glass. "A little music would give us all heart. There're faces around here as long as a wet Turn."

Timidly at first, because of the older injunction against singing in front of people, Menolly joined her voice to Harper Oharan's baritone.

"Yes, I like it, Menolly. You've got a sure sense of pitch," said Oharan so approvingly that she started to worry again.

If Yanus knew she was singing at the Weyr . . . But Yanus wasn't here and he would never know.

"Say, can you harmonize to this one?" And Oharan broke into one of the older ballads, one in which she had always sung a counter-tune against Petiron's melody.

Suddenly there were other voices humming along, softly but surely. Mirrim looked around, stared suspiciously at T'gellan, and then pointed at Beauty.

"She's humming in tune. Menolly, however did you teach her to do that? And the others . . . some of them are singing, too!" Mirrim was wide-eyed with amazement.

Oharan kept on playing, nodding at Mirrim to be quiet so they could all hear the fire lizards while T'gellan craned his head and cocked his ears, first at Beauty, then at Rocky and Diver and Brownie who were near him.

"I don't believe it," said T'gellan.

"Don't scare them! Just let them do it," said Oharan in a low voice as he modulated his chords into another verse.

They finished the song with the fire lizards humming obediently along with Menolly. Mirrim demanded then to know how on earth Menolly had gotten her lizards to sing with her.

"I used to play and sing for them in the cave, you know, to keep us company. Just little twiddles."

"Just little twiddles! I've had my three much longer, and I never even knew they liked music."

"Just shows that you don't know all there is to know, doesn't it, young Mirrim?" teased T'gellan.

"Now that isn't fair," Menolly interceded and then hiccuped.

To her embarrassment she hiccuped again.

"How much wine have you been giving her, T'gellan?" demanded Mirrim, frowning at the bronze rider.

"Certainly not enough to put her in her cups."

Menolly hiccuped again.

"Get her some water!"

"Hold your breath," Oharan suggested.

T'gellan brought water and, with quick sips, Menolly managed to stop her hiccuping. She kept insisting that she didn't feel the wine, but she was very tired. If someone would watch the eggs . . . it was so late . . . With solicitous help, T'gellan and Oharan supported her to her sleeping chamber, Mirrim fussing at them that they were two great big numbwits who hadn't a lick of sense between them.

Menolly was very glad to lie down and let Mirrim remove the slippers and the new clothes and cover her. She was asleep before the fire lizards had disposed themselves about her for the night.

CHAPTER 12

Dragonman, Dragonman,
Between thee and thine,
Share me that glimpse of love
Greater than mine.

Mirrim roused Menolly early the next morning, impatiently shushing the fire lizards who hissed at her rough shaking of their mistress.

"Menolly, wake up. We need every hand in the kitchen. The eggs will Hatch today and half Pern's invited. Turn over. Manora's coming to look at your feet."

"Ouch! You're too rough!"

"Tell Beauty . . . ouch . . . I'm *not* hurting you. Beauty! Behave or I'll tell Ramoth!"

To Menolly's surprise, Beauty stopped diving at Mirrim and retreated with a squeak to the far corner of the room.

"You were hurting me," said Menolly, too sleepy to be tactful.

"Well, I said I was sorry. Hmmm. Your feet really do look a lot better."

"We won't use such heavy bandages today," said Manora, entering at that moment. "The slippers give enough protection."

Menolly craned her head about as she felt Manora's strong gentle fingers turn first one foot and then the other.

"Yes, lighter bandages today, Mirrim, and salve. Tonight, no bandages at all. Wounds must have fresh air, too, you know. But you've done a good job. The fire lizard eggs are fine this morning, Menolly."

With that she left, and Mirrim quickly set about dressing the feet. When she'd finished and Menolly rose to put on her clothes, her fingers lingering in the soft folds of the overshirt, Mirrim sank onto the bed with an exaggerated sigh.

"What's the matter with you?" Menolly asked.

"I'm getting all the rest I can while I can," Mirrim replied. "You don't know what a Hatching is like, with all those holders and crafters stumbling about the Weyr, poking here and there where they're NOT supposed to be and getting scared of and scaring the dragons and the weyrlings and the hatchlings. And the way they eat!" Mirrim rolled her eyes expressively. "You'd think they'd never seen food and . . ." Mirrim flopped over on the bed and started to sob wildly.

"Mirrim, what's the matter? Oh, it's Brekke! Isn't she all right? I mean, won't she re-Impress? Sanra said that's what Lessa hoped . . ."

Menolly bent to comfort her friend, herself upset by those heart-rending sobs. Mirrim's words were garbled by her weeping, although Menolly gathered that Mirrim didn't want her foster-mother to re-Impress and the reason was obscure. Brekke didn't want to live, and they had to find some way to make her. Losing her dragon was like losing half herself, and it hadn't been Brekke's fault. She was so gentle and sensible, and she loved F'nor, and for some reason that was unwise, too.

Menolly just let Mirrim cry, knowing how much relief she had felt the day before when she'd wept, and hoping deep in her heart that there might be joyful tears, too, for Mirrim later that day. There had to be. She forgave Mirrim all her little poses and attitudes, aware that that was how Mirrim had masked her intense anxiety and grief.

There was a rattling of the cubicle's curtain, a squabble of fire lizard protest, and then Mirrim's Tolly crawled under the curtain, his eyes whirling with indignation and worry. He saw Menolly stroking Mirrim's hair and, raising his wings, made as if to launch himself at her when Beauty warbled sharply from the corner. Tolly sort of shook his wings, but when he leaped to the bed, he landed gently on the edge and remained there, his eyes first on Mirrim, then on Menolly. A moment later the two greens entered. They settled themselves on the stool, watchful but not obtrusive.

Beauty, in her corner, kept an eye on them all.

"Mirrim? Mirrim?" It was Sanra's voice from the living cavern. "Mirrim, haven't you finished Menolly's feet yet? We need both of you! Now!"

As Menolly rose obediently, Mirrim caught her hand and squeezed it. Then she rose, shook her skirts out and marched from the cubicle, Menolly following more slowly behind her.

Mirrim had by no means exaggerated the amount of work to be done. It was just past sunrise, but obviously the main cooks had already been up for hours, judging by the breads—sweet, spiced and sour—cooling on long tables. Two weyrmen were trussing a huge herdbeast for the main spit and at the smaller hearths, wild wherries were being cleaned and stuffed for roasting later.

For added protection in the busy kitchen, someone had placed the small table over her fire lizard egg basket. They were doing fine, the sand nice and warm all around. Felena caught sight of her, told her to feed herself quickly from the sauce hearth and did she know anything flavorful to do with dried fish? Or would she prefer to help pare roots?

Menolly instantly elected to cook fish, so Felena asked what ingredients she'd need. Menolly was a little dismayed to learn the quantity she'd have to prepare. She had had no idea that so many people came to a Hatching: the number coming was more than *lived* at Half-Circle Sea Hold.

The knack in making the fish stew tasty was in the long baking so Menolly applied herself to prepare the huge pots quickly, to give them enough time to simmer into succulence. She did so with such dispatch that there were still plenty of roots left to pare.

Excitement filled the air of the kitchen cavern. The mound of root vegetables in front of Menolly melted away as she listened to the chatter of the other girls and women. There was great speculation as to which of the boys, and the girls for the queen egg, would Impress the dragons to be hatched that day.

"No one has ever re-Impressed a dragon," said one woman wistfully. "D'you think Brekke will?"

"No one's ever been given the chance before."

"Is it a chance we should take?" asked someone else.

"*We* weren't asked," said Sanra, glaring at the last speaker. "It's Lessa's idea, but it wasn't F'nor's or Manora's . . ."

"Something has to help her," said the first woman. "It tears my heart to see her lying there, just lying, like the undead. I mind me of the way D'namal went. He sort of . . . well . . . faded completely away."

"If you'll finish that root quickly, we can put this kettle on," said Sanra, briskly rising.

"Will all of this be eaten?" asked Menolly of the woman beside her.

"Yes, indeed, and there'll be some looking for more," she said with a complacent smile. "Impression Days are good days. I've a fosterling and a blood son on the Hatching Ground today!" she added with understandable pride. "Sanra!" she turned her head to shout over her shoulder, "just one more largish kettle will take what's left."

Then white roots had to be sliced finely, covered with herbs and placed in clay pots to bake. The succulent odors of Menolly's fish concoction aroused compliments from Felena, who was in charge of the various hearths and ovens. Then Menolly, who was told to keep off her poor feet, helped decorate the spiced cakes. She giggled with the rest when Sanra distributed pieces of one cake about, saying they had to be certain the bake had turned out well, didn't they?

Menolly did not forget to turn the fire lizard eggs, or to feed her friends. Beauty stayed within sight of Menolly, but the others had been seen bathing in the lake and sunning themselves, scrupulously avoiding Ramoth, whose bugles punctuated the morning.

"She's always like that on Impression Day," T'gellan told Menolly as he grabbed a quick bite to eat at her table. "Say, will you get your fire lizards to hum along with you again this evening? I've been called a liar because I said you'd taught them to sing."

"They might turn difficult and shy in front of a lot of people, you know."

"Well, we'll wait till things get quiet, and then we'll give it a try, huh. Now, I'm to see you get to the Hatching. Mid-afternoon, I'd say, so be ready."

As it happened, she wasn't. She felt the thrumming before she heard it. She and everyone else in the cavern stopped working as one-by-one they became aware of the intensely exciting noise. Menolly gasped, because she recognized it as the same sort of sound the fire lizards had made when their eggs had hatched.

There was suddenly no time for her to return to her cubicle and change. T'gellan appeared at the cavern entrance, gesturing urgently to her. She made as much speed as her feet would permit because she could see Monarth waiting outside the entrance. T'gellan had already taken her hand when she exclaimed over the cooking stains and wet marks on her overshirt.

"I told you to be ready. I'll put you in a corner, pet, not that anyone will notice stains today," T'gellan reassured her.

A trifle resentful, Menolly noticed that he was dressed in new dark trousers, a handsomely overstitched tunic, a belt worked with metal and jewels, but she didn't resist.

"I have to get you in place first, because I'm to collect some visitors," T'gellan said, climbing nimbly into place in front of her on Monarth's neck ridges. "F'lar's filling the Hatching Ground with anyone who'll ride a dragon *between*."

Monarth was awing, slanting up from the Bowl floor to an immense opening, high up on the Weyr wall, which Menolly had not noticed before. Other dragons were angling toward it, too. Menolly gasped as they entered the mouth, with a dragon before them and one abaft, so close that she had momentary fears of collision. The dark core of the tunnel was lit at the far end, and abruptly they were in the gigantic Hatching Ground.

The whole north quadrant of the Weyr must be hollow, thought Menolly, awed. Then she saw the gleaming clutch of dragon eggs and gasped. Slightly to one side was a larger egg, and hovering over it was the zealous golden form of Ramoth, her eyes incredibly brilliant with the coming of Impression.

Monarth dropped with distressing abruptness, then back-winged to land neatly on a ledge.

"Here you are, Menolly. Best seat in the Ground. I'll be back for you afterward."

Menolly was only too glad to sit still after that incredible ride. She was in the third tier, by the outer wall, so she had a perfect view of the Hatching Ground and the entrance through which people were beginning to file. They were all so elegantly dressed that she brushed vainly at the stains and crossed her arm over her chest. At least the clothes were new.

Other dragons were arriving from the upper entrance, depositing their passengers, often three and four at a time. She watched the now steady stream of visitors coming in from the ground entrance. It was amusing to watch the elegant, and sometimes overdressed, ladies having to pick up their heavy skirts and run in awkward little steps across the hot sands. The tiers filled rapidly, and the excited thrumming of the dragons increased in pitch so that Menolly found it difficult to sit quietly.

A sudden cry announced the rocking of some of the eggs. Late arrivals began to hurry across the sands, and the seats beyond Menolly were filled with a group of minecraftsmen, to judge from their red-brown tunic devices. She crossed her arms again and then uncrossed them because she had to lean forward to see around the minecraftsmen's stocky bodies.

More eggs were rocking, all of them except the smallish gray egg that had somehow got shoved back against the inside wall.

Another rush of wings, and this time bronze dragons entered, depositing the girls who were candidates for the queen egg. Menolly tried to figure out which one was Brekke, but they all looked very aware and healthy. Hadn't the weyrwomen remarked that morning how Brekke just lay like someone dead? The girls formed a loose but incomplete semicircle about the queen egg while Ramoth hissed softly behind it.

Young boys marched in now from the Bowl, their expressions purposeful, their shoulders straight in the white tunics as they approached the main clutch.

Menolly did not see Brekke's entrance because she was trying to figure out which of the violently rocking eggs would hatch first. Then one of the miners exclaimed and pointed toward the entrance, to the slender figure, stumbling, halting, then moving onward, apparently insensitive to the hot sands underfoot.

"That would be the one. That would be Brekke," he told his comrades. "Dragonrider said she'd be put to the egg."

Yes, thought Menolly, she walks as if she's asleep. Then Menolly saw Manora and a man she didn't recognize standing by the entrance, as if they had done all they could in bringing Brekke to the Hatching Ground.

Suddenly Brekke straightened her shoulders with a shake of her head. She walked slowly but steadily across the sands to join the five girls who waited by the golden egg. One girl turned and gestured for her to take the space that would complete the semicircle.

The humming ceased so abruptly that a little ripple of reaction ran through those assembled. In the expectant silence, the faint crack of a shell was clear, and the pop and shatter of others.

First one dragonet, then another, awkward, ugly, glistening creatures, flopped and rolled from their casings, squawking and creeling, their wedge-shaped heads too big for the thin, sinuous short necks.

Menolly noticed how very still the boys were standing, as stunned as she'd been in that very little cave with those tiny fire lizards crawling from their shells, voracious with hunger.

Now the difference became apparent; the fire lizards had expected no help at their hatching, their instinct was to get food into their churningly empty stomachs as fast as possible. But the dragons looked expectantly about them. One staggered beyond the first boy who sidestepped its awkward progress. It fell, nose first at the feet of a tall, black-haired boy. The boy knelt, helped the dragonet balance on his shaky feet, looked into the rainbow eyes.

Emotion like a fist squeezed Menolly's heart. Yes, she'd Impressed her fire lizards, but to Impress a dragon . . . Startled, she wondered where Beauty, Rocky, Diver and the others were. She missed them acutely, wanted Beauty's affectionate nuzzling, even the choke-tight twist of the little queen's tail about her neck.

The crack of the golden egg was a summons for all attention to be centered on it. The egg split right down the center, and its inmate, protesting her abrupt birth, fell to the sand on her back. Three of the girls moved to assist it. They got the little queen to her four legs and then stepped back. Menolly held her breath as they all turned toward Brekke. She was unaware of anything. Whatever strength had sustained her to walk across the sands had now left her. Her shoulders sagged pathetically, her head listed to one side as if too heavy to hold upright. The queen dragonet turned her head toward Brekke, the glistening eyes enormous in the outsize skull. Brekke shook her head as if aware of the scrutiny. The dragonet lurched forward one step.

Menolly saw a bronze blur out of the corner of her right eye and for an unnerving moment thought it must be Diver. But it couldn't be, because the little bronze just hung above the dragonet's head, screaming defiantly. He was so close to her head that she reared back with a startled shriek and bit at the air, instinctively spreading her wings forward as protection for her vulnerable eyes.

Dragons bugled warnings from their perches at the top of the Hatching Ground, and Ramoth spread her wings, rising to her haunches as if to strike at the invader. One of the girls interposed her body between the queen and her small attacker.

"Berd! Don't!" Brekke, too, moved, her arm extended toward the irate bronze.

The dragonet queen creeled and hid her face in the girl's skirt. The two women faced each other for a moment, tense, worried. Then the other stretched her hand out to Brekke, and Menolly could see her smile. The gesture lasted only a moment because the young queen butted imperiously, and the girl knelt, her arms reassuringly encircling the dragonet's shoulders.

At the same instant, Brekke turned, no longer a somnolent figure, immersed in grief. She walked back to the entrance of the Cavern, the little bronze fire lizard whirring around her head, making noises that went from scolding to entreaty, just like Beauty when Menolly was doing something that had upset her.

Menolly didn't realize that she was weeping until tears dropped onto her arms. She glanced hastily to see if the miners had noticed, but they were concentrating on the main clutch. From their comments it seemed that a boy had been found on Search in one of their craftholds, and they were impatiently waiting for him to Impress. For a fleeting moment, Menolly was angry with them; hadn't they seen Brekke's deliverance? Didn't they realize how marvelous that was? Oh, think how happy Mirrim would be now!

Menolly sank wearily back against the stones, depleted by the emotionally laden miracle. And the look on Brekke's face as she passed under the arched entrance! Manora was there, her face radiant, her arms outstretched in a joyful gesture. The man, who was surely F'nor, swept Brekke up in his arms, his tired face mirroring his relief and gladness.

A cheer from the miners beside her indicated that their lad had Impressed although Menolly couldn't be certain which of the boys he was. There were so many now paired off with wobbly-legged hatchlings, all creeling with hunger, lurching and falling toward the entrance. The miners were urging their favorite on; and when a curly-haired, skinny lad passed by, with a grin for their cheering, she saw that he had done rather well, Impressing a brown. When the exultant miners turned to her to share their triumph, she managed to respond properly, but she was relieved when they scrambled down the tiers to follow the pair out of the Hatching Ground.

She sat there, glowing over the resurgence of Brekke, the determination and fierceness of bronze Berd, his courage in braving Ramoth's ire at such a moment. Now, why, Menolly wondered, didn't Berd want Brekke to Impress the new queen? At all events, the experiment had successfully roused Brekke from her lethargy.

The dragons were returning, landing in the Hatching Ground so that their riders could help the weyrlings, or to escort guests outside. The tiers were emptying. Soon there was only a man in holder colors on the first tier with two boys. The man looked as tired as she felt. Then one of the boys rose, pointing to the little egg on the sand that wasn't even rocking.

Idly Menolly thought that it might not hatch, remembering the uncracked egg left in the fire lizard's sand nest the morning after her fire lizards had hatched. She'd shaken it and something hard had rattled within. Sometimes hold babies were born dead, so she'd supposed that it could happen to other creatures, too.

The boy was running along the tier now. To Menolly's astonishment, he jumped to the Hatching Ground and began kicking at the little egg. His cries and his actions attracted the notice of the Weyrleader and the small knot of candidates who had not Impressed. The Holder halfrose, one hand extended in a cautionary gesture. The other boy was shouting at his friend.

"Jaxom, what are you doing?" shouted the Weyrleader.

The egg fractured then, and the boy began tearing at the shell, ripping out sections and kicking until Menolly could see the small body pushing at the thick inner membrane.

Jaxom cut at the membrane with his belt knife, and a small white body, not much larger than the boy's torso, fell from the sac. The boy reached out to help the creature to his feet.

Menolly saw the little white dragon lift his head, his eyes, brilliant with greens and yellows, fastened on the boy's face.

"He says his name is Ruth!" the boy cried in amazed delight.

With a strangled exclamation, the older man sank back to the stone seat, his face a mask of grief. The Weyrleader and the others who had rushed to prevent what had just occurred halted. To Menolly it was all too obvious that Jaxom's Impression of the little white dragon was unprecedented and unwelcome. And she couldn't imagine why: the boy and the dragon looked so radiant, who could deny them their joyous union?

CHAPTER 13

Harper, your song has a sorrowful sound,
Though the tune was written as gay.
Your voice is sad and your hands are slow
And your eye meeting mine turns away.

When it became obvious to Menolly that T'gellan had forgotten his promise to return, she slowly climbed down from the tiers and made her way out of the deserted Hatching Ground, over the hot sand.

Beauty met her at the entrance, demanding caresses and reassurance. She was swiftly followed by the others, all chittering nervously and with many anxious dartings to the entrance to see if Ramoth was about.

Although Menolly had not had far to walk on the sands, the heat had quickly penetrated the soles of her slippers. Her discomfort was acute by the time she stepped onto the cooler earth of the Bowl. She edged to one side of the entrance and sank down, her fire lizards grouping themselves about her while she waited for the pain to subside.

As everyone was on the kitchen cavern side of the Bowl, no one noticed her, for which she was grateful since she felt useless and foolish. It would be a long walk across the Bowl to the kitchens. Well, she'd just take it in small sections.

She heard the faint cries of the herdbeasts at the farthest end of the Bowl valley and saw Ramoth hovering for a kill. The weyrwomen had said that Ramoth hadn't eaten for the past ten days, which was partly the cause of her irascible temper.

By the lakeside, hatchlings were being fed and bathed, and their riders shown how to oil the fragile skin. Their white tunics stood out among the gleaming green, blue, brown and bronze hides. The little queen was slightly removed from the others, with two of the bronze dragons in attendance. She couldn't see where the white dragon was.

On the weyr ledges dotting the Bowl's face, some dragons were curled in what remained of the afternoon sun. Above and to the left of her, Menolly saw great bronze Mnementh on the ledge of the queen's weyr. He was seated on his haunches, watching his mate choose her meal. Menolly saw him move slightly, glancing over his left shoulder. Then Menolly caught a glimpse of a man's head as he descended the stairs from the queen's weyr.

Felena's voice, raised above the conversational babble, brought Menolly's gaze back to the kitchen cavern where tables were being erected for the evening's feasting. The dragonriders were doing it, for the bright colors of their best tunics were conspicuous, moving about while the soberer colors of Holder and Craft seemed to stay in stationary clumps at a polite distance from the workers.

The man had reached the Bowl floor now from the queen's weyr, and Menolly idly watched him start across. Auntie One and Two came sweeping down to her, chittering about something that had excited them and ducking their heads at her for reassurance. They needed to be oiled, and she felt guilty for not taking better care of them.

"Do you have *two* greens?" asked an amused voice, and the tall man was standing in front of her, his eyes friendly and interested.

"Yes, they're mine," she said and held up Two for him to inspect, responding to the kindness and good humor in his long face. "They like their eye ridges scratched, gently, like this," she added, showing him.

He dropped to one knee in the sand and obligingly caressed Two, who crooned and closed her eyelids in appreciation. Auntie One whistled at Menolly for attention, digging a jealous claw into her hand.

"Stop that, you naughty creature."

Beauty roused, and Rocky and Diver reacted as well, all three scolding Auntie One so fiercely that she took flight.

"Don't tell me the queen *and* the two browns are yours as well?" the man asked, startled.

"I'm afraid so."

"Then you must be Menolly," he said, rising to his feet and making such an elaborate bow that she blushed. "Lessa has just told me that I may have two eggs of that clutch *you* discovered. I'm rather partial to browns, you know, though I wouldn't actually object to a bronze. Of course the greens, like this lady here," and he smiled such a winning smile to the watching Two that she crooned responsively, "are such delicate darlings. That doesn't mean that I would object to a blue, however."

"Don't you want the queen?"

"Ah, now that would be greedy of me, wouldn't it?" He rubbed his face thoughtfully and gave her a wry half-smile. "All things considered, though, I'd be heartily embarrassed if Sebell—my Journeyman is to have possession of the other egg—

secured a queen instead. But . . ." and he threw his long fingered hand upward to signify his submission to chance. "Are you waiting here for some purpose? Or is the confusion on the other side of the Bowl too much for all your friends?"

"I should be there. The clutch must be turned; the eggs are in warm sand by the hearth; but T'gellan brought me into the Hatching Cavern and told me to wait . . ."

"And seems to have forgot you. Not surprising, considering today's surprises." The man hastily cleared his throat and extended his hand to her.

She accepted his aid because she couldn't have risen without it. He had taken three strides when he realized that she wasn't keeping up with him. Politely he turned. Menolly tried to walk normally, a feat she managed for about three strides when her heel came down so painfully on a patch of pebbles that she involuntarily cried out. Beauty whirled, scolding fiercely, and Rocky and Diver added their antics, which were of no help to anyone.

"Here's my arm, girl. Were you too long on the hot sands? Ah now, wait. You're a long child, but there's no meat on your bones."

Before Menolly could protest, he'd swung her up into his arms and was carrying her across the Bowl.

"Tell that queen of yours I'm helping you," he asked when Beauty disordered his silvering hair, diving at him. "After sober reflection, be sure you give me green eggs."

Beauty was too excited to harken to Menolly, so she had to wave her arms about his head and face to protect him. It was not astonishing then that their approach to the kitchen caverns attracted attention; but people made way so politely, bowing to them with such deference, that Menolly began to wonder who the man was. His tunic was a gray cloth with just a band of blue, so he must be a harper of some sort; probably weyrbound to Fort Weyr to judge by the yellow arm device.

"Menolly, did you hurt your feet?" Felena appeared before them, curious at the flurry of excitement. "Didn't T'gellan remember you? He's got no memory, drat the man. How good of you to rescue her, sir!"

"Think nothing of it, Felena. I discovered she was custodian of the fire lizard eggs. However, if you happened to have a cup of wine . . . This is thirsty work."

"I can stand, really I can, sir," Menolly protested, for something in Felena's manner told her that this man was too important to be toting sore-footed girls. "Felena, I couldn't stop him."

"I'm only being my usual ingratiating self," the man told her, "and do stop struggling. You're too heavy!"

Felena was laughing at his exaggeration as she led the way to Menolly's table above the egg basket.

"You're a terrible fellow, Master Robinton, indeed you are. But you'll have your wine while Menolly picks out the best of the clutch. Have you spotted the queen egg, Menolly?"

"After the way Menolly's queen has been attacking me, I'd be safer with any other color, Felena. Now do get that wine for me, there's a good woman. I'm utterly parched."

As he gently settled her into her chair, Menolly heard Felena's teasing remark, ". . . terrible fellow, Master Robinton . . . terrible fellow, Master Robinton . . ." She stared at him, disbelieving.

"Now, what's the matter, Menolly? Did my exercise bring out spots on my face?" He mopped at his cheeks and brow and examined his hand. "Ah, thank you, Felena. You've saved my life. My tongue was quite stuck to the roof of my mouth. And here's to you, young queen, and thank you for your courtesy." He raised his cup to Beauty, who was perched on Menolly's shoulder, her tail firmly entwined as she glared at him. "Well?" he asked kindly of Menolly.

"You're the Masterharper?"

"Yes, I'm Robinton." He sounded quite casual about it. "And I think you need some wine, too."

"No, I couldn't." Menolly held up her hands in refusal. "I get hiccups. And go to sleep." She hadn't meant to say that either, but she had to explain why she was discourteous enough to refuse his cup. She was also acutely aware now of her stained overshirt, her sandy clothes and slippers, her complete disarray. This wasn't how she imagined her first meeting with the Masterharper of Pern, and she hung her head in embarassment.

"I always advise eating *before* drinking," remarked Master Robinton in the nicest possible way. "I shouldn't wonder but that's half the problem right now," he added and then raised his voice. "This child is faint with hunger, Felena."

Menolly shook her head, denying his suggestion and trying to forestall Felena, but she was already ordering one of the lads to bring klah, a basket of breads, and a dish of sliced meats. When she was served, just as if she were one of the Weyrwomen, she kept her head bent over her cup, blowing to cool the contents.

"Do you think there's enough here for a starving man?" asked Masterharper Robinton, his voice so plaintive and faint with his pretended hunger that Menolly was startled into glancing up at him. His expression was at once so wistful, appealing and kind that, despite her deep chagrin, she smiled in response to his foolishness. "I'll need strength for this evening's work, and a base for my drinking," he added in a very quiet, worried voice.

She had the feeling that he had let her share his responsibilities, but she wondered at the sadness and anxiety. Surely everyone in the Weyr was happy today?

"A few slices of meat on a slab of that good bread," and Robinton made his voice quaver like a peevish old uncle's. "And . . ." his voice returned to his normal baritone range, "a cup of good Benden wine to wash it down . . ."

To her consternation, he rose then, bread and meat in one hand, the wine mug in the other. He bowed to her with great dignity and, with a smile, was off.

"But, Masterharper, your fire lizard eggs . . ."

"Later, Menolly. I'll come back later for them."

His tall figure, his head visible above the bustling activity, retreated across the cavern, away from her. She watched until he was out of sight amid the visitors, bewildered, and all too keenly aware that there was no way in which she would be able to ask Masterharper Robinton about her songs. Twiddles they were, as Yanus and Mavi had always said: too insignificant to be presented for serious consideration to such a man as Masterharper Robinton.

Beauty crooned softly and headstroked Menolly's cheek. Rocky hopped down from his wall perch to her shoulder. He nuzzled her ear, humming in a consoling tone.

Mirrim found her that way, and she roused from her apathy to rejoice with her friend.

"Oh, I'm so very happy for you, Mirrim. You see it did come right!" If Mirrim, with all her worries, had been able to keep a good face, surely Menolly, with much to be grateful for, could manage to follow her example.

"Did you see it? You *were* in the Hatching Ground? I was so terrified that I didn't dare watch," Mirrim said, no trace of terror now in her radiant face. "I made Brekke eat, the first food she's taken in just days. And she smiled at me, Menolly. She smiled at me, and she knew me. She's going to be perfectly all right. And F'nor ate every speck of the roast wherry I brought him." She giggled, all mischievous girl, not Mirrim-Felena, or Mirrim-Manora. "I snitched the best slices of the spiced wherry breast, too. And you know, he ate every bit of it! He'll probably eat himself sick at the Feast as well. Then I told him to take poor Canth down to feed because that dragon's just about transparent with hunger." Her voice dropped in awe. "Canth tried to protect Wirenth from Prideth, you know. Can you imagine that? A brown protecting a queen! It's because F'nor loves Brekke so. And now it's all right. It's well and truly all right. So tell me."

"Tell you? What?"

Irritation flashed across Mirrim's face. "Tell me exactly what happened when Brekke got on the Hatching Ground. I told you I didn't dare look myself."

So Menolly told her. And told her again until she ran out of answers to all the detailed questions Mirrim found to ask her.

"Now you tell me why everyone's so upset about this Jaxom Impressing the little white dragon. He saved his life, you know. The dragon would have died if Jaxom hadn't broken the shell and cut the sac."

"Jaxom Impressed a dragon? I didn't know!" Mirrim's eyes widened with consternation. "Oh! Now why would that kid do such a dreadful thing?"

"Why is it dreadful?"

"Because he's got to be Lord Holder of Ruatha Hold, that's why."

Menolly was a bit annoyed with Mirrim's impatience and said so.

"Well, he can't be Lord Holder *and* dragonrider. Didn't you learn anything in that Sea Hold of yours? And, by the way, I saw the Half-Circle Harper, I think his name is Elgion. Shall I tell him you're here?"

"No!"

"Well, no need to bite my head off." And with that Mirrim flounced off in a huff.

"Menolly, will you forgive me? I completely forgot to come back for you," T'gellan said, striding up to the table before Menolly had a chance to catch her breath. "Look, the Masterminer is supposed to have two eggs. He can't stay for the whole Feast, so we've got to fix something for him to carry the eggs home in. And the rest of the eggs as well. No, don't get up. Here, you, come be feet for Menolly," he ordered, beckoning to one of the weyrboys.

So Menolly spent most of that evening in the kitchen cavern sewing furry bags to carry eggs safely *between*. But she could hear all the jollity outside; and with no small effort, she made herself enjoy the singing. Five Harpers, two drummers and three pipers made music for the Impression Feast. She thought she recognized Elgion's strong tenor in one song, but it was unlikely he'd look for her at the back of the kitchen cavern.

His voice made her briefly homesick for seawinds and the taste of salty air; briefly, too, she longed for the solitude of her cave. Only briefly; this Weyr was the place for her. Her feet would heal soon; she'd no longer be Old-Auntie-Sit-by-the-Fire. So how would she make her place in the Weyr? Felena had enough cooks, and how often would the Weyr, used to meat when it wished, want to eat fish? Even if she knew more ways of preparing it than anyone else? When she came down to it, the only thing in which she excelled was gutting fish. No, she would not think about harpering anymore. Well, there had to be something she could do.

"Are you Menolly?" asked a man tentatively.

She looked up to see one of the minercraftsmen who'd shared her tier at the Impression.

"I'm Nicat, Masterminer of Crom Hold. Weyrwoman Lessa said that I was to have two fire lizard eggs."

Beyond his stiff manner, Menolly could see he was restraining an eager impatience to hold fire lizard eggs of his own.

"Indeed I have sir, right here," she said, smiling warmly at him and indicating the table-protected basket.

"Well, my word," and his manner thawed visibly, "you're taking no chances, are you."

He helped her move the table and watched anxiously as she brushed back the top layer of sand and exposed the first of the eggs.

"Could I have a queen egg?" he asked.

"Master Nicat, Lessa explained to you that there's no way of telling which is which among the fire lizard eggs," said T'gellan, joining them to Menolly's intense relief. "Of course, Menolly might have a way of telling . . ."

"She might?" Masterminer Nicat regarded her with surprise.

"She's Impressed nine, you know."

"Nine?" Master Nicat frowned at her now, and she could

practically read his mind: Nine for a child, and only two for the Masterminer?

"Pick Master Nicat two of the best, Menolly! We don't want him to be disappointed." Although T'gellan's face was sober, Menolly caught the expression in his eyes.

She managed to conduct herself with proper dignity and made a play of picking out just the right eggs for Masterminer Nicat, all the while being certain in her own mind that the queen egg was going to Masterharper Robinton only.

"Here you are, sir," she said, handing Masterminer Nicat the furry pouch with its precious contents. "You'd best carry them in your riding jacket, against your skin, on the way home."

"Then what do I do?" Master Nicat asked with humility as he held the sack in both hands against his chest.

Menolly looked at T'gellan, but both men were looking at her. She gulped.

"Well, I'd do exactly what we're doing here. Keep them near the hearth in a strong basket with either hot sand or furs. The Weyrwoman said they'd be hatching in about a sevenday. Feed them as soon as they break their shells, as much as they can eat, and talk to them all the time. It's important to . . ." She faltered; how could she tell this hard-faced man that you had to be affectionate and kind . . .

"You must reassure them constantly. They're nervous when they're first hatched. You saw the dragons today. Touch them and stroke them . . ." The Masterminer was nodding as he catalogued her instructions. "They must be bathed daily, and their skins must be oiled. You can always tell when a crack is developing from scaly patches on the hide. And they keep scratching themselves . . ."

Master Nicat turned questioningly to T'gellan.

"Oh, Menolly knows what to do. Why, she has her fire lizards singing tunes along with her and all . . ."

T'gellan's airy assurance did not sit too well with the Masterminer.

"Yes, but how do you get them to come to you?" he asked pointedly.

"You make them *want* to come back to you," Menolly said so firmly that she rated one of the Miner's daunting frowns.

"Kindness and affection, Master Nicat, are the essential ingredients," T'gellan said with equal force. "Now I see that T'gran is waiting to escort you, and your fire lizards, back to Crom." And he led the Masterminer off.

When T'gellan returned to Menolly, his eyes were dancing.

"I'll wager you my new tunic that one won't keep a fire lizard. Cold clod, that's what he is. Numbwit!"

"You shouldn't have said that about my fire lizards singing with me."

"Why not?" T'gellan was surprised at her criticism. "Mirrim hasn't done that much with her three, and she's had them longer. I told . . . Ah, yes, Craftmaster, F'lar did indeed say that you're to have a fire lizard egg."

And so the evening went, with lucky eager holders and crafts-men arriving to collect the precious fire lizard eggs. By the time only Masterharper Robinton's eggs remained in the warm sands of the basket, Menolly had become resigned to hearing T'gellan's wheeze that she had taught her fair of fire lizards to sing. Fortu-nately no one asked her to put it to the test, since her weary friends were curled up on their wall perches. They hadn't roused from sleep for all the singing and laughter at the merry tables in the Bowl.

• • •

Harper Elgion was thoroughly enjoying the Impression Feast. He hadn't realized how dour Half-Circle Hold was until this evening. Yanus was a good man, a fine Sea Holder to judge by the respect his holders accorded him, but he certainly knew how to take the joy out of living.

When Elgion had sat in the Hatching Ground, watching the young boys Impress, he'd determined that he'd find a fire lizard clutch of his own. That would alleviate the gloom at Half-Circle. And he'd see that Alemi got an egg, too. He'd heard from his neighbors in the tiers that the clutch being distributed this evening to the fortunate had been found down the coast from Half-Circle Sea Hold by T'gellan. Elgion had promised himself a chat with the bronze dragonrider; but T'gellan had had two passengers aboard Monarth when he'd collected Elgion at Half-Circle so there'd been no opportunity to talk. Elgion hadn't seen the man since the Hatching. But he'd bide his time.

Meanwhile, Oharan, the Weyr Harper, had Elgion playing gitar with him to amuse the visitors.

Elgion had just finished another tune with Oharan and some of the other visiting harpers when he caught sight of T'gellan, assisting a craftsman to mount a green dragon. It was then that Elgion noticed that the visitors were thinning out and this rare evening was drawing to a close. He'd speak with T'gellan, and then seek out the Masterharper, too.

"Over here, man," he said, beckoning to the bronze rider.

"Oh, Elgion, a cup of wine, please. I'm parched with talking. Not that it'll do those cold clods much good. They've no feeling for fire lizards at all."

"I heard you found the clutch. It wasn't in that cave by the Dragon Stones, was it?"

"By the Dragon Stones? No. Way down the coast in fact."

"Then there wasn't anything there?" Elgion was so bitterly disappointed that T'gellan gave him a long look.

"Depends on what you were expecting. Why? What did you think would be in that cave if it didn't hold fire lizard eggs?"

Elgion wondered briefly if he would be betraying Alemi's confidence. But it had become a matter of his professional honor to know if the sounds he'd heard from that cave had been made by pipes.

"The day Alemi and I saw the cave from the boat, I could have sworn I heard pipes. Alemi insisted it was wind over blowholes in the cliff, but there wasn't that much wind that day."

"No," T'gellan said, seeing a chance to tease the Harper, "you heard pipes. I saw 'em when I searched the place."

"You found pipes? Where was the player?"

"Sit down. Why're you so excited?"

"Where's that player?"

"Oh, here at Benden Weyr."

Elgion sat down again, so deflated and disappointed that T'gellan forbore to tease him further.

"Remember the day we rescued you from Thread? T'gran brought someone in as well."

"The lad?"

"That was no lad. That was a girl. Menolly. She'd been living in the cave . . . Now, what's the matter?"

"Menolly? Here? Safe? Where's the Masterharper? I've got to find Master Robinton. Come, T'gellan, help me find him!"

Elgion's excitement was contagious and though he was mystified, T'gellan joined the search. Taller than the young Harper, T'gellan spotted Master Robinton in deep conversation with Manora at a quiet table in the Bowl.

"Sir, sir, I've found her," Elgion cried, dashing up to them.

"Have you now? The love of your life?" asked Master Robinton amiably.

"No, sir. I've found Petiron's apprentice."

"Her? The old man's apprentice was a girl?"

Elgion was gratified by the Masterharper's surprise and grabbed at his hand, quite prepared to drag the man after him to search.

"She ran away from the Sea Hold, because they wouldn't let her make music, I think. She's Alemi's sister . . ."

"What's this about Menolly?" asked Manora, obstructing Elgion's flight with the Harper.

"Menolly?" Robinton raised his hand to silence Elgion. "That lovely child with the nine fire lizards?"

"What do you want of Menolly, Master Robinton?" Manora's voice was so stern that the Harper was brought up sharp.

He took a deep breath. "My much respected Manora, old Petiron sent me two songs written by his 'apprentice'; two of the loveliest melodies I've heard in all my Turns of harpering. He asked were they any good . . ." Robinton raised his eyes heavenward for patience, "I sent word back immediately, but the old man had died. Elgion found my message unopened when he got to the Sea Hold, and then he couldn't find the apprentice. The Sea Holder gave him some folderol about a fosterling who'd returned to his own hold. What's distressing you, Manora?"

"Menolly. I knew something had broken that girl's heart, but not what. She may not be able to play, Master Robinton. Mirrim says there's a dreadful scar on her left hand."

"She can, too, play," said T'gellan and Elgion together.

"I heard the sound of multiple pipes coming from that cave," Elgion said hurriedly.

"I saw her hide those pipes when we cleared out her cave," T'gellan added. "And furthermore, she's taught her fire lizards to sing, too."

"She has!" Bright sparks lit the Masterharper's eyes, and he turned purposefully toward the kitchen cavern.

"Not so fast, Masterharper," said Manora. "Go softly with that child."

"Yes, I saw that, too, when we were chatting this evening, and now I understand what was inhibiting her. So how to proceed cautiously?" The Masterharper frowned and gazed at T'gellan so long that the bronze rider wondered what he'd done wrong. "How do you know she's taught her fire lizards to sing?"

"Why, they were singing along with her and Oharan last night."

"Hmmm, now that's very interesting. Here's what we shall do."

Menolly was tired now, and most of the visitors had left. Still the Masterharper did not appear to collect his fire lizard eggs. She wouldn't leave until she'd seen him again. He'd been so kind; she hugged to herself the memory of their meeting. It was hard for her to believe that the Masterharper of Pern had carried her, Menolly of . . . Menolly of the Nine Fire Lizards. She propped her elbows up on the table and rested her head on her hands, feeling the rough scar against her left cheek and not even minding that at the moment.

She didn't hear the music at first, it was soft, as if Oharan was playing to himself at a nearby table.

"Would you sing along with me, Menolly?" asked Oharan

softly, and she looked up to see him taking a place at the table.

Well, no harm in singing. It would help keep her awake until the Masterharper arrived. So she joined in. Beauty and Rocky roused at the sound of her voice, but Rocky went back to sleep after a peevish complaint. Beauty, however, dropped down to Menolly's shoulder, her sweet soprano trill blending with Menolly's voice.

"Do sing another verse, Menolly," said Manora, emerging from the shadows of the darkened cavern.

She took the chair opposite Menolly, looking weary, but sort of peaceful and pleased. Oharan struck the bridging chords and started the second verse.

"My dear, you have such a restful voice," Manora said when the last chord died away. "Sing me another one and then I'm away."

Menolly could scarcely refuse, and she glanced at Oharan to see what she should sing.

"Sing this one along with me," the Weyr Harper said, his eyes intent on Menolly's as his fingers struck an opening chord. Menolly knew the song, which had such an infectious rhythm that she began to sing before she realized why it was so familiar. She was also tired and not expecting to be trapped, not by Oharan and certainly not by Manora. That's why she didn't real- ize at first what Oharan was playing. It was one of the two songs she'd jotted down for Petiron: the ones he'd said he'd sent to the Masterharper.

She faltered.

"Oh, don't stop singing, Menolly," Manora said, "it's such a lovely tune."

"Maybe she should *play* her own song," said someone standing just behind Menolly in the shadow; and the Masterharper walked forward, holding out his own gitar to her.

"No! NO!" Menolly half-rose, snatching her hands behind her back. Beauty gave a startled squawk and twined her tail about Menolly's neck.

"Won't you please play it . . . for me?" asked the Harper, his eyes entreating her.

Two more people emerged from the darkness: T'gellan, grinning fit to crack his face wide open, and Elgion! How did he know? From the gleam of his eyes and his smile, he was pleased and proud. Menolly was frightened and hid her face in confusion. How neatly she had been tricked!

"Don't be afraid now, child," said Manora quickly, catching Menolly's arm and gently pressing her back into her chair. "There's nothing for you to fear now: for yourself or your rare gift of music."

"But I can't play . . ." She held up her hand. Robinton took it in both of his, gently fingering the scar, examining it.

"You can play, Menolly," he said quietly, his kind eyes on hers, as he continued to stroke her hand, much as she would have caressed her frightened Beauty. "Elgion heard you when you were playing the pipes in the cave."

"But I'm a girl . . ." she said. "Yanus told me . . ."

"As to that," replied the Masterharper somewhat impatiently, though he smiled as he spoke, "if Petiron had had sense enough to tell me that that was the problem, you might have been spared a great deal of anguish: and I certainly would have been spared a great deal of trouble searching all Pern for you. Don't you *want* to be a harper?" Robinton ended on such a wistful, distressed note that Menolly had to reassure him.

"Oh yes, yes. I want music more than anything else in the world . . ." On her shoulder, Beauty trilled sweetly and Menolly caught her breath sharply in distress.

"Now what's the matter?" asked Robinton.

"I've got fire lizards. Lessa said I belong in the Weyr."

"Lessa will not tolerate *nine singing* fire lizards in her Weyr," said the Harper in a voice that brooked no contradiction. "And they *do* belong in my Harperhall. You've a trick or two to teach me, my girl." He grinned down at her with such mischief dancing in his eyes that she smiled timorously back at him. "Now," and he waggled a finger at her, in mock seriousness, "before you can think of any more obstacles, arguments or distractions, will you kindly bundle up my fire lizard eggs, get whatever you have, and let us be off to the Harperhall? This has been a day of many tiring impressions."

His hand pressed hers reassuringly, and his kind eyes urged her acquiescence. All Menolly's doubts and fears dissolved in an instant.

Beauty bugled, releasing the stranglehold of her tail about Menolly's neck. Beauty called again, rousing the rest of the fair, her voice echoing Menolly's joy. She rose slowly to her feet, her hand clinging to the Harper's for support and confidence.

"Oh, gladly will I come, Master Robinton," she said, her eyes blurred by happy tears.

And nine fire lizards bugled a harmonious chorus of accord!

TURN THE PAGE FOR A SNEAK PEEK
OF THE NEXT ADVENTURE IN
THE HARPER HALL OF PERN TRILOGY!

The little queen all golden
Flew hissing at the sea.
To stop each wave
Her clutch to save
She ventured bravely.

As she attacked the sea in rage
A holderman came nigh
Along the sand
Fishnet in hand
And saw the queen midsky.

He stared at her in wonder
For often he'd been told
That such as she
Could never be
Who hovered there, bright gold.

He saw her plight and quickly
He looked up the cliff he faced
And saw a cave
Above the wave
In which her eggs he placed.

The little queen all golden
Upon his shoulder stood
Her eyes all blue
Glowed of her true
Undying gratitude.

When Menolly, daughter of Yanus Sea Holder, arrived at the Harper Craft Hall, she came in style, aboard a bronze dragon. She was seated on Monarth's neck between his rider, T'gellan, and the Masterharper of Pern, Robinton. For one who had been told that girls could not become harpers, who had run away and actually lived holdless because she could not continue life without music, this was something of a triumphal success.

Yet it was also frightening. To be sure, music would not be denied her at the Harper Hall. True, she had written some songs that the Masterharper had heard and liked. But they were just tunings, not anything important. And what could a girl, even one who had taught her Hold's youngsters their Teaching Songs and Ballads, do at a Harper Hall from which all teaching songs originated? Especially a girl who had inadvertently Impressed nine fire lizards when everyone else on Pern would give a left arm to own just one? What *had* Master Robinton in mind for her to do here in the Harper Hall?

She couldn't think, she was so tired. She'd had a busy, exciting day at Benden Weyr on the opposite side of the continent where night now was well advanced. Here in Fort Hold, the sky was just darkening.

"Just a few minutes more," said Robinton in her ear. She heard him laugh because just then bronze Monarth trumpeted a greeting to the Fort Hold watch dragon. "Hang on, Menolly. I know you must be exhausted. I'll put you in Silvina's care the moment we land. See, there," and she followed the line of his pointing finger and saw the lighted quadrangle of buildings at the foot of the Fort Hold cliff. "That's the Harper Hall."

She shivered then, with fatigue, the cold of their passage *between* and apprehension. Monarth was circling now, and figures were pouring out of the Harper Hall into the courtyard, waving wildly to cheer the Masterharper's return. Somehow, Menolly hadn't expected that there'd be so many people in the Harper Craft Hall.

They kept well back, though their shouts of welcome didn't abate, while the big bronze dragon settled in the courtyard, giving him plenty of wingroom.

"I've got two fire lizard eggs!" shouted Master Robinton. Hugging the earthen pots tightly against his body, he slid from bronze Monarth's shoulder with the ease of considerable practice in dismounting dragons. "Two fire lizard eggs!" he repeated joyfully, holding the precious egg pots above his head and striding quickly to show off his prizes.

"My fire lizards!" Anxiously Menolly glanced up and about her. "Did they follow us, T'gellan? They're not lost *between*."

"No chance of that, Menolly," T'gellan replied, pointing to the slated roof behind them. "I asked Monarth to tell them to perch there for the time being."

With infinite relief, Menolly saw the unmistakable outlines of her fire lizards on the rooftop against the darkening sky.

"If only they don't misbehave as they did at Benden . . ."

"They won't," T'gellan assured her easily. "You'll see to that. You've done more with your fair of fire lizards than F'nor has with his one little queen. And F'nor's a trained dragonrider." He swung his right leg over Monarth's neckridge and dropped to the ground raising his arms to her. "Bring your leg over. I'll steady you so you won't jar those sore feet of yours," and his hands braced her as she slid down Monarth's shoulder. "That's the girl, and here you are, safe and sound in the Harper Hall." He gestured broadly as if only he could have accomplished this mission.

Menolly looked across the courtyard, where the Masterharper's tall figure and presence dominated those surrounding him. Was Silvina one of them? Wearily Menolly hoped that the Harper would find her quickly. The girl could put no reliance on T'gellan's glib assumption that her fire lizards would behave. They'd only just got used to being at Benden Weyr, among people who had some experience with winged antics.

"Don't worry so, Menolly. Just remember," said T'gellan, gripping her shoulder in awkward reassurance, "every harper on Pern has been trying to find Petiron's lost apprentice . . ."

"Because they thought that apprentice was a boy . . ."

"That made no difference to Master Robinton when he asked you to come here. Times are changing, Menolly, and it'll make no difference to the others. You'll see. In a sevenday you'll have forgotten you've ever lived anywhere else." The bronze dragonrider chuckled. "Great shells, girl, you've lived holdless, outrun Thread, and Impressed nine fire lizards. What's to fear from harpers?"

"Where *is* Silvina?" The Masterharper's voice rose above the others. There was a momentary lull and someone was sent to the Hall to find the woman. "And no more answers now. You've the bones of the news, I'll flesh it out for you later. Now, don't drop these egg pots, Sebell. Right now, I've more good news! I've found Petiron's lost apprentice!"

Amid exclamations of surprise, Robinton broke free of the crowd and beckoned T'gellan to bring Menolly forward. For a brief second, Menolly fought the urge to turn and run, impossible as it was with her feet barely healed from trying to outrun Thread and with T'gellan's arm about her. His fingers squeezed on her shoulder as if he sensed her nervousness.

"There's nothing for you to fear from harpers," he repeated in her ear as he escorted her across the court.

Robinton met them halfway, beaming with pleasure as he took her right hand. He flung up his other arm to command silence.

"This is Menolly, daughter of Yanus Sea Holder, late of Half-Circle Sea Hold, and Petiron's lost apprentice!"

Whatever response the harpers made was covered by an explosion of fire lizard cries from the rooftop. Fearful that the fair might wing down on the harpers, Menolly turned, saw that their wings were indeed spread and sternly commanded them to stay where they were. Then she had no excuse for not confronting the sea of faces: some smiling, some with mouths ajar in surprise at her fire lizards, but too many, many people.

"Yes, and those fire lizards are Menolly's," Robinton went on, his voice easily projecting above the murmurs. "Just as that lovely song about the fire lizard queen is Menolly's. Only it wasn't a *man* who saved the clutch from the sea, it was Menolly. And when no one would let her play or sing in Half-Circle Sea Hold after Petiron died, she ran away to the fire lizard queen's cave and Impressed nine of the eggs before she realized what she was doing. Furthermore," and he raised his volume above the ragged cheers of approval, "furthermore, she found another clutch, which provided *me* with two eggs!"

The second cheer was more wholehearted, reverberating in the courtyard and answered by shrill whistles from the fire lizards. Under cover of good-natured laughter at that response, T'gellan muttered, "I told you so" in her ear.

"And where is Silvina?" asked the Harper again, a note of impatience audible.

"Here I am and you ought to be ashamed of yourself, Robinton," said a woman, pushing through the ring of harpers. Menolly had an impression of very white skin and large expressive eyes set in a broad-cheeked face framed by dark hair. Then strong but gentle hands took her from Robinton's grasp. "Subjecting the child to such an ordeal. No, no, you lot calm down. All this noise. And those poor creatures up there too scared out of their wits to come down. Haven't you any sense, Robinton? Away! The lot of you. Into the Hall. Carry on all night if you've the energy but I'm putting this child to bed. T'gellan, if you'd help me . . ."

As she upbraided everyone impartially, the woman was also making her way, with Menolly and T'gellan, through the crowd which parted respectfully but humorously before her.

"It's too late to put her with the other girls at Dunca's," said Silvina to T'gellan. "We'll just bed her in one of the guest rooms for the night."

Unable to see clearly in the shadows of the Hall, Menolly barked her toes on the stone steps, cried out involuntarily at the pain and grabbed at the supporting hands.

"What happened, child?" asked Silvina, her voice kind and anxious.

"My toes . . . my feet!" Menolly choked back tears that the unexpected pain had brought to her eyes. Silvina mustn't think her a coward.

"Here! I'll carry her," said T'gellan and swung Menolly up into his arms before she could protest. "Just lead the way, Silvina."

"That dratted Robinton," Silvina said, "*he* can go on all day and night without sleep but forgets that others—"

"No, it's not his fault. He's done so much for me . . ." Menolly began.

"Ha! He's deeply in *your* debt, Menolly," said the dragonrider with a cryptic laugh. "You'll have to have your healer see to her feet, Silvina," T'gellan continued as he carried Menolly up the broad flight of stairs that led from the main entrance of the Hall. "That's how we found her. She was trying to outrun the leading edge of Threadfall."

"She was?" Silvina stared over her shoulder at Menolly, her green eyes wide with respectful astonishment.

"She nearly did, too. Ran her feet raw. One of my wingmen saw her and brought her back to Benden Weyr."

"In this room, T'gellan. The bed's on the left-hand side. I'll just open the glow baskets . . ."

"I see it," and T'gellan deposited her gently in the bed. "I'll get the shutters, Silvina, and let those fire lizards of hers in here before they do get into trouble."

Menolly had let herself sink into the thick mattress of sweet rushes. Now she loosened the thong holding the small bundle of belongings to her back but she hadn't the energy to reach for the sleeping fur folded at the foot of the bedstead. As soon as T'gellan had the second shutter open, she called her friends in.

"I've heard so much about the fire lizards," Silvina was saying, "and had only the glimpse of Lord Groghe's little queen that. . . . Gracious goodness!"

At Silvina's startled remark, Menolly struggled out of the

thick mattress to see the fire lizards dipping and wheeling about the woman.

"How many did you say you have, Menolly?"

"There are only nine," replied T'gellan, laughing at Silvina's confusion. She was twisting about, trying to get a good look at one or another of the gyrating creatures.

Menolly told them to settle down quickly and behave. Rocky and Diver landed on the table near the wall while the more daring Beauty took up her accustomed perch on Menolly's shoulder. The others came to rest on the window ledges, their jeweled eyes whirling with the orange of uncertainty and suspicion.

"Why, they're the loveliest creatures I've ever seen," said Silvina, peering intently at the two bronzes on the table. Rocky chirped back, recognizing that remarks were being made about him. He flipped his wings neatly to his back and cocked his head at Silvina. "And a good evening to you, young bronze fire lizard."

"That bold fellow is Rocky," said T'gellan, "if I remember correctly, and the other bronze is Diver. Right, Menolly?" She nodded, relieved in her weariness that T'gellan was ready to speak for her. "The greens are Aunties One and Two," and the pair began to chatter so like old women that Silvina laughed. "The little blue is Uncle but I haven't got the three browns sorted out . . ." and now he turned inquiringly to Menolly.

"They're Lazybones, Mimic and Brownie," Menolly said pointing at each in turn, "and this . . . is Beauty, Silvina," Menolly spoke the woman's name shyly because she didn't know her title or rank in the Harper Hall.

"And a Beauty she is, too. Just like a miniature queen dragon.

And just as proud, I see." Then Silvina gave Menolly a hopeful look. "By any chance, will one of Robinton's eggs hatch a queen?"

"I hope so, I really do," said Menolly fervently. "But it's not easy with fire lizard eggs to tell which is the queen."

"I'm sure he'll be just as thrilled no matter what the color. And speaking of queens, T'gellan," and Silvina turned to the dragonrider, "do please tell me, did Brekke re-Impress the new queen dragon at your Hatching today? We've been so worried about her here, since her queen was killed."

"No, Brekke didn't re-Impress," and T'gellan smiled quickly to reassure Silvina. "Her fire lizard wouldn't let her."

"No?"

"Yes. You should have seen it, Silvina. That little bronze midget flew at the queen dragon, scolding like a wherry hen. Wouldn't let Brekke near the new queen. But she snapped out of that depression, and she'll be all right now, F'nor says. And it was little Berd who pulled the trick."

"Well, that really is interesting." Silvina regarded the two bronzes with thoughtful respect. "So they've a full set of wits . . ."

"They seem to," T'gellan went on. "F'nor uses his little queen, Grall, to send messages to the other Dragon Weyrs. Of course," and T'gellan chuckled disparagingly, "she doesn't always return as promptly as she goes . . . Menolly's trained hers better. You'll see." The dragonrider had been edging toward the door and now gave a huge yawn. "Sorry . . ."

"I'm the one who should apologize," replied Silvina, "indulging my curiosity when you two are all but asleep. Get along with you now, T'gellan, and my thanks for your help with Menolly."

"Good luck, now, Menolly. I know you'll sleep well," said T'gellan with a jaunty wink of farewell. He was out of the door, his boot heels clicking on the stone floor before she could thank him.

"Now, let's just have a quick look at these feet you ran ragged . . ." Silvina gently tugged off Menolly's slippers. "Hmmm. They're all but healed, Manora's clever with her nursing, but we'll have Master Oldive look at you tomorrow. Now, what's this?"

"My things, I don't have much . . ."

"Here, you two watch that and keep out of mischief," Silvina said, putting the bundle on the table between Rocky and Diver. "Now, slip off your skirt, Menolly, and settle down. A good long sleep, that's what you need. Your eyes are burned holes in your head."

"I'm all right, really."

"To be sure you are, now you're here. Living in a cave, did T'gellan say? With every harper on Pern looking for you in holds and crafthalls." Silvina deftly tugged at skirt tapes. "Just like old Petiron to forget to mention you being a girl."

"I don't think he forgot," Menolly said slowly, thinking of her father and mother and their opposition to her playing. "He told me girls can't be harpers."

Silvina gave her a long hard look. "Maybe under another Masterharper. Or in the old days, but surely old Petiron knew his own son well enough to—"

"Petiron was Master Robinton's father?"

"Did he never tell you that?" Silvina paused as she was spreading the sleeping fur over Menolly. "The old stubborn fool! Determined not to advance himself because his son was elected Masterharper . . . and then picking a place halfway to nowhere. . . . I beg your pardon, Menolly . . ."

"Half-Circle Sea Hold *is* halfway to nowhere."

"Not if Petiron found *you* there," said Silvina, recovering her brisk tone, "and sponsored you to this Craft. Now that's enough talking," she added, closing the glow basket. "I'll leave the shutters open . . . but you sleep yourself out, you hear me?"

Menolly mumbled a reply, her eyelids closing despite her effort to remain politely awake while Silvina was in the room. She let out a soft sigh as the door banged softly shut. Beauty immediately curled up by Menolly's ear, and the girl felt other small hard bodies making themselves comfortable against her. She composed herself for sleep, aware now of the dull throbbing of her feet and the aching of her banged toes.

She was warm, she was comfortable; she was so tired. The bag that enclosed the thick rushes was stout enough to keep stray edges from digging into her flesh, but she couldn't sleep. She also couldn't move because, while her mind turned over all the day's incredible events, her body wasn't hers to command but in some nether region of unresponsiveness.

She was conscious of the spicy odor of Beauty, of the dry sweet scent of the rushes, the earthy smell of wet fields borne in by the night wind, accented occasionally by the touch of acrid blackstone smoke. Spring was not advanced enough to dispense with evening fires.

Strange not to have the smell of sea in her nostrils, Menolly thought, for sea and fish odors had dominated all but the last sevenday of her fifteen Turns. How pleasant to realize that she had done with the sea, and fish, forever. She'd never have to gut another packtail in her life, or risk another infected cut. She couldn't use her injured hand as much as she wanted to yet, but she would. Nothing was impossible, not if she could get to the Harper Hall in spite of all the odds against it. And she'd play gitar again and harp. Manora had assured her she'd use the fingers properly in time. And her feet were healing. It amused Menolly, now, to think that she'd had the temerity to try to outrun the leading edge of Threadfall. Running had done more than save her skin from Threadscoring: it had brought her to Benden Weyr, to the attention of the Masterharper of Pern and to the start of a completely new life.

And her dear old friend, Petiron, had been Master Robinton's father? She'd known the old Harper had been a good musician, but it had never occurred to her before to wonder why he had been sent to Half-Circle Sea Hold where only she had profited from his ability as a teacher. If only her father, Yanus, had let her play gitar when the new Harper first arrived . . . but they'd been so afraid that she'd disgrace the Sea Hold. Well, she hadn't, and she wouldn't! One day her father, and yes, her mother, too, would realize that Menolly was no disgrace to the Hold of her birth.

Menolly drifted on thoughts of triumph until sound invaded her reflections. Male voices, laughing and rumbling in conversation, carried on the clear night air. The voices of harpers; tenor, bass and baritone, in amused, argumentative, cajoling tones, and one querulous, sort of quavery, older, whiny voice. She didn't like that one. Another, a velvet-soft, light baritone, rose above the cranky tenor, soothing. Then the Masterharper's deeper baritone dominated and silenced the others. Though she couldn't understand what he was saying, his voice lulled her to sleep.

Harper, tell me of the road
That leads beyond this Hold,
That wends its way beyond the hill . . .
Does it go further on until
It ends in sunset's gold?

Menolly roused briefly, reacting to an inner call that had nothing to do with the sun's rising on this side of Pern. She saw dark night and stars through the window, felt the sleeping fire lizards tucked about her, and gratefully went back to sleep again. She was so tired.

Once the sun had cleared the roof of the outer side of the rectangle of buildings that comprised the main Harper Craft Hall, it shone directly at her windows, set in the eastern side of the Hall. Gradually the light penetrated the room, and the unusual combination of light and warmth on her face woke Menolly.

She lay, her body not yet responsive, wondering where she was. Remembering, she was uncertain what to do next. Had she missed some general waking call? No, Silvina had said that she was to sleep herself out. As she pushed back the sleeping furs, she heard the sound of voices chanting. The rhythm was familiar. She smiled, identifying one of the long Sagas. Apprentices were being taught the complicated timing by rote, just as she had taught the youngsters in Half-Circle Sea Hold when Petiron was sick, and later after he died. The similarity reassured her.

As she slid from the bed, she clenched her teeth in anticipation of touching the cool hard stones of the floor, but to her surprise, her feet only felt stiff, not painful, this morning. She glanced out the window at the sun. It was well into morning by the cast of shadow: she'd really slept. Then she laughed at herself, for, to be sure she had: she was halfway round Pern from Benden Weyr and Half-Circle Hold, and she had had at least six hours more rest than usual. Fortunately the fire lizards had been as tired as she or they'd have wakened her with their hunger.

She stretched and shook out her hair, then hobbled carefully to the jar and basin. After washing with soapsand, she dressed and brushed her hair, feeling able to face new experiences.

Beauty gave an impatient chirp. She was awake. And very hungry. Rocky and Diver echoed the complaint.

Menolly would have to find them food and right soon. Having nine fire lizards would prejudice enough people against her, without having unmanageably hungry ones who would irritate even the most tolerant of people.

Resolutely, Menolly opened the door to a silent hallway. The aromatic odors of *klah,* baking breads and meats filled the air. Menolly decided she need only follow the smells to their source to satisfy her friends.

On either side of the wide corridor were doors; those on the outside of the Hall were open to let sun and air flood the inside. She descended from the uppermost level into the large entranceway. Directly in front of the staircase were dragon-high metal doors with the most curious closings she'd ever seen: on the back of the doors were wheels, which evidently turned the heavy bars into floor and ceiling. At Half-Circle Sea Hold there had been the heavy horizontal bars, but this arrangement would be easier to lock and looked much more secure.

To the left was a double-doored entrance into a Great Hall, probably the room where the Harper had been talking last night. To the right, she looked into the dining hall, almost as large as the Great Hall, with three long tables parallel to the windows. Also to her right, by the stairwell, was an open doorway, leading to shallow steps and the kitchen, judging by the appetizing odors and familiar sounds.

The fire lizards creeled in hunger, but Menolly couldn't have the whole fair invading the kitchen and upsetting the drudges. She ordered them to perch on the cornices in the shadows above the door. She'd bring them food, she promised them, but they had to behave. Beauty scolded until the others settled meekly into place, only their glowing, jewel-faceted eyes giving evidence of their positions.

Then Beauty assumed her favorite perch on Menolly's shoulder, her head half-buried in Menolly's thick hair, and her tail wrapped securely about Menolly's throat like a golden necklace.

As Menolly reached the kitchen, the scene with the drudges and cooks scurrying about preparing the midday meal fleetingly revived memories of happier days at Half-Circle. But here, it was Silvina who noticed her and smiled, as Menolly's mother would not have done.

"You're awake? Are you rested?" Silvina gestured imperatively at a slack-featured, clumsy-looking man by the hearth. "Klah, Camo, pour a mug of klah, for Menolly. You must be famished, child. How are your feet?"

"Fine, thank you. And I don't want to bother anyone . . ."

"Bother? What bother? Camo, pour the klah into the mug."

"It's not for myself I'm here . . ."

"Well, you need to eat, and you must be famished."

"Please, it's my fire lizards. Have you any scraps . . ."

Silvina's hands flew to her mouth. She glanced about her head as if expecting a swarm of fire lizards.

"No, I've told them to wait," Menolly said quickly. "They won't come in here."

"Now, you are a thoughtful child," Silvina said in so firm a tone that Menolly wondered why and then realized that she was the object of a good deal of furtive curiosity. "Camo, here. Give me that!" Silvina took the cup from the man, who was walking with exaggerated care not to slop an overfull container. "And get the big blue bowl from the cold room. The big blue bowl, Camo, from the cold room. Bring it to me." Silvina deftly handed the cup to Menolly without spilling a drop. "The cold room, Camo, and the blue bowl." She turned the man by the shoulders and gave him a gentle shove in the proper direction. "Abuna, you're nearest the hearth. Do dish up some of the cereal. Plenty of sweetening on it, too, the child's nothing but skin and bones." Silvina smiled at Menolly. "No use feeding the fowl and starving the servant, as it were. I saved meat for your friends when we trussed up the roast," and Silvina nodded toward the biggest hearth where great joints of meat were turning on heavy spits, "since meat's what the Harper said fire lizards need. Now, where would the best place . . ." Silvina glanced about her undecidedly, but Menolly had noticed a low door that led up a short flight of steps to the corner of the courtyard.

"Would I disturb anyone out there?"

"Not at all, you are a considerate child. That's right, Camo. And thank you." Silvina patted the half-wit's arm kindly, while he beamed with the pleasure of a job properly done and rewarded. Silvina tipped the edge of the bowl toward Menolly. "Is this enough? There's more . . ."

"Oh, that's a gracious plenty, Silvina."

"Camo, this is Menolly. Follow Menolly with the bowl. She can't carry it *and* her own breakfast. This is Menolly, Camo, follow Menolly. Go right out, dear. Camo's good at carrying things . . . at least what doesn't spill."

Silvina turned from her then, speaking sharply to two women chopping roots, bidding them to slice, not stare. Very much aware of scrutiny, Menolly moved awkwardly to the steps, cup in one hand, bowl of warm cereal in the other, and Camo shuffling behind her. Beauty, who had remained discreetly covered by Menolly's hair, now craned her neck about, smelling the raw meat in the bowl Camo carried.

"Pretty, pretty," the man mumbled as he noticed the fire lizard. "Pretty small dragon?" He tapped Menolly on the shoulder. "Pretty small dragon?" He was so anxious for her answer that he almost tripped on the shallow steps.

"Yes, she is like a small dragon, and she is pretty," Menolly agreed, smiling. "Her name is Beauty."

"Her name is Beauty." Camo was entranced. "Her name is Beauty. She pretty small dragon." He beamed as he loudly declared this information.

Menolly shushed him, not wanting either to alarm or distract Silvina's helpers. She put down her mug and bowl and reached for the meat.

"Prettty small dragon Beauty," Camo said, ignoring her as she pulled the bowl so firmly clutched in his huge, thick-fingered hands.

"You go to Silvina, Camo. You go to Silvina."

Camo stood where he was, bobbing his head up and down, his mouth set in a wet, wide grimace of childish delight, too entranced by Beauty to be distracted.

Beauty now creeled imperiously, and Menolly grabbed a handful of meat to quiet her. But her cries had alerted the others. They came, some of them from the open windows of the dining hall above Menolly's head, others, judging by the shrieks of dismay, through the kitchen and out the door by the steps.

"Pretty, pretty. All pretty!" Camo exclaimed, turning his head from side to side, trying to see all the flitting fire lizards at once.

He didn't move a muscle as Auntie One and Two perched on his forearms, snatching gobblets of meat directly from the bowl. Uncle secured his talons to the fabric of Camo's tunic, his right wingtip jabbing the man in the neck and chin as the littlest fire lizard fought for his fair share of the meat. Brownie, Mimic, and Lazybones ranged from Camo's shoulders to Menolly's as she tried to distribute the meat evenly.

Alternating between embarrassment at her friends' bad manners and gratitude for Camo's stolid assistance, Menolly was acutely aware that all activity had ceased in the kitchen to watch the spectacle. Momentarily, she expected to hear an irate Silvina order Camo back to his ordinary duties, but all she heard was the buzz of whispered gossiping.

"How many does she have?" she heard one clear whisper out of the general mumble.

"Nine," Silvina answered, imperturbable. "When the two the Harper was given have hatched, the Harper Hall will have eleven." Silvina sounded smugly superior. The buzz increased in volume. "That bread's risen enough now, Abuna. You and Kayla shape it."

The fire lizards had cleared the bowl of meat, and Camo stared into its hollow, his face contorted by an expression of dismay.

"All gone? Pretties hungry?"

"No, Camo. They've had more than enough. They're not hungry anymore." In fact, their bellies were distended, they'd gorged so. "You go to Silvina. Silvina wants you, Camo," and Menolly followed Silvina's example: she took him by the shoulders, turned him down the steps, and gave him a gentle shove.

Menolly sipped the good hot klah, beginning to think that Silvina's marked attentions and kindness were deliberate. Or was that foolish? Silvina was just a kind, thoughtful person: look how she treated dull-witted Camo. She was patience itself with his inadequacy. Nonetheless, Silvina was obviously the headwoman at the Harper Craft Hall and, like serene Manora at Benden Weyr, undoubtedly wielded a good deal of authority. If Silvina was friendly, others would follow her lead.

Menolly began to relax in the warm sun. Her dreams last night had been troubled though she couldn't remember details now in the bright morning, only a sense of uneasiness and helplessness. Silvina had done much to dissipate the lingering misgivings. *Nothing to fear from harpers.* T'gellan had repeatedly told her.

Across the courtyard, young voices broke into a lusty rendition of the Saga previously chanted. The fire lizards rose at the eruption of sound, settling again as Menolly laughingly reassured them.

Then a pure sweet trill from Beauty soared in delicate descant above the apprentices' male voices. Rocky and Diver joined her, wings half-spread as they expanded their lungs for breath. Mimic and Brownie dropped from the window ledge to add their voices. Lazy would not put himself to any such effort, and the two Aunties and blue Uncle were at best indifferent singers, but they listened, heads cocked, jeweled eyes whirling. The five singers rose to their haunches now, their throats thickening, their cheeks swelling as their jaws relaxed to emit the sweet pure notes. Their eyes were half-lidded as they concentrated, as good singers will, to produce the fluting descant.

They were happy then, Menolly thought with relief, and picked up the melody of the Saga, not that the fire lizards needed her voice with the apprentices supplying the tune and harmony.

They were on the last two measures of the chorus when Menolly suddenly realized that it was only herself and the fire lizards singing, that the male voices had ceased. Startled, she looked up and saw that almost every window about the courtyard was filled with faces. The exceptions were the windows of the hall from which the voices had come.

"Who has been singing?" demanded an irate tenor, and a man's head appeared at one of the empty windows.

"Why, that's a grand way to wake up, Brudegan," said the clear baritone of the Masterharper from some point above Menolly and to her left. Craning her head up, she saw him leaning out of his window on the upper story.

"Good morning to you, Masterharper," said Brudegan courteously, but his tone indicated that he was disgruntled by the intervention.

Menolly tried to sit small, heartily wishing herself *between:* she was certainly frozen motionless.

"I didn't know your fire lizards could sing," Silvina said, appearing on Menolly's right and absently retrieving mug and bowl from the steps. "A nice compliment to your chorus, eh, Brudegan," she added, raising her voice to carry across the courtyard. "You'd be wanting your klah now, Robinton?"

"It would be welcome, Silvina." He stretched, leaned farther out to peer down at Menolly. "Enter a fair of fire lizards singing! A lovely way to be wakened, Menolly; and a good morning to you, too." Before Menolly could respond, a look of dismay crossed his face. "*My* fire lizard. My egg!" and he disappeared from sight.

Silvina chuckled and she regarded Menolly. "He'll be of no use to anyone until it's hatched and he's got one of his own."

At that point, Brudegan's singers renewed their song. Beauty chirruped questioningly at Menolly.

"No, no, Beauty. No more singing, not now."

"*They* need the practice," and Silvina gestured at the hall. "Now I've the Harper's meal to see to and you to settle . . ." She paused, glancing about at the fire lizards. "But what to do with them?"

"They usually sleep when they're as full as they are right now."

"All to the good . . . but where? Mercy!"

Menolly tried not to laugh at Silvina's astonishment, because all but Beauty, who took her usual perch on Menolly's shoulder, had disappeared. Menolly pointed to the roof opposite and the small bodies landing there, apparently out of thin air.

"They do go *between*, don't they?" Silvina said more than asked. "Harper says they're much like dragons?" That was a question.

"I don't know that much about dragons, but fire lizards can

go *between*. They followed me last night from Benden Weyr."

"And they're obedient. I could wish the apprentices were half so willing." Then Silvina motioned Menolly to follow her back into the kitchen. "Camo, turn the spit. Camo, now turn the spit. I suppose the rest of you have been watching the yard instead of the food," she said, scowling indiscriminately about the kitchen. The cooks and drudges alike pretended industry, clanging, banging, splashing or bending with assiduous care over quieter tasks of paring and scraping. "Better yet, Menolly, *you* take the Harper his klah, and check that egg of his. He'll be roaring for you soon enough, so we might as well anticipate. Then I shall want Master Oldive to see your feet, not that Manora hasn't all but healed them anyway. And . . ." Silvina caught Menolly's left hand and scowled at the red mark. "Wherever did you get such a fierce wound? And who bungled the healing of it? There now, can you grip with that hand?" Silvina had been assembling on a small tray the various items of the Harper's breakfast, the last of which was a heavy pot of klah. Now she gave the tray to Menolly. "There now. His room is the second door on the right from yours, Menolly. Turn the spit, Camo, don't just hold on to it. Menolly's fire lizards are fed and sleeping. You'll have another gawk at them later. Turn the spit now!"

As briskly as Menolly could move on her stiff feet, she made her way out of the kitchen and up the broad steps to the second level. Beauty hummed softly in her ear, a gently disobedient descant to the Saga that Brudegan's pupils were singing lustily.

Master Robinton hadn't sounded annoyed about the fire lizards' singing, Menolly thought. She'd apologize to Journeyman Brudegan when she got the chance. She simply hadn't realized she'd cause a distraction. She'd been so pleased that her friends were relaxed enough to want to sing.

Second door on her right. Menolly tapped. Then rapped, then knocked, hard enough to make her knuckles sting.

"Come. Come. And, Silvina . . . oh, Menolly, you're just the person I wanted to see," the Harper said, throwing open the door. "And good morning to you, proud Beauty," he added, grinning at the little queen who chirped an acknowledgment as he took the tray from Menolly. "Silvina's forever anticipating me. . . . Would you please check my egg? It's in the other room, by the hearth. It feels harder to me . . ." He sounded anxious as he pointed to the farther door.

Menolly obediently entered the room, and he walked with her, setting the tray down as he passed the sandtable by the window and pouring himself a mug of klah before he joined her by the hearth in the next room where a small fire burned gently. The earthen pot had been set at the edge of the hearth apron.

Menolly opened it, carefully brushing aside the warm sand that covered the precious fire lizard egg. It was harder, but not much more so than when she had given it to the Masterharper at Benden Weyr the previous evening.

"It's fine, Master Robinton, just fine. And the pot is warm enough, too," she said, running her hands down the sides. She replaced the sand and the top and rose. "When we brought the clutch back to Benden Weyr two days ago, Weyrwoman Lessa said it would take a sevenday for them to hatch, so we've five days more."

The Harper sighed with exaggerated relief. "You slept well, Menolly? You're rested? Awake long?"

"Long enough."

The Harper burst out laughing as she realized how much chagrin she'd put into her tone.

"Long enough to set a few people by the ears, huh? My dear child, did you not notice the difference in the chorus the second time? Your fire lizards have challenged them. Brudegan was only gruff with surprise. Tell me, can your fire lizards improvise descants to any tune?"

"I don't really know, Master Robinton."

"Still not sure, are you, young Menolly?" He didn't mean the fire lizards' abilities. There was such kindness in his voice and eyes that Menolly felt unexpected tears behind her eyes.

"I don't want to be a nuisance . . ."

"Allow me to differ both to statement and content, Menolly . . ." Then he sighed. "You're overyoung to appreciate the value of nuisance, although the improvement in that chorus is a point in my argument. However, it's much too early in the morning for me to expound philosophy." He guided her back into the other room, quite the most cluttered place she had ever seen and in direct contrast to the neatness of his bedchamber. While musical instruments were carefully stored on hook and shelf in cases, piles of record skins, drawings, slates—wax and stone—littered every surface and were heaped in corners and against the walls of the room. On one wall was a finely drawn map of the Pern continent, with smaller detailed drawings of all the major Holds and Crafthalls pinned here and there on the borders. The long sandtable by the window was covered with musical notations, some of them carefully shielded by glass to prevent erasure. The Harper had set the tray on the center island, which separated the sandtable into two halves. Now he pulled a square of wood to protect the sand and positioned the tray so he could eat comfortably. He smeared a thick slice of bread with soft cheese and picked up his spoon to eat his cereal, motioning with the spoon for Menolly to seat herself on a stool.

"We're in a period of change and readjustment, Menolly," he said, managing to speak and eat simultaneously without choking on food or garbling his words. "And you are likely to be a vital part of that change. Yesterday I exerted an unfair pressure on you to join the Harper Hall. . . . Oh yes, I did, but you belong here!" His forefinger stabbed downward at the floor and then waggled out at the courtyard. "First," and he paused to swallow klah, washing down bread and cereal, "we must discover just how well Petiron taught you the fundamentals of our craft and what you need to further your gifts. And . . ." he pointed now to her left hand, ". . . what can be done to correct that scar damage. I'd still like to hear you *play* the songs you wrote." His eyes fell to her hands in her lap so that she was aware of her absentminded kneading of her left palm. "Master Oldive will set that right if anyone can."

"Silvina said I was to see him today."

"We'll have you playing again, more than just those pipes. We need you, when you can craft songs like those Petiron sent me and the ones Elgion found stuck away at the back of the harper's shelves in Half-Circle. Yes, and that's a matter I'd better explain . . ." he went on, smoothing the hair at the back of his neck and, to Menolly's amazement, appearing to be embarrassed.

"Explain?"

"Yes, well, you obviously hadn't finished *writing* that song about the fire lizard queen . . ."

"No, I hadn't actually . . ." Menolly felt that she was not hearing his words properly. For one thing, why did the Masterharper have to explain anything to *her*? And she'd only jotted down the little tune about the fire lizard queen, yet last night. . . . Now she remembered that he'd mentioned the song, as if all the harpers knew about it. "You mean, Harper Elgion sent it to you?"

"How else would I have got it? We couldn't find you!" Robinton sounded annoyed. "When I think of you, living in a cave, with a damaged hand, and you hadn't been *allowed* to finish that charming song. . . . So I did."

He got up, rummaged among the piles of waxed slates under the window, extracted one and handed it to her. She looked at the notations obediently but, although they were familiar, she couldn't make her mind read the melody.

"I had to have something about fire lizards, since I believe they're going to be far more important than anyone has yet realized. And this tune . . ." his finger tapped the hard wax surface approvingly, ". . . was so exactly what I needed, that I just brushed up the harmonics, and compressed the lyric story. Probably what you'd've done yourself if you'd had the chance to work on it again. I couldn't really improve on the melodic line without destroying the integral charm of. . . . What's the matter, Menolly?"

Menolly realized that she'd been staring at him, unable to believe that he was praising a silly tune she'd only scrawled down. Guiltily, she examined the slate again.

"I never did get a chance to *play* it. . . . I wasn't supposed to play my own tunes in the Sea Hold. I promised my father I wouldn't . . . so you see—"

"Menolly!"

Startled, she looked up at his stern tone.

"I want you to promise me—and you're now my apprentice—I want you to promise me to write down any tune that comes into your mind: I want you to play it as often as necessary to get it right . . . do you understand me? That's why I brought you here." He tapped the slate again. "That was a good song even before I tampered with it. I need good songs badly.

"What I said about change affects the Harper Hall more than any other craft, Menolly, because we are the ones who effect change. Just as we teach with our songs, so we also help people accept new ideas and necessary changes. And for that we need a special kind of harpering.

"Now, I still have to consider Craft principles and standards. Especially in your unusual situation, the conventional procedure must be observed. Once we've dispensed with the formalities, we can proceed with your training as fast as you want to go. But this is where you belong, Menolly, you and your singing fire lizards. Bless me but that was lovely to hear this morning. Ah, Silvina, good morning and to you, as well, Master Oldive . . ."

Menolly knew it was impolite to stare at anyone and looked away as soon as she realized that she was staring, but Master Oldive required a long look. He was shorter than herself but only because his head was awry on his neck. His great lean face tilted up from its permanent slant, and she had the impression of enormous dark eyes under very shaggy brows taking in every detail of herself.

"I'm sorry, Master Robinton, have we interrupted you?" Silvina paused on the threshold indecisively.

"Yes, and no. I don't think I've convinced Menolly but that will take time. Meanwhile, we'll get on with the basics. We'll speak again, Menolly," said the Harper. "Go along with Master Oldive now. Let him do his best, or his worst, for you. She must play again, Oldive." The Harper's smile as he gestured to Menolly to follow the man implied complete faith in his ability. "And Silvina, Menolly says the egg's safe enough for four or five days, but you'll please arrange to have someone—"

"Why not Sebell? He's got his egg to check, too, doesn't he? And with Menolly here in the Hall . . ." Silvina was saying as Master Oldive, ushering Menolly out of the room before him, closed the door.

"I'm to see to your feet as well, Silvina tells me," was the man's comment as he indicated Menolly should lead the way to her room. The Master's voice was unexpectedly deep. And while he might be shorter than herself in the torso, he'd as long a leg and arm and matched her stride down the corridor. As he pushed wider her door, she realized that his stature was due to a terrible malformation of his spine.

"By my life!" Oldive exclaimed, stopping abruptly as Menolly preceded him into the room. "I thought for a moment you were as blighted as myself. It is a fire lizard on your shoulder, isn't it?" He chuckled. "Now, there's one on me, so it is. Is the creature friendly?" He peered up at Beauty, who chirruped pleasantly back, since Oldive was patently addressing her. "As long as I'm friendly to your Menolly, I take it? You'll have to write another verse to your fire lizard song, proving the rewards of kindness," he added, gesturing her to sit on the window side of the bed as he pulled up the stool.

"Oh, that's not my song . . ." she said, removing her slippers.

Master Oldive frowned. "Not your song? But Master Robinton assigns it to you—constantly."

"He rewrote it . . . he told me so."

"That's not unusual," and Master Oldive dismissed her protest. "Proper mess you made of your feet," he said, his voice taking on a distant, thoughtful quality as he looked at first one, then the other foot. "Running, I believe . . ."

Menolly felt reproved. "I was caught out during Threadfall, you see, far from my cave and had to run . . . oooh!"

"Sorry, did I hurt? The flesh is very tender. And will remain that way awhile longer."

He began to smooth on a pungent-smelling substance, and she couldn't keep her foot still. He grabbed her ankle firmly to complete the medication, countering her embarrassed apology by remarking that her twitching proved that she'd done the nerves no harm with the pounding she'd given her feet.

"You're to keep off them as much as possible. I'll tell Silvina so. And use this salve morning and night. Aids healing and keeps the skin from itching." He replaced Menolly's slippers. "Now, this hand of yours."

She hesitated, knowing that his opinion of the bungled wound was likely to echo Manora's and Silvina's. Perversely she was afflicted by an obscure loyalty to her mother.

Oldive regarded her steadily, as if divining some measure of her reluctance, and extended his own hand. Compelled by the very neutrality of his gaze, she gave him her injured hand. To her surprise, there was no change of expression on his face, no condemnation or pity, merely interest in the problem the thick-scarred palm posed for a man of his skill. He prodded the scar tissue, murmuring thoughtfully in his throat.

"Make a fist."

She could just about do that but, when he asked her to extend her fingers, the scar pulled as she tried to stretch the palm.

"Not as bad as I was led to believe. An infection, I suppose . . ."

"Packtail slime . . ."

"Hmm, yes. Insidious stuff." He gave her hand another twist. "But the scar is not long healed, and the tissue can still be stretched. A few more months and we might not have been able to do anything to flex the hand. Now, you will do exercises, tightening your fingers about a small hard ball, which I will provide you, and extending the hand." He demonstrated, forcing her fingers upward and apart so that she cried out involuntarily. "If you can discipline yourself to the point of actual discomfort, you are doing the exercise properly. We must stretch the tightened skin, the webbing between your fingers, and the stiffened tendons. I shall also provide a salve, which you are to rub well into the scar tissue to make it softer and more pliable. Conscientious effort on your part will determine the rate of progress. I suspect that you will be sufficiently motivated."

Before Menolly could stammer her thanks, the astonishing man was out of the room and closing the door behind him. Beauty made a sound—half quizzical chirp, half approving burble. She'd come loose from Menolly's neck during the examination, watching the proceedings from a depression in the sleeping furs. Now she walked over to Menolly and stroked her head against Menolly's arm.

From the apprentices' hall across the courtyard, the singing was renewed, with vigor and volume. Beauty cocked her head, humming with delight and then, when Menolly shushed her, looked wistfully up at the girl.

"I don't think we should sing again just now, but they do sound grand, don't they?"

She sat there, caressing Beauty, delighting in the music. Very close harmony, she realized approvingly, the sort only trained voices and well-rehearsed singers can achieve.

"Well," said Silvina, entering the room briskly, "you have stirred them up. It's good to hear that old rooter sung with some spirit."

Menolly had no time to register astonishment at Silvina's comment, for the headwoman poked at Menolly's bundle of things on the table, and twitched the sleeping rug into neat folds.

"We might just as well get you settled in Dunca's cottage now," Silvina continued. "Fortunately, there's an outside room unoccupied . . ." The headwoman wrinkled her nose in a slightly disparaging grimace. "Those holder girls are impossible about being outside, but it oughtn't to worry you." She smiled at Menolly. "Oldive says you're to keep off your feet, but some walking's got to be done. Still, you won't be in a chore section . . . another good reason to keep you at Dunca's, I suppose . . ." Silvina frowned and then looked back at Menolly's small bundle. "This is all you brought with you?"

"And nine fire lizards."

Silvina laughed. "An embarrassment of riches." She glanced out the window, peering across the courtyard to the far roof where the fire lizards were still sunning themselves. "They *do* stay where they're told, don't they?"

"Generally. But I'm not sure how good they are with too many people about or unusual noise."

"Or fascinating diversions . . ." Silvina smiled again at Menolly as she nodded toward the windows and the music issuing from the apprentices' hall.

"They always sang along with me . . . I didn't realize we shouldn't—"

"How should you? Not to worry, Menolly. You'll fit in here just fine. Now, let's wrap up your bundle and show you the way to Dunca's. Then Robinton wants you to borrow a gitar. Master Jerint is sure to have a spare usable one in the workshop. You'll have to make your own, you know. Unless you made one for Petiron at the Sea Hold?"

"I had none of my own." Menolly was relieved that she could keep her voice steady.

"But Petiron took his with him. Surely you . . ."

"I had the use of it, yes." Menolly managed to keep her tone even as she rigidly suppressed the memory of how she had lost the use, of the beating her father had given her for forbidden tuning, playing her own songs. "I made myself pipes . . ." she added, diverting Silvina from further questions. Rummaging in her bundle, she brought out the multiple pipes she had made in her cave by the sea.

"Reeds? And done with a belt knife by the look of them," said Silvina, walking to the window for more light as she turned the pipes in a critical examination. "Well done for just a belt knife." She returned the pipes to Menolly with an approving expression. "Petiron was a good teacher."

"Did you know him well?" Menolly felt a wave of grief at her loss of the only person in her home hold who had been interested in her.

"Indeed I did." Silvina gave Menolly a frown. "Did he not talk of the Harper Hall at all to you?"

"No. Why should he?"

"Why shouldn't he? He taught you, didn't he? He encouraged you to write. . . . Sent Robinton those songs . . ." Silvina stared at Menolly in real surprise for a long moment, then she shrugged with a little laugh. "Well, Petiron always had his own reasons for everything he did, and no one the wiser. But he was a good man!"

Menolly nodded, unable for a moment to speak, berating herself for ever once doubting, during those lonely miserable days at Half-Circle after Petiron's death, that he'd done what he said he'd do. Though the old Harper's mind had taken to wandering. . . .

"Before I forget it," Silvina said, "how often do your fire lizards need to be fed?"

"They're hungriest in the morning, though they eat any time, but maybe that was because I had to hunt and catch food for them, and it took hours. The wild ones seemed to have no trouble . . ."

"Fed 'em once and they're always looking to you, is that it?" Silvina smiled, to soften any implied criticism. "The cooks throw all scraps into a big earthen jar in the cold room . . . most of it goes to the watchwhers, but I'll give orders that you're to have whatever you require."

"I don't mean to be a bother . . ."

Silvina gave her such a look that Menolly broke off her attempt to apologize.

"Be sure that when you *do* bother me, I'll inform you." Silvina grinned. "Just ask any of the apprentices if I won't."

Silvina had been leading Menolly down the steps and out of the cliffhold of the Harper Hall as she talked. Now they passed under an arch that gave onto a broad road of paving stones, never a blade of grass or spot of moss to be seen anywhere.

For the first time Menolly had a chance to appreciate the size of Fort Hold. Knowing that it was the oldest and largest Hold was quite different from seeing it, being outside the towering cliff.

Thousands of people must live in the cliffholds and cottages that hugged the rock palisade. Awed, Menolly's steps slowed as she stared at the wide ramp leading to the courtyard and main entrance of Fort Hold, higher in the cliff face than the Harper

Craft Hall, and with rows of windows extending upward in sheer stone, almost to the fire heights themselves. In Half-Circle Sea Hold, everyone had been in the cliff, but at Fort Hold, stone buildings had been built out in wings from the cliff, forming a quadrangle similar to the Harper Craft Hall. Smaller cottages had been added onto the original wings, on either side of the ramp. There were dwellings bordering the sides of the broad paved road that led in several well-traveled directions; south to the fields and pastures, east down the valley toward the low foothills and west around to the pass in the cliff that would lead to the higher mountains of the Central Fort Range.

Silvina guided Menolly now toward a cottage, a good-sized one with five windows, all of them shuttered tight, on the upper floor. The cottage nestled against the slope of the ramp. As they got close enough, Menolly realized that the little cot was also quite old. And the cottage door was metal, too! Incredible! Silvina opened it, calling out for Dunca. Menolly had just time to notice that the metal door closed as the one at the Harper Hall did, with a small wheel throwing the thick rods into grooves in ceiling and floor.

"Menolly, come and meet Dunca who holds the cottage for the girls who study at the Harper Hall."

Menolly dutifully greeted the short, dumpy little woman with bright black eyes and cheeks like a puffbelly's sides. Dunca gave Menolly a raking look, at odds with her jolly appearance, as if measuring up Menolly to the gossip she'd already heard. Then Dunca saw Beauty peeking around Menolly's ear. She gave a shriek, jumping back.

"What's that?"

Menolly reached up to calm Beauty, who was hissing and

raising her wings, getting one entangled in Menolly's hair.

"But, Dunca, surely you knew—" Silvina's voice chided the woman, "—that Menolly had Impressed fire lizards."

Menolly's sharp ear caught the edge to Silvina's voice, and so did the little queen, for Beauty thrummed softly and warningly in her throat as her eyes whirled at Dunca. Menolly silently called her to order.

"I'd *heard,* but I don't always credit things I'm *told,*" said Dunca, standing as far away from Menolly and Beauty as the hall permitted.

"Very wise of you," replied Silvina. The set of the head-woman's lips and the wary amusement in her glance told Menolly that Silvina was not overly fond of the little cotholder. "Now you've a windowed room vacant, have you not? I think it's best if we settled her there."

"I don't want another hysterical girl who'll panic during Threadfall and scare us all with imagining that Thread is actually *in* the cottage!"

Silvina's eyes danced with suppressed laughter as she glanced Menolly's way. "No, Menolly won't panic. She is, by the way, the youngest daughter of Yanus Sea Holder of Half-Circle Sea Hold, beholden to Benden Weyr. The sea breeds stern souls, you know."

Dunca's bright little eyes were almost lost in the folds of her eye flesh as she peered up at Menolly.

"So you knew Petiron, did you?"

"Yes, I did, Dunca."

The cotholder gave a disgusted snort and turned so quickly her full skirt followed in hasty swirls as she made for the stone steps carved into the wall at the back of the hallway. She kept twitching her skirt, grunting at the steepness of the risers as she heaved her small fat person upward.

Two narrow corridors, lit at either end by dimming glows, went left and right from the stairwell. Dunca turned right, led them to the far end and threw open the last door on the outside.

"Lazy sluts," she said truculently, fumbling at the catch of the glowbasket. "They've cleared the glows."

"Where are they kept?" asked Menolly, wishing to ingratiate herself with the cotkeeper. Fleetingly she wondered if she'd always be trotting up and down narrow steps after glows.

"Where's your drudge, Dunca? It's her task to bring glows, not Menolly's," said Silvina as she walked past Dunca and flipped open first one, then a second set of shutters, flooding the room with sunlight.

"Silvina! What are you doing?"

"Threadfall's not for two more days, Dunca. Be sensible. The room's fusty."

Dunca's answer was a shriek as the other fire lizards swooped in through the opened window, diving about the room, chittering excitedly. There was nothing for them to cling to, since the walls were bare of hangings and the bed a frame, empty of rushes, the sleeping fur rolled up on the small press. The two green Aunties and blue Uncle fought for landing space on the stool and then zoomed out the window again as Dunca's screams startled them. The little cotholder cowered in the corner, skirts about her head, shrieking.

Menolly ordered the browns to stop diving, told Auntie One and Two and Uncle to stay on the window ledge, got Rocky and Diver to settle on the bedstead while Silvina calmed Dunca and led her from the corner. By the time the cotholder had been cajoled into watching Silvina handle Lazybones, who'd let anyone caress him so long as it involved no effort on his part, Menolly realized that Dunca would never be comfortable in their presence and that the woman disliked Menolly intensely for witnessing her fearfulness. For a long, sad moment, Menolly wished that she could have stayed at the Weyr where everyone could accept fire lizards equably.

She sighed softly to herself as she stroked Beauty, absently listening to Silvina's reassurances to Dunca that the fire lizards wouldn't harm anyone, not her, not her charges; that Dunca'd be the envy of every other cotholder in Fort to have nine fire lizards . . .

"Nine?" Dunca's protest came out in a terrified squeak, and she reached for her skirts to throw over her head. "Nine of those beastly things flitting and diving about *my* home—"

"They don't like to stay inside, except at night," said Menolly, hoping to reassure Dunca. "They're rarely all with me at one time."

From the horrified and malicious look Dunca gave her, Menolly realized that she herself would be rarely with Dunca if the cotholder had anything to say in the matter.

"We can stop here no longer now, Menolly. You've to pick a gitar from the workshop," said Silvina. "If you need more rushes, Dunca, you've only to send your woman to the Hall," she added as she motioned Menolly to precede her from the room. "Menolly will be more closely involved with the Hall than the other girls . . ."

"She's to be back here at shutter time, same as the others, or stay at the Hall," said Dunca as Silvina and Menolly went down the steps.

"She's strict with the girls," Silvina remarked as they emerged into the bright midday sun and started across the broad paved square, "but that's to the good with all those lads vying for their attention. And take no heed to her grumbles over Petiron. She'd hoped to wed him after Merelan died. *I'd* say Petiron resigned as Fort Hold Harper as much to get free of Dunca as to clear the way for Robinton. He was so very proud that his son was elected Masterharper."

"Half-Circle Sea Hold is a long way from Fort Hold."

Silvina chuckled. "And one of the few places isolated enough to prevent Dunca from following him, child. As if Petiron would ever have taken another woman after Merelan. She was the loveliest person, a voice of unusual beauty and range. Ah, I miss her still."

More people were about: field workers coming in for their midday meal; a party of men on leggy runners, slowing to an amble through the crowd. An apprentice, intent on his errand, ran right into Menolly. He was mouthing an apology when Beauty, peering through Menolly's hair, hissed at him. He yelped, ducked with an apprentice's well-developed instinct, and went pelting back the way he'd come.

Silvina laughed. "I'd like to hear his tale when he gets back to his hall."

"Silvina, I'm—"

"Not a word, Menolly! I will not have you apologizing for your fire lizards. Nor will Master Robinton. There will always be fools in the world like Dunca, fearful of anything new or strange." They had entered the archway of the Harper Hall. "Through that door, across the stairhall, and you'll find the workshop. Master Jerint is in charge. He'll find you an instrument so you can play for Master Domick. He'll meet you there." With an encouraging pat and a smile, Silvina left her.

THE
EPIC
TALE
OF
TWO
YOUNG
MEN:

the greatest warrior of his age, and a good-natured con man. Together, they led a rebellion against a tyrannical emperor who had betrayed the gods and his people. These two men were once brothers in arms, but will fidelity and noble goals fall to bitter and tragic actions as they become rival kings battling to rule the seven islands?

This is an epic fantasy novel debut from Ken Liu, one of the most lauded fantasy and science fiction writers of his generation and the winner of the Hugo, Nebula, and World Fantasy Awards.

TWO SISTERS GROWING UP
IN A POST—WWIII POW
CAMP IN MANHATTAN . . .

A HARROWING ESCAPE . . .

AND A STARTLING TRUTH
THAT WILL CHANGE EVERYTHING.

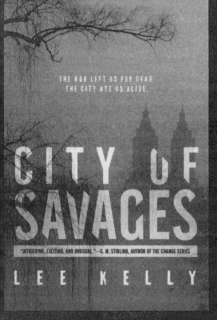

THE WAR LEFT US FOR DEAD.
THE CITY ATE US ALIVE.

CITY OF
SAVAGES

"INTRIGUING, EXCITING, AND UNUSUAL."—S. M. STIRLING, AUTHOR OF THE CHANGE SERIES

LEE KELLY

PRINT AND E-BOOK EDITIONS AVAILABLE
SAGAPRESS.COM